XANDER STEELE

Tempting the Enemy's Daughter

A Love Born from Rivalry

First published by Xander Steele 2025

Copyright © 2025 by Xander Steele

All rights reserved. No part of this publication may be reproduced, stored or transmitted in any form or by any means, electronic, mechanical, photocopying, recording, scanning, or otherwise without written permission from the publisher. It is illegal to copy this book, post it to a website, or distribute it by any other means without permission.

This novel is entirely a work of fiction. The names, characters and incidents portrayed in it are the work of the author's imagination. Any resemblance to actual persons, living or dead, events or localities is entirely coincidental.

Xander Steele asserts the moral right to be identified as the author of this work.

Xander Steele has no responsibility for the persistence or accuracy of URLs for external or third-party Internet Websites referred to in this publication and does not guarantee that any content on such Websites is, or will remain, accurate or appropriate.

Designations used by companies to distinguish their products are often claimed as trademarks. All brand names and product names used in this book and on its cover are trade names, service marks, trademarks and registered trademarks of their respective owners. The publishers and the book are not associated with any product or vendor mentioned in this book. None of the companies referenced within the book have endorsed the book.

First edition

This book was professionally typeset on Reedsy. Find out more at reedsy.com

Contents

Introduction		1
1	Chapter 1	3
2	Chapter 1: A Dangerous Alliance	6
3	Chapter 2: The Enemy's Daughter	21
4	Chapter 3: A Tempting Proposition	41
5	Chapter 4: Crossing Enemy Lines	52
6	Chapter 5: The Masquerade Ball	68
7	Chapter 6: Secrets and Lies	79
8	Chapter 7: A Dangerous Game	93
9	Chapter 8: Betrayals and Alliances	106
10	Chapter 9: The Web of Deception	125
11	Chapter 10: A Daring Escape	140
12	Chapter 11: Running from the Past	153
13	Chapter 12: Finding Sanctuary	167
14	Chapter 13: Unlikely Allies	182
15	Chapter 14: The Truth Unveiled	197
16	Chapter 15: A Heart in Conflict	207
17	Chapter 16: The Ultimate Betrayal	221
18	Chapter 17: A Race Against Time	231
19	Chapter 18: Confronting the Enemy	245
20	Chapter 19: The Convergence	259
21	Chapter 20: A New Dawn	273
Epilogue		294

Introduction

In a world where kingdoms are bound by fragile alliances and ancient secrets, Lord Valerius of Aeridor seeks to secure his power through an unexpected alliance with Duke Alaric of Solara. When Valerius proposes a marriage to the Duke's stunning daughter, Lady Lyra, the lines between diplomacy and desire blur. But Lyra is no innocent pawn. Her beauty is renowned, her loyalty, uncertain. As their kingdoms teeter on the edge of war, Lyra's true motives remain shrouded in mystery.

As she travels to Aeridor under the guise of diplomatic negotiations, Lyra becomes entangled in a web of intrigue, betrayal, and forbidden attraction. At a grand masquerade ball, an exchange of secret messages sets the stage for a dangerous game of power, as Valerius and Lyra engage in a high-stakes chess match, each move a calculated play for control. But as the hidden past of their kingdoms unravels, neither can ignore the sizzling tension that builds between them.

With an ancient pact broken and a catastrophic magical event threatening to fracture reality, Lyra must navigate treacherous alliances and her growing feelings for Valerius.

Tempting the Enemy's Daughter

Her heart torn between loyalty to her father and an undeniable attraction to the man she was supposed to manipulate, she finds herself caught in a race against time to save not only her kingdom but the very fabric of existence itself.

As the ultimate betrayal is revealed and the true enemy comes to light, Lyra, Valerius, and their unlikely allies must unite their powers to prevent history from being rewritten. In the end, the price of victory may be greater than they ever imagined—and the future of Aeridor and Solara uncertain.

Tempting the Enemy's Daughter: A Love Born from Rivalry is a thrilling tale of passion, power, and betrayal, where love blooms in the unlikeliest of places, and loyalty is the most dangerous weapon of all.

One

Chapter 1

XANDER STEELE

Tempting the Enemy's Daughter

A Love Born From Rivalry

Chapter 1

Two

Chapter 1: A Dangerous Alliance

The air in the grand hall of Aeridor's Keep was thick with anticipation. The flickering torches cast long shadows against the stone walls, and the grand oak table at the center of the room was covered in maps, parchments, and ink pots. The kingdom of Aeridor had always prided itself on its strength, but the winds of war were shifting in ways no one had anticipated. After years of uneasy peace, the ancient pact between Aeridor and Solara was in danger of shattering, and Lord Valerius knew that every decision he made in the coming weeks would determine whether his kingdom stood firm or crumbled under the weight of its enemies.

Lord Valerius stood at the head of the table, his hands resting lightly on the edge as he gazed at the map of the two kingdoms. His dark eyes were focused, unreadable—yet his thoughts were far from clear. Solara, once a trusted ally, was becoming increasingly unpredictable. The Solarian Duke,

Chapter 1: A Dangerous Alliance

Alaric, had always been an enigmatic figure. His movements in the past year had been strange, his diplomacy laced with hidden agendas, and it was clear to Valerius that the time had come to act before things escalated beyond repair.

A soft rustling behind him broke his reverie. He turned to find his trusted advisor, Seraphine, stepping into the room. Her long cloak swirled behind her, and her eyes were sharp, assessing the situation as always. Seraphine had been with him through battles, betrayals, and moments of triumph. Her loyalty was unquestionable, but even she seemed unsettled today.

"Lord Valerius," she began, her voice low but tinged with curiosity, "are you certain about this course of action? Duke Alaric is no fool. An alliance, especially one forged in such secrecy, may not sit well with him—or with his daughter."

Valerius turned back to the map, studying the borders of the two kingdoms. "I'm aware of the risks. But if we don't act swiftly, we may find ourselves at the mercy of forces beyond our control." He met her gaze. "The alliance with Solara is not just about territory or power. It's about securing the future of Aeridor. Without it, we'll fall prey to a greater enemy—one that neither of our kingdoms can afford to ignore."

Seraphine's expression softened, but only slightly. "I hope you know what you're doing. There's a saying among the people of Solara: *Those who make deals with the devil often find themselves burned by the flames.*" She hesitated, then added, "And speaking of the devil, there is the matter of his daughter."

Valerius's jaw tightened. Lady Lyra. The daughter of Duke Alaric, a woman whose beauty had captivated kingdoms and whose charm had won the favor of many. But beneath that porcelain face lay a mind as sharp as any blade, and the rumors surrounding her were dangerous. Some said she was a spy, others claimed she was the true power behind her father's throne. Valerius did not know the truth—but he knew that to secure the alliance, he would have to navigate her carefully.

"I have no intention of being burned," he said firmly. "The marriage alliance is the key. If I can secure her hand in marriage, the Duke will have no choice but to agree. She is his most prized possession, after all. A powerful pawn."

Seraphine raised an eyebrow. "And if she refuses? What then?"

Valerius smiled grimly, his fingers tapping lightly on the table. "Then we find another way. We cannot afford to fail. Solara's future, and our own, depends on it."

The next day, the royal court of Aeridor was a flurry of activity. Servants scurried to prepare the grand hall for an important visitor, and nobles murmured in hushed tones as they passed by Valerius's chambers. He had sent word to Duke Alaric that he wished to discuss a matter of mutual importance, and Alaric had agreed to send his daughter, Lady Lyra, as his emissary. It was a delicate balance. The meeting would be a game of diplomacy and seduction, a dance of words where every gesture, every glance, would be scrutinized.

As the hour approached, Valerius stood before the mirror, adjusting his tunic and smoothing the silver clasp of his cloak. His appearance was deliberate, designed to project authority while still hinting at the charisma that lay beneath the surface. He was no stranger to the art of influence, and he would need every ounce of it today.

The door to his chambers opened, and Seraphine entered, her eyes immediately searching his face for signs of doubt.

Chapter 1: A Dangerous Alliance

"You look prepared," she remarked, her voice dry.

"Don't I always?" Valerius replied, his tone light but carrying an edge.

A knock at the door interrupted them. The time had come.

Lady Lyra entered the room with the grace of a queen. Her dark hair cascaded down her back in soft waves, and her eyes—pale as winter ice—met Valerius's with an almost predatory calm. She wore the colors of Solara: deep reds and golds, the fabric rich and luxurious. Her presence was commanding, even without words.

"Lord Valerius," she said, her voice smooth as velvet, "I am honored by your invitation."

Valerius offered a small, courteous bow, though his eyes never left hers. "The honor is mine, Lady Lyra. I trust your journey here was pleasant?"

"Quite. The roads between our kingdoms are well-traveled," she replied, her gaze never wavering. "Though I must admit, I am curious as to the nature of this... *important* matter you wished to discuss."

Valerius smiled, gesturing toward a pair of chairs near the fire. "Shall we sit? I think the discussion is best held in comfort, given its importance."

Lyra hesitated for a moment, as though assessing whether the invitation was genuine or another subtle test. Then, with a fluid movement, she took a seat.

"As you know, the old pact between our kingdoms is not what it once was," Valerius began, his tone measured but laced with an underlying urgency. "The winds of war are stirring, and it is becoming clear that Solara may soon be facing threats from beyond its borders. I propose an alliance—one that will secure both our futures."

Lyra's eyes narrowed slightly, a flicker of something unreadable crossing her features. "An alliance, you say? How… convenient."

Valerius leaned forward, his expression earnest. "This is not just diplomacy, Lady Lyra. This is survival. Together, we could secure not only the future of our kingdoms but our people as well. But there is a condition, one that I hope you will consider seriously."

She tilted her head, intrigued despite herself. "And what condition is that?"

"A marriage between you and I," he said, his voice steady but carrying the weight of finality. "It would unite our houses and solidify the pact. We would become not only allies by treaty, but by blood."

Lyra's lips curved into a smile, but it was one that did not reach her eyes. "A tempting proposition, Lord Valerius. But you must understand, marriage is not a trivial matter in Solara. There is more at stake than you might think. My father's loyalty to his allies… and to you, may not be as steadfast as you hope."

Valerius did not flinch. He had expected this. "Then let us ensure that it is."

The game had begun.

The fire crackled in the hearth, casting an orange glow across the stone walls of the chamber, but the warmth of the flames seemed distant. Lady Lyra's icy gaze remained fixed on Valerius, the pause between them thick with unspoken thoughts. She was calculating, her mind sharp enough to cut through the layers of diplomacy, intrigue, and subterfuge that filled the room. Valerius could feel her studying him,

Chapter 1: A Dangerous Alliance

evaluating every word, every gesture.

She leaned back in her chair, the silk of her gown pooling around her like a shadow. Her fingers, long and delicate, drummed lightly on the armrest, the only indication of her contemplation. "A marriage," she repeated softly, as if tasting the word, savoring its implications. "And you think that such a union would be enough to convince my father? A marriage of convenience to seal a political alliance, is that your proposal?"

Valerius held her gaze steadily, unwilling to show any sign of discomfort. "Indeed. A union that benefits both of us. Solara's power would remain unchallenged, and Aeridor's borders would be protected. The pact, once fractured, could be mended. But we need more than just words. We need action, Lady Lyra. And this marriage could serve as that action."

Her lips quirked, but it was not a smile. "And if I refuse?" she asked, her voice laced with a quiet challenge. "What then, Lord Valerius? Are you prepared to risk everything on the whims of a woman's decision?"

Valerius allowed a flicker of uncertainty to pass through his mind, though he swiftly masked it. He had expected her to resist, but the intensity of her resistance took him by surprise. *She is not like other noblewomen,* he realized. *She is a strategist in her own right.*

"If you refuse," Valerius replied, his tone cool but unwavering, "then I will find another way. There are always other paths. But I am not blind to the power that lies in this union, Lady Lyra. The marriage between us would be more than a mere joining of two people; it would be a message to the world that our kingdoms stand united. It would send a signal to every rival, every enemy, that Aeridor and Solara are forces to be reckoned with. Together, we are stronger."

She regarded him for a long moment, her eyes glinting with something unreadable. Then, she sat up straighter, folding her hands in her lap. "But what of me, Lord Valerius? What if I have no interest in strengthening your position? What if I prefer to see my own kingdom rise, unburdened by the ties of a broken alliance? And what if I do not wish to be a mere pawn in your game of power?"

The sharpness of her words was like a blade's edge, and for a moment, Valerius felt a slight chill, though he did not flinch. He had suspected as much—Lyra was not the kind of woman to be easily manipulated or coerced. She was not some naïve princess waiting for a suitor's proposal to shape her destiny. She was a force in her own right, a political entity with her own ambitions.

"I am not asking you to be a pawn," Valerius said, his voice softer now, measured. "I am asking you to become a queen— not just by title, but by your own will. In our union, you would hold the power to shape both our fates. Your influence in Solara would grow immeasurably, and you would have the ear of the most powerful man in Aeridor. Together, we could achieve things far beyond what either of us could accomplish alone."

Lyra's expression softened imperceptibly, but the walls around her emotions remained firmly in place. "You speak of power," she said slowly, almost thoughtfully. "But power is a dangerous thing, Lord Valerius. One misstep, one wrong word, and it crumbles. Do you truly think we can control it? Do you think you can control me?"

Her question hung in the air, a dare wrapped in velvet. Valerius could sense the shifting currents between them,

Chapter 1: A Dangerous Alliance

the delicate balance of diplomacy teetering on the edge of something more volatile. He had come to this meeting with a clear goal, but now he understood that winning Lyra's favor—if not her agreement—would be far more complex than he had anticipated.

"I don't seek to control you, Lady Lyra," Valerius said, his voice lower now, more sincere. "I seek to align our interests. The strength of Aeridor and Solara is undeniable—together, we could secure our future. But we need each other, and I need you. Not just as the daughter of Duke Alaric, but as a woman capable of great things. Together, we can craft a new destiny."

She tilted her head slightly, a faint smile playing on her lips, though it did not reach her eyes. "Destiny, hmm?" she mused. "Such lofty ideals, Lord Valerius. And yet, destiny is often shaped by those who are willing to make sacrifices. What are you willing to sacrifice for this… alliance?"

He had expected her to ask this question, though not with such precision. *She is testing me,* he thought. *Testing my resolve.*

"I am willing to sacrifice whatever is necessary to ensure Aeridor's future," he said, his voice steady. "I will not let it fall to chaos—not when there is a chance to restore what was lost. If that means binding myself to you in marriage, then so be it. We must all make sacrifices in pursuit of something greater."

Lyra studied him for a long moment, her eyes sharp and calculating. Then, to Valerius's surprise, she leaned back in her chair with a soft laugh, the sound as cold and beautiful as winter's breath.

"How quaint," she said, her voice teasing but tinged with an underlying darkness. "You speak of destiny, of alliances, and of sacrifices. But in the end, Lord Valerius, we are all pawns in a game far larger than ourselves. You speak of strength, but strength is not always the key to victory. Sometimes, it is patience, deception, and timing."

Valerius met her gaze, his heart a beat too fast. There was something in her words—something ominous—that he couldn't quite grasp. Was she playing him, or was she merely speaking truths he had yet to understand? His instincts told him it was both. Lyra was far more than she appeared, and this meeting had already become a chess game, each word a calculated move.

"Then I suggest we both be patient," Valerius said, rising from his chair and offering his hand. "Let us take the first step together, and see where it leads us."

Lyra did not immediately take his hand, but her eyes never left his. "We shall see," she said softly, her voice now a quiet promise. "We shall see."

As she left the room, her dark figure disappearing into the hallway, Valerius let out a breath he hadn't realized he'd been holding. The encounter had been everything he had expected—and more. Lady Lyra was a dangerous force, and he had only begun to understand the depth of her power.

He turned back to the map of the kingdoms, his mind racing. The alliance with Solara was not just a political maneuver—it was a battle for control over the future of both kingdoms. And Lyra... she was not just the Duke's daughter. She was the key to it all.

Outside, the wind howled against the castle's stone walls, a harbinger of the storm that was to come. Neither Aeridor nor Solara would remain untouched by the coming tides.

Chapter 1: A Dangerous Alliance

And as Valerius stood there, staring out into the darkness, he realized that he was already caught in the web of Lyra's designs—whether he knew it or not.

The dangerous alliance had begun.

As Lady Lyra disappeared into the hallway, the sound of her soft footsteps echoing against the stone corridors, Valerius stood at the window of the chamber, staring out over the darkening landscape of Aeridor. His mind was racing, sifting through the implications of their conversation. Lady Lyra had been an enigma from the moment she entered the room, and though the meeting had concluded without a clear agreement, something in her gaze—a flicker of recognition, perhaps—told him that she was not as opposed to the idea of an alliance as she had let on.

She was playing a game, just as he was. But unlike most of the women he had dealt with in the past, Lyra wasn't moved by flattery or promises of grandeur. She was far more calculating, and Valerius had to respect that.

Still, the idea of marrying her, of binding himself to the daughter of his kingdom's most dangerous enemy, made his stomach twist. It wasn't the prospect of a marriage that troubled him—after all, he had seen many political unions forged out of necessity. It was the mystery that surrounded Lyra. Her beauty was only the surface; her mind was sharp, and she wielded power like a hidden blade. The rumors whispered about her in both Aeridor and Solara spoke of a woman who was more than her father's daughter—she was said to have her own secret allegiances, her own designs on power.

Valerius's fingers clenched around the cold stone of the window ledge. *What do you want, Lyra? What do you really want from this?*

The evening passed in a blur of muted conversation and fleeting thoughts. Valerius's council had convened, and though he was present in body, his mind kept drifting back to Lyra. Seraphine noticed his distraction, her keen eyes never missing a flicker of his expression.

"You've gone quiet," she remarked as the meeting broke for the night. "What's on your mind, my lord?"

Valerius turned to her, his face a mask of controlled thought. "Lady Lyra," he said briefly, his voice low. "Her response was… as expected, but I still don't know if she's fully on board. Or if she's playing me."

Seraphine studied him for a long moment, her arms folded across her chest. "She is playing you, Valerius. And she's playing everyone. But that's not necessarily a bad thing."

He shot her a sharp glance. "You make it sound as if you approve of her manipulation."

Seraphine smirked. "I don't approve or disapprove. But I do recognize strategy when I see it. And right now, you're both vying for the same thing—control of the future. Whether you like it or not, that makes you allies of a sort."

Valerius frowned. "I wouldn't call her an ally—not yet."

"No," she agreed, her voice turning more serious, "but she *could* be. And you *must* be prepared for that, Lord Valerius. If she is to be your bride—if you plan to make that happen— you'll need more than just diplomacy. You'll need to find a way to earn her trust. She's not the type of woman who can be coerced into submission."

"I didn't intend to coerce her," Valerius replied, his voice hardening. "I want her to see that this alliance is in her best

Chapter 1: A Dangerous Alliance

interest."

Seraphine gave him an appraising look. "Do you? Or do you simply want her to bend to your will, just like everyone else who stands before you?"

Valerius was quiet for a moment, the words striking deeper than he cared to admit. It was true that he had always prided himself on his ability to control the flow of events, to guide outcomes with deft strategy and unyielding will. But Lyra— she was different. She wasn't someone he could just sway with promises of power or manipulation.

Her independence unsettled him.

The next morning, Valerius stood on the balcony of his chambers, overlooking the bustling courtyard as his servants prepared for the day. The sounds of metal clanging, horses whinnying, and the occasional laugh or shout filled the air, but he was hardly aware of it. His thoughts were still tangled in the previous night's conversation with Lyra. He had expected resistance, but not the degree of cold calculation she had shown.

She was no naïve princess. *She's been trained for this,* he thought. *She's as much a player in this game as I am. And if I'm going to win her trust, I'll need to outmaneuver her at every turn.*

He was so lost in his thoughts that he didn't hear the soft knock on his door. It was only when the door creaked open that he realized Seraphine had entered, her expression unreadable.

"You're thinking about her again, aren't you?" she said, her tone light but with a knowing edge.

Valerius turned to face her, trying to force his mind back to the matters at hand. "I need to be sure that I'm making the right move. You were right about one thing—this alliance isn't just a matter of politics. It's a matter of trust, and I can't afford to misstep."

Seraphine nodded, her sharp gaze never leaving him. "Trust is a fickle thing, especially with someone like Lyra. She plays a long game. She's not looking for quick victories. She's looking for something she can control."

"Control," Valerius muttered under his breath. "I understand that. I need to figure out what she wants—what she's really after. Once I know that, I can offer her something more than just a marriage contract."

Seraphine raised an eyebrow. "And how do you plan to learn that?"

Valerius's lips curled into a faint smile, though it didn't quite reach his eyes. "The same way I always do. I'll get close enough to figure it out."

Later that afternoon, as the sun began to dip behind the hills, casting a golden light across the sprawling estate, Valerius received word that Lady Lyra would be attending a formal dinner at the castle. It was a rare occasion, as she had been spending most of her time within the confines of her own quarters, refusing to attend public gatherings. But the invitation had been extended—and accepted.

The dinner was to be held in one of the grandest halls of Aeridor Keep, with long tables covered in silken cloth and lined with silver and crystal. The nobles in attendance whispered excitedly about the possibility of seeing the Solarian princess up close, but Valerius's attention was fixed on the entrance.

And then, as if on cue, she entered.

Chapter 1: A Dangerous Alliance

Lady Lyra was as striking in person as she had been during their private meeting. The room seemed to hush for a moment as she glided across the floor, her presence commanding the attention of every person in the hall. Her gown shimmered with delicate threads of gold, accentuating her graceful form. But it was her eyes, cold and calculating, that drew Valerius's gaze.

She didn't look at him immediately—didn't acknowledge him with the faintest gesture—but Valerius could feel her eyes on him, even from across the room. He smiled faintly to himself. *Let's see how she plays this game.*

As Lyra took her seat, her posture elegant, yet unyielding, Valerius moved toward her, navigating through the crowds of courtiers with practiced ease. When he finally reached her side, he bowed slightly, his voice smooth but laced with intent.

"Lady Lyra," he said, offering her a smile that was both respectful and knowing, "I'm glad you could join us this evening. It's an honor."

She tilted her head, her lips curling into a small, enigmatic smile. "The pleasure is mine, Lord Valerius," she replied, her voice soft but sharp as a knife's edge. "I do hope the food is as… intriguing as your proposal."

Valerius's eyes sparkled, a momentary glint of amusement flashing through him. "I trust it will be," he said, taking the seat next to her. "But as we've already learned, Lady Lyra, it is not the surface that matters most. It's what lies beneath."

She met his gaze without flinching. "And what do you think lies beneath, Lord Valerius?"

Valerius leaned in slightly, his voice lowering to a near-whisper. "Only time will tell. But I think we both have much to uncover about each other."

She smiled again, but it was a smile that made his skin prickle with unease. "Indeed. Time has a way of revealing secrets, doesn't it?"

As the conversation continued, both of them aware of the games they were playing, the feeling of tension between them only deepened. This alliance, this delicate dance of words and gestures, was far from over. And for Valerius, it was becoming clear that winning Lyra's trust—if that was even possible—would be the greatest challenge he had ever faced.

Three

Chapter 2: The Enemy's Daughter

The sun hung low over the horizon, casting the castle of Solara in a golden glow. The towering spires of Duke Alaric's stronghold pierced the sky, its massive stone walls adorned with banners of deep crimson and gold, fluttering gently in the evening breeze. It was a fortress of old, with history carved into its very foundation—a history that now held the weight of a thousand whispered secrets and unspoken alliances.

Inside the grand hall, Lady Lyra moved with the grace of a shadow, her presence barely noticed by the courtiers who buzzed with idle chatter. She was not like the others—neither the giggling debutantes nor the scheming noblewomen, nor even the courtiers who lingered in the background, hoping to curry favor with the powerful. Lyra was an enigma in her own right: a force that demanded attention without seeking it.

Her gown was a deep shade of emerald, the fabric flowing

effortlessly around her as she walked, the intricate embroidery glinting like stars under the torchlight. Her dark hair, pinned up with a single silver comb, framed a face that was both striking and inscrutable. But it was her eyes—the cold, calculating eyes—that commanded the most attention. Her gaze, sharp as a dagger, took in everything and everyone around her, never missing a detail, yet never betraying a hint of emotion.

In the court of Solara, she was known for her beauty—rumors of her allure had traveled far beyond the borders of the kingdom—but few truly understood the power that lay behind her poised exterior. The daughter of Duke Alaric, the ruler of Solara, Lyra was more than just a noblewoman. She was a player in a game far greater than any of her peers could comprehend.

And that game was about to take an unexpected turn.

Lyra entered her private chamber later that evening, her mind a whirlwind of thoughts and calculations. Her father's realm was vast, stretching across a landscape of untamed beauty and rich resources, but it was also filled with enemies and rivals—some old, some new. And now, with the arrival of Lord Valerius of Aeridor and his proposal for an alliance, she was faced with a choice. A dangerous choice.

The fire crackled in the hearth, the warm glow contrasting with the chill in the room. Lyra moved to the window, her fingers brushing lightly against the cold glass as she gazed out over the darkened landscape of Solara. The kingdom was beautiful, but it was not safe. Not anymore.

Her thoughts lingered on the conversation she had shared with Valerius the night before. There had been a certain

Chapter 2: The Enemy's Daughter

quiet intensity to him—a man driven by ambition, yes, but not without a measure of respect for those he sought to manipulate. He had offered her something far more enticing than a mere political alliance. He had offered her power, the kind of power that could change the course of history.

But Lyra wasn't easily swayed by promises of power, not when she knew that such promises often came with a heavy price.

What does he want? she wondered. *And what does he think I want?*

There had been a moment during their conversation when she had almost believed him—when she had thought that perhaps, just perhaps, this alliance could work in her favor. But then the mask had slipped for a second, and she had seen the truth beneath the polished exterior: Valerius was not interested in a true partnership. He was interested in control.

And control was something Lyra was not willing to give up.

A soft knock at the door interrupted her thoughts. Lyra turned, her expression unreadable, and nodded for the visitor to enter.

Her personal attendant, Mira, stepped into the room, her face a mixture of respect and curiosity. "Lady Lyra," she said, her voice low. "You've received word from Aeridor."

Lyra's eyebrows rose slightly. She had expected Valerius to be persistent, but she hadn't anticipated him to move so quickly. "What does it say?"

Mira handed her a sealed letter, the wax bearing the emblem of Aeridor—two crossed swords and a crown. Lyra took it with a slow, deliberate motion, breaking the seal with practiced ease. As she read the letter, her lips curled into a small, almost imperceptible smile.

"So it begins," she murmured to herself. "The game, I mean."

The letter was formal, written in the crisp, precise handwriting of Valerius himself. He requested a meeting, one in which they could discuss the potential terms of the alliance in more detail. The message was courteous, even respectful, but it was also clear in its intent: Aeridor's position was strong, and Valerius was confident that Lady Lyra would eventually see the wisdom of the marriage.

Confidence, Lyra thought. *How charmingly naive.*

She placed the letter on the table and turned back to the window, the weight of her father's kingdom pressing down on her shoulders. As much as she hated to admit it, there was a certain logic to Valerius's proposal. If the ancient pact between their kingdoms could be restored, then the peace between Solara and Aeridor would be guaranteed—at least for a time. But there were too many unknowns. Too many risks.

The alliances in both kingdoms were fragile, teetering on the edge of collapse. If she were to marry Valerius, she would have to tread carefully. But there was something else to consider—something far more dangerous than the political landscape of Aeridor and Solara.

Her mind drifted back to the fragments of whispers she had caught in the hallways of the castle. *Magic,* they said. *Strange happenings at the borders.* There had been reports of odd occurrences in the wilds that separated their two kingdoms—things that defied explanation, things that spoke of a deeper, darker force at work.

And it wasn't just the physical world that seemed to be fray-

Chapter 2: The Enemy's Daughter

ing at the edges. The pact that had once bound their kingdoms had been broken for reasons no one truly understood. It was as if reality itself had been torn asunder.

Lyra shook her head. She could not let herself become distracted by rumors and half-truths. There was no room for such things if she was to succeed. She had her own power to wield—and she would use it, whether it meant allying herself with Valerius or betraying him. But first, she would need to find out what game he was really playing.

That night, after the banquet, Lyra sat alone in her chamber, poring over maps of both Solara and Aeridor. Her fingers traced the borders, the strategic strongholds, the weak points—every detail she had memorized long ago. She was calculating her next move, as she always did, but something gnawed at her—a feeling of unease that she couldn't shake.

The shadows seemed deeper tonight, as if the very air around her was thick with unseen dangers. *If there's a fracture in reality,* she thought, *then perhaps the true enemy is not what we expect.*

The flickering candlelight cast dancing shapes on the walls, but for a moment, Lyra thought she saw something more. Something moving in the dark—a shadow that didn't belong.

Her pulse quickened, but she refused to acknowledge the fear creeping into her chest. It was nothing.

Still, the unsettling feeling remained, gnawing at the edges of her thoughts as she turned back to the maps and the letter from Valerius, her mind set on the delicate dance ahead.

Lyra had always known that power was fleeting. It could be gained in an instant, but it could also be lost just as quickly. *I will not lose it,* she vowed to herself. *Not to him. Not to anyone.*

She reached for a quill and began to write her response to Valerius, her hand steady and sure. The message was simple, but it would send a clear signal: **The game was on.**

The next morning, the air was thick with anticipation as Lyra prepared for her reply to Lord Valerius. Her chamber was lit by the soft glow of the rising sun, and the scent of jasmine from the gardens below drifted through the window, mingling with the scent of parchment and ink. She sat at her writing desk, the quill poised above the paper, but her mind remained sharp and unsettled. The night had been long, filled with restless thoughts and fleeting dreams that felt too real— dreams of shifting landscapes and fractured realities, of voices calling from distant places, and of shadowy figures watching her from the dark.

She dismissed the thoughts as mere distractions. This was not the time for fantasy. The stakes were far too high. She had to focus, and focus she did, her gaze unwavering as she wrote her response to Valerius.

To Lord Valerius of Aeridor,

The proposal you extended last night has not gone unnoticed, and I appreciate your candor. I, too, believe that the future of our kingdoms may well depend on the actions we take now.

Your suggestion of a meeting is prudent. We will arrange to discuss the terms of this alliance in more detail. However, I must make it clear that the path to such a union is not one that is easily walked, nor one that can be forged in haste.

I suggest we convene in a week's time, in a location neutral to both our lands, where we may have the space to discuss

Chapter 2: The Enemy's Daughter

the full implications of this proposal, and what it may cost us both.

I look forward to your response.

Lady Lyra Alaric,

Daughter of Duke Alaric of Solara

She signed the letter with a flourish, the seal of her house—a soaring phoenix—pressed into the warm wax with careful precision. She knew Valerius would understand the weight behind her words. His invitation for an immediate meeting had been a calculated move, no doubt designed to test her willingness to bend to his will. But Lyra was not a woman to be rushed into decisions, especially when it came to matters of such importance. She would play her part, but on her terms.

With the letter sealed and dispatched, Lyra turned to the mirror hanging on the far wall of her chamber. The reflection that stared back at her was one she knew all too well: the poised, composed daughter of Duke Alaric, the figurehead of Solara's nobility. But beneath that mask of perfection, beneath the delicate layers of silk and gold, Lyra was far more than her father's dutiful child.

She had inherited more than his looks—she had inherited his ambition.

The world of court politics, where alliances were forged and broken with a mere word, was a place where Lyra excelled. She had been trained for this all her life, taught to read people's intentions before they spoke a word, to see the cracks in their armor before they realized they were exposed. She had seen it all: fathers, brothers, kings, and queens who thought they could control everything around them, only to be undone by their own hubris.

Tempting the Enemy's Daughter

And now, Valerius. The Lord of Aeridor was no different.

Her gaze shifted to the map of Solara spread out on the table in the center of the room. It was carefully drawn, every border marked, every stronghold noted. Lyra's fingers grazed the map, touching the delicate lines that separated her kingdom from that of Aeridor. She thought of the power Valerius wielded, the strategic positions of his armies, and the advantages they might have if they formed an alliance.

But then she thought of the cost.

To give up the independence of Solara, to share control of her father's realm with a man like Valerius… it would be a dangerous gamble.

Her eyes narrowed. *I don't trust him.* Not yet. And not just because of his position. There was something about him—something beneath his polished exterior—that unsettled her. He was not the typical ambitious lord, driven only by greed or the desire for power. There was something darker about him, something she had sensed during their brief conversation the night before. But she would need more than a fleeting impression to fully understand him.

And she would.

Later that afternoon, as the sun began to dip below the horizon, Lyra made her way to her father's study. Duke Alaric's private chambers were located in a high tower of the castle, a place where only the most trusted of his advisers were ever invited. As she entered the room, the low light of the setting sun cast long shadows across the room, where her father sat at his desk, poring over papers with a furrowed brow.

The Duke was a formidable man, with broad shoulders and

Chapter 2: The Enemy's Daughter

a stern face that betrayed little emotion. His dark hair was streaked with silver, a testament to the years he had spent at the helm of Solara's rule. Despite his age, he still commanded respect, and when he spoke, people listened. He was a man of few words, but each one carried weight.

"Father," Lyra said, her voice respectful yet firm, "there is news from Aeridor."

The Duke's eyes flicked up from the papers. His expression remained impassive, but Lyra could sense his interest. "I assume it's about the proposal from Lord Valerius?"

Lyra nodded. "Yes. He's eager to meet. I've replied, but I need to know how you want me to proceed. The terms of this alliance are not something we can take lightly."

The Duke's lips tightened into a thin line, and for a moment, Lyra could almost see the conflict beneath his calm exterior. "We don't have the luxury of being selective, Lyra. The situation between our kingdoms has become… precarious." His voice was low, tinged with something that almost sounded like regret. "The borders are unstable. The peace we've had for the last decade is fragile. Aeridor is a powerful neighbor, and it's clear that Valerius is ambitious. If we refuse him outright, we risk war."

Lyra watched her father closely. She knew him well enough to see when he was trying to downplay his concerns. He was not one to admit vulnerability, not even to his own daughter. But the truth was clear: Duke Alaric was as wary of this marriage as she was.

"You think he's after more than just an alliance," she said softly, stepping closer to his desk.

Her father didn't answer right away. He placed the papers he had been reading to the side and looked up at her, his expression unreadable. After a long pause, he finally spoke, his voice low and measured. "I think he is. And I think it's our job to find out what that is before we decide how to proceed."

Lyra nodded, understanding the weight of his words. "So, you want me to proceed with the meeting?"

"I want you to proceed," he said, his voice firm. "But tread carefully. If Valerius thinks he can manipulate you, he will. You must remain in control of this situation, no matter what."

Lyra met her father's gaze, her eyes cold and calculating. "Don't worry, Father. I can handle him."

Later that evening, as the final traces of sunlight faded into dusk, Lyra sat in her chambers, lost in thought. Her father's words lingered in her mind, but they only fueled her determination. She would not let herself be manipulated. If she had to play the role of the dutiful daughter to secure Solara's future, then so be it. But she would do it on her terms.

The letter had been sent, and the countdown had begun. In a week, she would meet Valerius in a neutral location. There, the game would truly begin.

Let's see how well you play, Lord Valerius, she thought, her lips curling into a faint smile. *Because I don't intend to lose.*

The days leading up to the scheduled meeting were an uneasy mix of anticipation and silence, as both Solara and Aeridor prepared for what was sure to be a pivotal moment in their tense relations. The news of the forthcoming alliance—or rather, the possibility of it—had already begun to ripple through the courts and noble houses, igniting a whirlwind of speculation. Whispers filled the halls, servants exchanged furtive glances, and emissaries made their discreet reports to their respective masters. The atmosphere in Solara was one

Chapter 2: The Enemy's Daughter

of wary caution.

In her private quarters, Lyra continued to refine her strategies. Each decision she made had consequences, and she knew the stakes were as high as they had ever been. It was a delicate game—one that required not just intellect but a deep understanding of human nature. The final outcome, though uncertain, would hinge on her ability to read those around her, to discern their hidden motives, and, ultimately, to remain a step ahead.

As the days passed, Lyra found herself drawn not only to the strategic intricacies of her father's realm but also to the increasingly vivid dreams that had begun to haunt her. They were no ordinary dreams—they felt real, tangible, like fleeting glimpses of a world that had been altered. There were landscapes she did not recognize, faces she could not place, and an overwhelming sense that time itself was unraveling, fragmenting into pieces that could never be reassembled.

One night, in the quiet stillness of her chamber, Lyra stood by the window, looking out at the expanse of the Solaran plains, shrouded in mist under the pale moonlight. Her hand rested against the cold stone as she stared out, lost in thought. A sharp knock on her door broke her reverie.

"Enter," she called without turning.

Mira, her ever-loyal attendant, stepped inside, her expression strained. The younger woman hesitated, as if unsure whether to speak the words on her mind. "Lady Lyra," she began, her voice uncharacteristically soft, "there is word from Lord Valerius. He has sent an advance party ahead of his own, to begin preparations for the upcoming meeting."

Lyra turned, her brow furrowing slightly. "And what of it? His party is expected, is it not?"

"Yes," Mira replied, still cautious. "But... there is something unusual. One of his men, a knight named Sir Aldric, is known to be... involved in matters beyond the typical duties of Aeridor's nobility. He has ties to a secretive group, one that few in the court speak of openly. It's said they deal with... darker things. Things that have no place in our kingdoms."

Lyra felt the hairs on the back of her neck stand on end. *Darker things?*

"What do we know of this Sir Aldric?" she asked, her voice cool despite the rising tension within her.

Mira glanced over her shoulder, lowering her voice. "It is whispered that he is not merely a knight, but a... protector of sorts. An enforcer of Lord Valerius's will. Some say he has a hand in shadowy dealings, manipulating events in the background. He is trusted by Valerius—perhaps too trusted."

Lyra considered this information carefully. It was not uncommon for powerful men to surround themselves with such figures, but something about this Sir Aldric struck her as significant. "Where is he now?" she asked.

"Already within the walls of Solara, Lady Lyra," Mira replied, her voice barely above a whisper. "He arrived this morning. No one seems to know where he is staying, but it is said that he is quietly inspecting the defenses and ensuring that everything is in order for the coming talks."

Lyra's eyes narrowed. The mention of "inspecting the defenses" was not a casual remark. There was an underlying implication—a subtle threat. Aeridor was coming prepared, and Sir Aldric was likely here to ensure the security of not just the upcoming talks, but of Valerius's interests.

She knew then that the meeting would be no mere diplomatic exchange. There were deeper currents at play, currents

Chapter 2: The Enemy's Daughter

she had yet to fully understand.

"I will need to meet with him," Lyra said, her voice steady. "Make the arrangements, Mira. Discreetly."

Later that evening, Lyra found herself walking through the castle's winding corridors toward a hidden section of the stronghold, far from the public eye. The meeting had been arranged under the pretense of a casual conversation between two noble representatives—nothing out of the ordinary. But Lyra was no fool. She had heard enough to know that the stakes were much higher than mere diplomacy. The shadows that clung to Sir Aldric were not to be ignored.

She arrived at a small, unassuming study—its stone walls covered with tapestries depicting scenes of battles long past. The fire crackled softly in the hearth, casting an orange glow across the room as Sir Aldric turned from the window when she entered.

He was taller than most men, with broad shoulders and the build of someone accustomed to physical conflict. His face was sharply defined, a hardened jaw and eyes that seemed to see everything and nothing all at once. His dark armor was immaculate, as if he had never worn it into battle, and his cloak billowed like a shadow behind him. There was a quiet menace in his presence, a sense that he carried with him not just the weight of his title, but something far darker.

"Lady Lyra," Sir Aldric greeted her with a low bow, though there was no mistaking the coldness in his tone. "I trust the day has treated you well?"

Lyra regarded him coolly, her posture regal, but her eyes sharp. "It has, Sir Aldric. Though I must admit, I am curious as to why Aeridor has sent its... enforcers ahead of the Lord himself. Is there something you are not telling us?"

A flicker of a smile appeared on Sir Aldric's lips, but it was a smile that held no warmth. "I assure you, my lady, Aeridor's intentions are purely diplomatic. As for my role…" He paused, letting the words hang in the air. "I am here to ensure the safety and success of the negotiations. A man like Lord Valerius cannot afford to be vulnerable. And I, as his most trusted knight, have a duty to see that no harm comes to him—or to our interests."

"And those interests," Lyra said evenly, "extend beyond mere diplomacy, do they not?"

Sir Aldric's smile faltered, just for a moment. It was as if he was assessing whether to speak further, whether to reveal more than he intended. But then, with a casual shrug, he leaned back against the stone wall, his gaze unwavering. "Perhaps," he admitted softly. "But one must always be prepared for the unexpected, Lady Lyra. In this world, power is not simply handed over. It must be claimed."

Lyra met his gaze without flinching, though her heart skipped a beat. There was something in his words that sent a ripple of unease through her. This was not just about politics. It was about control. And there were forces at work here—forces she could not yet see clearly.

"You speak of power as though it's a thing that can be seized without consequence," she said, her voice laced with quiet warning. "But be careful, Sir Aldric. Those who seek too much often end up losing everything."

The knight's expression darkened, but his voice remained smooth. "I am well aware of the consequences, my lady. I have seen them firsthand."

Lyra's eyes narrowed slightly. There was something hidden

Chapter 2: The Enemy's Daughter

in that simple statement, something buried deep within Sir Aldric's past. A past that, if properly uncovered, might reveal far more than she wanted to know.

"I would advise caution, Sir Aldric," she said, her voice now as sharp as a blade. "Not just for the sake of this meeting, but for the sake of Aeridor's future as well."

For a brief moment, she thought she saw something flicker in his eyes—something like recognition. But then it was gone, replaced by that same cold indifference.

"Of course, my lady," Sir Aldric said, straightening his posture. "I will keep that in mind."

As Lyra turned to leave, she could feel the weight of his gaze upon her, as if he were sizing her up, measuring her resolve. She did not trust him, but she would not show weakness. She was the daughter of Duke Alaric, and she would play this game on her terms.

The meeting with Valerius was a week away, but Lyra knew one thing for certain: the shadows in the corners of her kingdom were growing deeper—and they would not let her go unchallenged.

The game was no longer just about kingdoms and alliances. It was about survival.

Lyra exited the study, her steps measured and deliberate, as though her mind were still spinning from the exchange. Sir Aldric's presence had unsettled her in a way that she hadn't anticipated. There was a coldness to him, yes, but more than that—there was a sense of deep calculation, as if every word, every glance, every gesture had been rehearsed for some grander purpose. She had been in the presence of many men who were skilled in the art of diplomacy, of power plays and subtle manipulations. But Sir Aldric was something

Tempting the Enemy's Daughter

else entirely. His focus was not just on the present, but on the future—on what lay beyond the fragile veneer of politics.

As Lyra passed through the quiet corridors of the castle, her thoughts drifted back to her father's earlier warning: *"Tread carefully. If Valerius thinks he can manipulate you, he will."* The same could be said of Sir Aldric, perhaps even more so. The knight's unsettling poise, his knowledge of darker matters, and the unspoken weight behind his words all pointed to something she hadn't yet fully grasped.

What exactly are they after?

She knew it was not just an alliance between their kingdoms that Valerius sought—there was something more beneath the surface, something hidden behind the façade of diplomacy. She could feel it in the pit of her stomach, that subtle unease that had been growing ever since the initial proposal had been made.

The firelight flickered in the grand hall as Lyra entered her chamber, her hand instinctively reaching for the heavy velvet curtain that shielded her from the rest of the castle. She wanted to be alone with her thoughts, to process the gravity of what she had just learned.

It was then that her gaze fell upon the strange relic on her writing desk. The small, smooth stone, dark as night with strange symbols etched into its surface, had been given to her by her mother years before—before she had passed, leaving Lyra to carry on in her stead. Her mother had never fully explained the stone's significance, only that it was a gift passed down through generations, and that one day, Lyra would understand its true meaning.

For a moment, Lyra simply stared at it, her fingers hovering above the stone but not touching it. Then, something inside

Chapter 2: The Enemy's Daughter

her stirred, a silent beckoning that urged her to pick it up, to hold it in her hand and listen to whatever it had to say.

She did.

The moment her fingers closed around the smooth, cold surface, a strange tingling sensation spread up her arm, a brief but powerful surge of energy. The stone hummed, almost imperceptibly, as though it recognized her touch, as though it had been waiting for her. Lyra's pulse quickened, but she did not pull away. She had felt this before, but never so strongly—this was no ordinary trinket.

Her breath caught in her throat as her mind was flooded with fragmented visions. She saw flashes of her mother—her face, so vivid, yet distant—whispering something about *time*, about *destinies intertwined*, and the *fracturing of realms*. She saw images of the kingdoms of Solara and Aeridor, but not as they were now. They were... broken, torn apart by forces neither kingdom had understood. And at the center of it all, a shadowed figure, shrouded in darkness, pulling the strings.

She jerked her hand away, the vision dissolving in an instant. The room was quiet again, the stone no longer humming with energy. Lyra's breath came in shallow bursts, her heart racing. She felt as though she had glimpsed something ancient, something powerful, something that had been hidden from her for reasons she could not yet fathom.

What was that?

The stone lay still on the desk before her, its surface smooth and unremarkable once again. Lyra blinked, trying to clear the lingering dizziness from her mind. She had to regain her composure. *There is no time for distractions*, she reminded herself.

She was no stranger to strange dreams or prophetic

visions—her mother had warned her, after all. But this... this was different. It was more vivid, more real. The symbols on the stone—she couldn't quite make sense of them, but they were somehow connected to the growing tensions between the two kingdoms. Perhaps it was not just politics or war that threatened them. Perhaps there was something deeper, something magical, that lay beneath the surface of their conflict.

Before she could dwell on it any longer, a knock at the door broke her reverie.

"Lady Lyra," came Mira's soft voice from the other side. "The meeting with Lord Valerius's emissary has been confirmed for tomorrow afternoon. They are expecting you."

Lyra stood slowly, brushing off the lingering unease. She had no time for distractions—tomorrow was crucial. The negotiations would begin in earnest, and she needed to be at the top of her game. No matter what she'd seen, no matter what strange forces might be stirring beneath the surface, she had her role to play.

With a decisive motion, she returned the stone to its place and moved toward the door. "I will be there shortly, Mira," she said, her voice steady once again.

As she passed through the corridors toward the designated meeting room, Lyra's thoughts lingered on Sir Aldric. Something told her that tomorrow's discussions would not be as straightforward as they seemed. And that, perhaps, it was not just the fate of the kingdoms at stake—but something far more ancient, and far more dangerous, than she could yet comprehend.

The following afternoon, the castle's great hall was filled

Chapter 2: The Enemy's Daughter

with the rustle of silks and the murmur of low voices as the emissaries from Aeridor took their places. Lyra entered with the practiced grace of someone who had spent years learning how to command a room without saying a word. She was a vision of composed elegance, her dark hair pulled back into a simple yet regal braid, her green eyes flashing with a fire that only the keenest would notice.

At the head of the table sat a man she had only seen from a distance—Lord Valerius's chief emissary, a tall, thin man with sharp features and a calculating smile. His eyes locked onto hers the moment she entered, and Lyra couldn't help but feel the weight of his gaze. There was something predatory in his stare, though he hid it well behind his smile.

She greeted him with a small but polite nod. "Lord Valerius's representative, I presume?"

The emissary inclined his head. "Indeed, my lady. It is an honor to finally make your acquaintance. Lord Valerius has spoken of you often."

"I trust it is all in the spirit of cooperation?" she asked coolly, taking her seat across from him.

His smile widened, though it didn't reach his eyes. "Of course, Lady Lyra. Cooperation is the only way forward for both our kingdoms."

Lyra didn't respond immediately, her gaze sweeping across the room. Sir Aldric was nowhere in sight, but she knew he was there—perhaps watching from the shadows, assessing every word, every move. The games had only just begun.

"I trust Lord Valerius is prepared to make a fair offer," she said, keeping her tone neutral. "And that he understands the value of Solara's sovereignty."

"Indeed, Lady Lyra," the emissary replied smoothly. "Lord

Valerius believes that a union between our two great houses will ensure peace and prosperity for both our peoples. And we are prepared to offer terms that are fair to both sides."

Lyra's lips curled into the faintest of smiles. She could feel the tension building—feel the quiet undercurrent of ambition, of secrets, and of power struggles just below the surface of their words. They were playing a game, and she was more than ready to participate.

But beneath the surface of this seemingly innocent negotiation, something darker was stirring—something neither she nor Valerius fully understood yet.

And Lyra was determined to find out what it was—before it was too late.

Four

Chapter 3: A Tempting Proposition

The room was bathed in the soft glow of candlelight, the flickering flames casting long shadows against the high stone walls of the Solaran palace. Outside, the wind howled through the narrow streets of the capital, carrying with it the chill of a coming winter. Inside, however, the air was warm, heavy with the scent of fresh lavender and the tension that hung between Lyra and the emissaries of Aeridor.

After their formal introductions, the delegation had settled into a tense silence, the usual pleasantries exchanged with minimal enthusiasm. The emissary from Aeridor, a man named Lord Maeron, had made his intentions clear: the time for negotiations had come. His master, Lord Valerius, had a proposal to offer. A proposal that would ensure the future prosperity of both kingdoms, he claimed. But Lyra was not so easily swayed by honeyed words.

She sat at the head of the long, oval table, her posture

impeccable, her green eyes glinting with determination. At her side, her trusted aide Mira stood, ever watchful, her gaze scanning the room as she discreetly observed the movements of the Aeridorian emissaries. For all their charm, Lyra knew that these men were not here to simply offer peace—they were here to secure something far more valuable.

The silence stretched for several moments, broken only by the soft clink of goblets being set down on the polished wood of the table. Then, Lord Maeron leaned forward, his voice low but firm.

"Lady Lyra," he began, his tone respectful but tinged with an underlying urgency, "Lord Valerius believes that a union between our two houses is not only desirable—it is essential. The strength of Aeridor, with its military prowess and resources, paired with Solara's political influence and strategic position, could change the course of history."

Lyra raised a brow but did not interrupt. She knew the script well enough by now. They were laying the groundwork for something much more significant.

"A union?" she asked, her voice deliberately neutral, though she couldn't entirely conceal the skepticism that lingered behind her words. "And how do you propose this union should come about? By what means, Lord Maeron?"

Maeron's lips curved into a smile, one that was as calculated as it was charming. "Through marriage, Lady Lyra. A marriage between you and Lord Valerius himself."

The words hung in the air like a challenge, and for a long moment, Lyra said nothing. Her gaze did not falter, though inside her heart quickened with a mixture of surprise, anger, and something else—something far more dangerous.

She had expected many things in this meeting, but this

Chapter 3: A Tempting Proposition

proposition… this was unexpected, even for Lord Valerius.

"The Lord of Aeridor wishes to marry me?" she asked, her tone measured, though the edge of incredulity was unmistakable. "And why would he choose me? I am, after all, the daughter of your enemy."

Lord Maeron did not flinch at her words. He was clearly prepared for the question. "Because, my lady, your value to our kingdom is not only in your bloodline but in your strategic mind. You are known throughout both kingdoms for your intellect, your political acumen, and your ability to maneuver in the most treacherous of courts. Lord Valerius recognizes these qualities and believes that together, your combined strength would be unmatched."

Lyra's mind raced as she carefully considered his words. The flattery, of course, was a part of the game, a tactic designed to soften her resistance. But she had long since learned how to see through such gestures. There was no genuine admiration in the air, only the cold, calculated drive for power.

"I see," she said, her voice calm but cool. "So, you would have me marry Lord Valerius to solidify a political alliance, a union of two kingdoms." She leaned back in her chair, her fingers drumming lightly on the armrest. "And what would Solara gain from this? What assurances can you give me that such a marriage would not mean the dissolution of our sovereignty?"

Lord Maeron's smile faltered for just a moment, but he quickly regained his composure. "In exchange for your hand, Lady Lyra, Solara would be granted the full protection of Aeridor's forces. A mutual defense pact would ensure that no external threat could destabilize either kingdom. In addition, a shared military command would allow for joint control of strategic territories."

Tempting the Enemy's Daughter

Lyra absorbed the offer, weighing it in her mind. A defense pact, joint military control... These were tempting incentives for any ruler. But she wasn't merely a pawn in this game of geopolitics. She had her own stakes to consider—her father's legacy, her people's freedom, and the fragile peace that still existed between the two nations. She would not sacrifice any of these without careful thought.

"And you believe," she said slowly, her voice laced with quiet challenge, "that I would agree to marry a man whose kingdom is responsible for the suffering of our people? A kingdom whose troops have ravaged our borders, whose spies have infiltrated our courts?"

Lord Maeron's expression darkened slightly, but he did not back down. "I believe that Lord Valerius is a man of vision, Lady Lyra. He seeks not war, but peace—a peace that can only be achieved through strength. By marrying him, you would not only secure Solara's future, but your own. You would be positioned as the true ruler of both kingdoms, with a say in every matter of consequence."

Her gaze sharpened. *Positioned as the true ruler of both kingdoms*—there it was, the real temptation. The offer was not just a union of two people. It was the promise of unparalleled power.

But at what cost?

Lyra's fingers tightened around the edge of the chair, her mind swirling with possibilities, each one darker than the last. She could play the game, rise to the top, shape the future of both kingdoms. But could she trust Lord Valerius? Could she trust Aeridor? Or was this simply another in a long line of manipulations designed to force her hand?

"I have heard your proposition, Lord Maeron," she said

Chapter 3: A Tempting Proposition

finally, her voice measured but cold. "And I will consider it. But understand this—my decision will not be made in haste. I will not be swayed by promises of power or protection alone. If Lord Valerius seeks my hand, he will have to prove that his intentions are true. Only then will I consider his offer."

Maeron bowed his head, his expression unreadable. "Of course, Lady Lyra. We would expect nothing less."

As the emissary turned to leave, Lyra's thoughts turned inward. *Marriage.* The word felt foreign on her tongue. She had always known that her fate, as the daughter of the Duke, would be tied to political alliances. But this… this was different. Lord Valerius, for all his power and ambition, was still a stranger to her. She could not allow herself to be swept away by the grandeur of his promises. Not without knowing what lay behind them.

But one thing was certain: Lord Valerius had just placed a dangerous card on the table. And she would need to decide how to play it—before the game consumed her.

Later that night, in the solitude of her chambers, Lyra stood before the mirror, her reflection barely visible in the candlelight. Her mind raced, torn between the weight of duty and the pull of something darker. She could feel the pressure building, the sense that the stakes were higher than ever before. Aeridor's offer was seductive, but it was also fraught with risks. She could not afford to be naïve.

Her gaze shifted to the small relic on her desk—the stone from her mother. The one that had hummed with strange energy when she had touched it earlier. The one that had shown her glimpses of something beyond time itself.

Perhaps, just perhaps, the answer lay not in the kingdoms,

Tempting the Enemy's Daughter

but in the secrets that had been hidden from her. The same secrets that Aeridor and Solara both seemed determined to keep buried.

And if she could uncover those secrets, perhaps she could decide not just the fate of Solara—but her own.

Lyra stared at the relic on her desk, the stone gleaming softly in the dim light. Her fingers hovered above it once again, but this time, she hesitated. The visions it had shown her earlier—those cryptic glimpses of fractured timelines and ancient betrayals—had left her unsettled. But she could not deny that the relic called to her. As much as it disturbed her, it also offered a deeper understanding, a way to peer beyond the immediate political games unfolding before her.

She had long suspected that the conflict between Solara and Aeridor was not as simple as it appeared, and now she had a sense that the answers she sought lay not in the halls of her father's court, but in forces beyond her understanding. If the stone held the key to those forces, she would take the risk.

Taking a deep breath, she placed her hand upon the stone once more.

The moment her fingers made contact, the faint hum returned, sending a wave of warmth through her arm, then quickly spreading across her chest. For a moment, it was like being immersed in a dream. The world around her seemed to blur, and the air itself thickened with an almost tangible energy.

The images returned, clearer this time—fragments of a story she had not yet fully grasped.

She saw her mother, standing in the ruins of an ancient temple, her expression grim but determined. Around her, glowing runes flared in the air like fireflies, illuminating the

Chapter 3: A Tempting Proposition

dark stone. Lyra could feel her mother's presence strongly, as though she were standing beside her in that very room.

"You must understand, my daughter," her mother's voice echoed in Lyra's mind, *"The kingdoms are bound by more than just blood or alliances. The fracture in our world runs deeper, and it is not just the politics of men that keep us apart."*

The vision shifted, and Lyra saw a rift in the fabric of reality itself—like a tear in the sky, a crack that pulsed with dark energy. She saw figures moving through it—figures neither fully human nor fully something else. They were cloaked in shadow, their features indiscernible, but their presence was unmistakable. They were not of Aeridor, not of Solara. They were… otherworldly.

"The fracture is not just between us and Aeridor," her mother's voice continued, *"It is between this world and another. And it was caused by a betrayal—a betrayal that must never be uncovered, or else all of us will fall."*

The vision flickered again, and Lyra saw a man she did not recognize—tall, with sharp features and dark eyes that gleamed with an unnatural intelligence. He stood at the center of a great hall, surrounded by noblemen and women, but he was not one of them. There was something wrong about him, an aura of unease that made her heart race.

The vision faded as quickly as it had come, leaving Lyra breathless, her skin tingling with the aftereffects of the strange energy. She pulled her hand back from the stone, feeling disoriented, as if she had just woken from a long, unsettling dream.

Her mind was awash with questions. The fracture her mother had spoken of—the tear between worlds—could this be the true cause of the discord between Aeridor and Solara?

Was the conflict between their kingdoms merely a surface conflict, a way to hide something much larger, much more dangerous? And what had her mother meant by betrayal?

Lyra looked down at the stone, her thoughts racing. She had learned more than she had bargained for, but there was still so much left unexplained. She couldn't afford to ignore these revelations, not when they could hold the key to everything—the political game, her potential marriage to Valerius, the fate of her kingdom, and perhaps even her own survival.

Suddenly, there was a knock at the door.

Lyra quickly pulled herself together, wiping any trace of the vision from her face before turning to answer. "Enter," she called.

The door creaked open, and Mira stepped inside, her sharp eyes immediately assessing the scene. Lyra had no doubt that her aide had sensed something was off, even without knowing exactly what had transpired.

"My lady," Mira said softly, her voice carrying the weight of unspoken concerns. "You requested to be informed when Lord Valerius's emissary had returned to the castle. He has arrived, and the meeting is set for this evening."

Lyra nodded, her mind already returning to the task at hand. The strange vision had left her shaken, but there was little time for distractions. She had to be sharp. The stakes had just been raised.

"I'm ready," Lyra replied, her voice steady once more. She would deal with whatever had just surfaced later. For now, she had a kingdom to save—and a dangerous proposition to consider.

The grand hall was alive with anticipation as Lyra entered, her

Chapter 3: A Tempting Proposition

steps purposeful and deliberate. The Aeridorian emissaries had gathered in a corner of the room, speaking in low voices as they awaited her arrival. Lord Maeron stood at the front, his usual confident demeanor in place, though his eyes betrayed a certain wariness when they met hers.

"Lady Lyra," Maeron said, bowing low. "It is an honor to have you join us this evening."

Lyra's gaze swept across the room, taking in the figures gathered. Lord Valerius was conspicuously absent, as she had expected. It was one of his emissaries who had been sent to negotiate the finer details. Still, the weight of his absence was palpable. The true power of Aeridor was never far behind.

"I trust the preparations are to your satisfaction?" Lyra asked, her tone polite but laced with an edge. "I was not informed that this meeting would require such secrecy."

Maeron smiled, though it did not reach his eyes. "Secrecy, Lady Lyra, is a necessary element of diplomacy. It is in these moments, when trust has yet to be established, that our words hold the most weight."

Her lips pressed together in a thin line, but she said nothing. She had no intention of letting the emissaries control the tempo of the discussion. She was the one who would decide if the marriage proposal was worth considering.

"As we discussed earlier," Maeron continued, "Lord Valerius has every intention of strengthening the ties between our kingdoms. The marriage alliance is merely the first step toward securing that future."

"I understand," Lyra replied coolly. "But I must admit, Lord Maeron, that I find this proposal... sudden. The timing is curious, especially given the current state of affairs."

Maeron's eyes gleamed with a knowing look. "Ah, Lady

Tempting the Enemy's Daughter

Lyra, your wisdom precedes you. I had a feeling you would see the complexities involved. But I assure you, this is the only way forward."

She narrowed her eyes. "And what, precisely, is it that you believe I must do to make this union work?"

Maeron's gaze flickered toward the other emissaries, a subtle signal for them to remain quiet. "Lord Valerius is not without his share of enemies, as you are no doubt aware. This marriage, if you accept it, will not only solidify the strength of Aeridor, but it will secure your position as a true power broker, not only in Solara but in the future of both our realms."

His words were measured, but Lyra could hear the veiled threat behind them. Accepting this marriage would not be a simple matter of duty. It would change everything—her role, her power, her future. She would become more than just the daughter of the Duke of Solara. She would become a queen in the making, a queen whose very existence could tip the balance of power between the two kingdoms.

But what would be the cost of such a union? And could she trust Lord Valerius—and the forces behind him—enough to take that step?

"I will consider your offer," Lyra said finally, her voice even. "But as I told your emissary earlier, I will not make any decisions in haste."

Maeron bowed once more, but there was a flicker of frustration behind his carefully composed demeanor. "Of course, Lady Lyra. We will give you the time you need. But know this: Lord Valerius's offer is not one that can be made twice."

And with that, the emissary withdrew, leaving Lyra alone with her thoughts. The game had begun in earnest, and it was

Chapter 3: A Tempting Proposition

clear that neither side would back down without a fight.

As Lyra turned toward the window, her thoughts again turned to the stone on her desk. The relic that had whispered of something greater.

A union between kingdoms. A marriage for power. But in the end, perhaps there was something else at stake—a far greater prize that neither Aeridor nor Solara fully understood.

And Lyra would be the one to uncover it, no matter the cost.

Five

Chapter 4: Crossing Enemy Lines

The dawn light filtered through the high windows of the Solaran palace, casting a pale glow across the stone floors. Lyra stood before the mirror in her chambers, her fingers brushing over the intricate embroidery of her gown—deep blue silk, with threads of silver that shimmered as she moved. She had dressed carefully this morning, for today was a day of negotiation, but also of strategy. The choices she made today could alter the course of her life and the future of her kingdom.

Mira entered quietly, her usual expression unreadable. Her eyes lingered for a moment on the gown, noting its significance, before she approached Lyra with the customary report.

"The carriage is prepared, my lady," Mira said, her tone neutral but sharp. "Your father has authorized the diplomatic visit to Aeridor, though he remains… cautious. I trust you

Chapter 4: Crossing Enemy Lines

have everything you need?"

Lyra nodded, her expression distant. "Everything," she murmured, but her thoughts were elsewhere, shifting between the weight of her mother's cryptic words and the dangerous allure of Lord Valerius's proposition.

She had agreed to travel to Aeridor, not because she was eager for the alliance—or the marriage—but because she understood that it was the next move in a game far larger than she had anticipated. She needed answers, and she would find them within the walls of Aeridor Castle. There were whispers of secrets buried deep in the castle's bowels, rumors of forgotten treaties and betrayals that stretched back centuries. If she could uncover them, perhaps she could understand the true nature of the forces that shaped this fractured world—and her place in it.

As Lyra made her way to the courtyard, Mira in tow, the carriage was already waiting. The horses were restless, as though they, too, could sense the tension in the air. The road to Aeridor was long, and the journey itself would be filled with subtle challenges. Every move would be watched, every word scrutinized. She could not afford to show weakness—not to Aeridor's emissaries, and certainly not to Lord Valerius himself.

She stepped into the carriage, and Mira settled beside her, the door closing behind them with a soft thud. The world outside the window seemed to blur as they passed through the streets of Solara, heading toward the border and the kingdom that had once been their enemy.

The journey was longer than Lyra had anticipated. Days passed in a haze of travel, interrupted only by brief stops at outlying villages and forts, where her father's banner flew high and proud, reminding the people that their Duke's daughter was en route to secure peace for them all. The countryside of Solara was rugged, its terrain as wild and unpredictable as the political landscape Lyra now navigated. She had always been a student of politics, but the deeper she delved into this game, the more she realized how little she truly understood of the forces at play.

Each night, after the carriage had made its way into temporary lodgings, Lyra would retire to her quarters, where she poured over maps of the borderlands, ancient texts her mother had left behind, and reports from her father's spies. The names of generals, lords, and advisers were listed, some familiar, others unfamiliar but still important. But it was the notes about strange occurrences—rumors of shadowy figures moving between the kingdoms, strange sights in the sky—that captured her attention most.

She couldn't shake the feeling that something far more sinister than political maneuvering was at work. The fracture her mother had mentioned. The rift between worlds. Was it truly a magical event, or something else entirely? Lyra was beginning to believe that the answer lay in Aeridor itself, hidden in the secrets they kept buried under layers of history.

On the fourth night of their journey, as they passed into the rolling hills near the border, Mira approached Lyra's carriage with a concerned expression. "My lady, there are rumors reaching us from the local villages. Word is that Aeridor's forces are... preparing for something. Something large."

Lyra turned to Mira, arching an eyebrow. "What kind of preparations?"

"Unclear," Mira replied, her voice low. "Some say it is

Chapter 4: Crossing Enemy Lines

military in nature. Others say it involves... something else. The spies report that something strange has been happening in the western provinces, near the border."

Lyra's pulse quickened. *Something strange*—it was the same kind of vague report she had seen in the intelligence her father's spies had gathered about Aeridor. She couldn't ignore it.

"Keep your eyes open," Lyra instructed. "And don't speak of this to anyone else. Not yet."

By the time they reached the border, the atmosphere had shifted. Aeridor's lands were not as grand as Solara's, but there was a weight to the air here—something ancient and oppressive, like the very ground they walked upon had borne witness to wars and bloodshed long before either kingdom's history had been written. The people they encountered were reserved, their expressions wary. Lyra couldn't help but notice how few smiled, even as they greeted her with polite bows.

The border crossing was a quiet affair, and the moment Lyra passed into Aeridor's territory, she felt a chill settle over her. She had crossed into enemy territory—not just as the daughter of Duke Alaric, but as a representative of a kingdom that had been at war with Aeridor for generations. She was keenly aware of the danger she faced, but more than that, she felt the weight of history pressing down on her.

As they drew closer to Aeridor Castle, Lyra's thoughts grew heavier. The castle loomed ahead, a fortress of dark stone perched high on a jagged hill. The towers were tall, their spires piercing the sky, and the walls, though well-maintained, carried the marks of age—small cracks and weathered stones that spoke of centuries of conflict. She had heard rumors of

Tempting the Enemy's Daughter

secret rooms, hidden passages, and forgotten halls beneath the castle. It was said that Aeridor's rulers had secrets buried deep within these walls, some of them far older than the kingdom itself.

The carriage came to a halt at the castle gates, and Lyra felt a tightening in her chest. This was no longer just about a political marriage, a mere diplomatic gesture—it was about uncovering the truth. The truths that had been kept hidden, even from her, despite all her father's efforts to guard his own kingdom's history.

Lord Valerius was waiting for her. He stood at the foot of the stairs leading up to the grand entrance, his figure outlined against the backdrop of the castle, the tall stone archway above him framing his presence like a king awaiting his guest. His dark hair was neatly combed, his cloak flowing regally behind him. He looked every inch the lord of Aeridor, confident, composed, and entirely in control.

For a moment, their eyes met, and something passed between them—a flicker of recognition, of mutual understanding. But it was quickly masked by the formalities that followed.

"Lady Lyra," he greeted her, his voice warm, though there was an edge to it. "I trust your journey was comfortable?"

"It was," Lyra replied, stepping out of the carriage, her gaze never leaving his. "But it is not comfort I seek in Aeridor, Lord Valerius. I seek answers."

Valerius gave a slight, knowing smile, though his eyes held a hint of something darker. "Answers, you say? You have come to the right place, then. Aeridor holds many secrets. But they are not easily uncovered."

Lyra studied him carefully, her mind already formulating

Chapter 4: Crossing Enemy Lines

her next move. She had crossed into enemy lines, yes—but she was no longer just the daughter of a Duke. She was a player in a game that was larger than either of them could fully comprehend.

And in this game, there would be no room for hesitation. Not if she was to uncover the truths that lay beneath the surface of Aeridor's stone walls—and not if she was to survive what lay ahead.

As the heavy gates of Aeridor Castle creaked shut behind them, Lyra felt a quiet foreboding settle in her chest. She had crossed the boundary of a kingdom once considered an enemy—now an uneasy ally. The chill of the air seemed to deepen as they ascended the long, winding stairs to the castle's main courtyard, and she could hear the distant clang of blacksmiths and the low murmurs of soldiers stationed at various posts. The vast stone walls of the castle seemed to close in around her, their sheer weight making the air feel heavy, almost suffocating.

Lord Valerius had already turned toward the entrance, leading the way up to the grand double doors. The soldiers stationed there bowed low as he passed, their demeanor respectful but guarded. Lyra could sense their watchful eyes following her every movement, sizing her up as she stepped into their fortress.

Inside the castle, the atmosphere was somber. The high ceilings, adorned with tapestries of ancient battles and heraldry, echoed with each footstep. The large hallways were dimly lit by flickering torches, casting long shadows that seemed to stretch and twist along the stone floors. The coldness of the air was palpable, but it was the silence that struck Lyra the most. Here, in the heart of Aeridor, the tension was not just political—it was something older, something that lingered in the very walls.

Lord Valerius led her down the corridor to a large, ornately carved door. As he opened it, Lyra took in the room before her. It was grand, yet stark in its simplicity—a long wooden table sat at the center, surrounded by high-backed chairs, each one worn from use. A few maps were spread out across the table, and several books and scrolls were scattered in organized chaos.

"This is where our most important meetings are held," Valerius said, gesturing to the room with a sweep of his hand. "I hope you find it to your liking, though I suspect your interest is less in our decor and more in our discussions."

Lyra took a moment to absorb the room's austere elegance before answering. "I've never been one for frills, Lord Valerius. I prefer the substance of a conversation over the appearance of its setting."

He smiled slightly, though his eyes remained guarded, as though assessing her words carefully. "Then I'm glad to hear it. Perhaps you'll find our talks to be just as direct."

Valerius waved a hand to the far side of the room, where a fire crackled in a hearth, offering the only warmth in the otherwise chilly space. "Please, make yourself comfortable. There's no need for formality between us—at least, not yet."

Lyra moved toward the fire, letting its warmth sink into her bones, though her mind remained focused. The air here felt different, charged. There was an almost oppressive weight in the atmosphere, a sense that things were not as they seemed. If anything, she had only grown more convinced that there was something deeper at play in Aeridor than a mere political alliance.

Chapter 4: Crossing Enemy Lines

As she approached the fire, she allowed her gaze to linger on the maps laid across the table. They seemed to chart not just the familiar borders of Aeridor and Solara, but other areas—regions further to the east, where the terrain grew more inhospitable, the maps marked with cryptic symbols that piqued her curiosity.

Lord Valerius watched her closely. "You're sharp, Lady Lyra," he said, his voice betraying a hint of amusement. "I see you've noticed the maps. Those are of areas we've recently… explored. There are places, beyond the borderlands, where the land itself behaves differently. Strange phenomena. Not quite magic, but something that defies understanding. We're investigating it."

Her heart skipped a beat at his words. *Strange phenomena? Beyond the borders?* It sounded like something from her mother's cryptic warnings. She studied the map more intently, wondering if the strange occurrences Mira had heard about in the borderlands were connected to these uncharted areas. Were these the same "fractures" her mother had spoken of— the disturbances in the fabric of reality that had somehow been linked to the ancient pact between the two kingdoms?

"I was unaware that Aeridor had interests beyond its borders," Lyra said carefully, keeping her voice neutral. "I thought your kingdom had enough on its plate with internal matters, let alone delving into the unknown."

Valerius' eyes glinted with a knowing look, as though he could see through her feigned disinterest. "That's the thing about kingdoms like mine, Lady Lyra. We don't just protect our borders; we push them. Sometimes, the answers we need aren't within the walls of our own castle or on the maps we know. Sometimes, they lie in places that others might

Tempting the Enemy's Daughter

consider... too dangerous to explore."

Dangerous? Lyra felt a tightening in her chest, but she masked it with a thin smile. "And you believe these... explorations could hold the key to peace between our kingdoms?"

Valerius' gaze lingered on her for a moment, and Lyra could sense he was weighing his response. Finally, he nodded slowly. "I believe that in order to truly secure a lasting peace between Solara and Aeridor, we must look beyond our petty grievances and the borders that separate us. The fractured state of our world is not just a political issue—it's a matter of survival. And if you're willing to entertain the possibility, Lady Lyra, I believe you and I can uncover truths that will change the future of both our kingdoms."

Her thoughts raced, the tension mounting. He was offering her something more than just an alliance or a marriage contract—he was offering her an opportunity to uncover the very forces that might shape the world itself. But it felt dangerous. What was he truly asking of her? Was he simply playing a game of diplomacy, or did he have a deeper, more personal stake in these explorations?

"Truths, you say?" Lyra repeated, her voice carefully controlled. "And what kind of truths would those be, Lord Valerius?"

He turned away from the table and moved toward the large window that overlooked the sprawling lands of Aeridor. The sun had begun to set, casting an orange glow over the hills. As he spoke, his voice softened, a hint of something almost... wistful in his tone.

"Truths about the pact," he said quietly. "The ancient pact that has bound our kingdoms for centuries. It was broken long before the first sword was drawn between us, Lady Lyra.

Chapter 4: Crossing Enemy Lines

And the consequences of that breach are still unfolding, even now."

Lyra's heart beat faster. The ancient pact. She had known the basics of it—how the two kingdoms had once been united in a powerful bond, only to fracture after a betrayal that neither kingdom would ever fully admit. But the details had always been shrouded in secrecy. Could Valerius be offering her a glimpse into those hidden truths? And if so, what was he really hoping to gain from her involvement?

"And what exactly are you hoping to uncover, Lord Valerius?" she asked, her voice low but sharp. "The truth about the pact? Or something far more dangerous?"

Valerius turned back to face her, his gaze intense. "Perhaps both, Lady Lyra. But sometimes, the only way to uncover the truth is to embrace danger. Will you embrace it, Lady Lyra? Will you cross the lines, not just of kingdoms, but of history itself?"

His words hung in the air like a challenge, one that Lyra could not ignore. She felt the weight of his gaze on her, the magnetism of his presence drawing her in. There was something dangerous about this man, something that both intrigued and unsettled her.

But it was not just Lord Valerius who posed a danger to her now—it was the secrets buried beneath Aeridor's stone walls, the ones she had come here to uncover.

And if she was to navigate this treacherous game, she would need to decide just how far she was willing to go to uncover the truth—*and whether she could trust Valerius enough to walk that line with him.*

Her heart heavy with uncertainty, Lyra met his gaze and replied quietly, "I will not turn away from the truth, Lord

Valerius. But beware—some truths are not meant to be uncovered."

He smiled, though it was edged with something darker, something that made her skin prickle. "We shall see, Lady Lyra. We shall see."

And as the shadows deepened around them, Lyra knew that this was only the beginning of a far more dangerous game—a game that would test her loyalty, her cunning, and perhaps even her very soul.

The fire crackled in the hearth, casting flickering light across the room. Lyra felt the heat, but it did little to ease the tension creeping up her spine. The walls of Aeridor Castle seemed to pulse with an energy of their own, as though they, too, were watching, waiting for something to happen. Perhaps that was the price of power—everything, even the stones beneath your feet, conspiring to remind you of the weight of the decisions you made.

Lord Valerius's words hung in the air, dense with unspoken implications. *Truths about the pact*. It was a subject that Lyra had been both taught and warned against, her father's words always cautioning her to tread lightly when it came to the ancient alliance that had once bound Aeridor and Solara. It was the source of their mutual animosity, the origin of every betrayal, every war that had followed. Yet, here was Valerius, suggesting they could rewrite that history, unearth the truth—whatever it was—and perhaps even change the fate of both kingdoms.

But *what* truth was he really after? And what would it cost them to uncover it?

Her mind raced as she tried to piece together the puzzle. Valerius had opened a door, but she couldn't yet see what lay

Chapter 4: Crossing Enemy Lines

beyond it. She had always trusted her instincts, and right now, her instincts were screaming that this wasn't just about securing peace between their kingdoms. This was something deeper—something darker—and the more she pushed, the more she might end up losing.

She took a slow breath, trying to steady herself. "You speak of truths, Lord Valerius," she said, her voice steady, "but truth, like history, is often subject to the eyes of the beholder. What you see as the 'truth' might not align with the interests of my kingdom—or even your own."

Valerius gave a slight, contemplative nod, as if considering her words carefully. He moved to stand beside the table, his back to her for a moment as he glanced over the scattered maps and the ancient tomes that lay open. When he finally spoke again, his voice was quieter, more contemplative, as if the weight of the subject had shifted in his mind.

"You are right, of course. History is written by the victors, and truth is often twisted to serve the agenda of the powerful. But there is a deeper truth beneath the surface, one that both our kingdoms have forgotten in their obsession with borders and crowns. What we have fought for, what we have lost... it was never meant to be this way."

Lyra's curiosity piqued despite herself, but she held her ground. "What do you mean? What was it meant to be?"

Valerius turned toward her, his gaze direct but shrouded in something unspoken. "There was a time—before the wars, before the betrayal—that the kingdoms of Aeridor and Solara were united, not just in alliance, but in purpose. The pact wasn't merely a treaty of peace; it was a promise to protect something far greater. Something powerful enough to change the fate of this world. But something happened. A fracture. A corruption that twisted the very essence of our lands."

His eyes darkened, and for a moment, Lyra could see the weight of his words settling on him. This was more than just a story. This was personal. Whatever had happened, whatever had broken the pact, had clearly marked Valerius in a way that no mere politician's speech could convey.

"I've heard the legends," Lyra said softly, her voice guarded. "The pact was broken by a betrayal. Some say it was your ancestor who struck the first blow. Others claim it was a failure of magic, a mistake that shattered the balance of both kingdoms."

Valerius's lips twitched, but there was no smile in his expression. He moved toward the window again, his back to her. "The truth is far more complicated than any of those stories, Lady Lyra. Yes, there was a betrayal. But it wasn't a simple matter of one kingdom against the other. It was… something else entirely. The pact was broken because the magic that bound us together was never meant to be contained by kingdoms. It was older, far older. It was tied to the very fabric of this world."

Lyra's mind raced as she processed his words. *The magic*—she had known it was part of the pact, but she had never considered its true nature. The magic wasn't just a binding force between two nations; it was something primordial, something tied to the land itself. And if what Valerius was suggesting was true, then the breach of that pact wasn't just a political failure—it was a rupture in the very order of the world.

"And now you believe you can restore it," Lyra said, her voice cutting through the silence.

Valerius turned toward her again, his expression inscrutable.

Chapter 4: Crossing Enemy Lines

"I do. And I believe you can help me."

Lyra's heart skipped a beat. She had anticipated many things—diplomatic games, marriage proposals, political alliances—but this was something entirely different. She had come to Aeridor to understand the motivations behind the proposed marriage alliance, to secure her position and her kingdom's future. But now, it seemed she was being asked to take part in something far more dangerous: a quest to heal a wound that had festered for centuries.

"I don't know how I can help," she replied slowly, her mind still struggling to comprehend the magnitude of his words. "What role do you think I can play in restoring this... ancient magic?"

Valerius walked toward her, his steps measured, as though carefully choosing his words. "Your bloodline, Lady Lyra, is not as distant from the magic of the pact as you might think. The line of Duke Alaric was once intertwined with the very forces that governed the peace between our kingdoms. Your mother—she knew more than she ever let on. I suspect she was closer to understanding the truth than anyone realized."

Lyra's breath caught in her throat. Her mother? She had always been told that her mother's death was a tragedy of politics, a result of the ever-shifting tides of war and diplomacy. But Valerius's words cast a new light on things. *Her mother had known something...* What had she hidden from her? What had she kept from her own daughter?

Before Lyra could respond, a soft knock on the door interrupted the conversation. A servant entered, bowing low before speaking quickly, "My lord, the Council has requested your presence. There are urgent matters they wish to discuss regarding the borderlands."

Valerius sighed and gave a curt nod. "I see. The Council's timing is impeccable, as always. Please, tell them I will be there shortly."

Turning back to Lyra, his demeanor shifted slightly, but the intensity in his gaze remained. "This conversation is far from over, Lady Lyra. I trust you'll give some thought to what I've shared. The truth I speak of… it's not just about healing the past. It's about saving the future."

Lyra nodded, though her mind was spinning with a hundred questions. She needed time to think, to process everything he had said—and, more than that, she needed to understand her mother's connection to this world-altering secret. The more Valerius spoke, the more she realized that she had been living with half of the story her entire life. Now, it seemed, it was time to uncover the rest.

"I will think on it," she said, though in her heart, she knew that the more she discovered, the harder it would be to walk away from this.

Valerius's smile returned, but it was enigmatic, as though he knew something she didn't. "Good. I look forward to hearing your thoughts. Until then, Lady Lyra, I must attend to other matters. But I hope you find your stay here… enlightening."

With that, he turned and walked toward the door, leaving Lyra alone in the quiet, dimly lit room. She stared at the crackling fire, her thoughts swirling with the weight of what she had just learned—and what it meant for her future.

The fire was warm, but the world she had just stepped into was colder than anything she had ever known. And the deeper she ventured, the harder it would be to retreat.

A voice in the back of her mind urged caution. But another voice—the voice of curiosity, the voice of ambition—

Chapter 4: Crossing Enemy Lines

whispered that some doors, once opened, could never be closed again.

And Lyra was certain that the door she had just stepped through led to a truth far darker than anything she had ever imagined.

Six

Chapter 5: The Masquerade Ball

The night of the masquerade arrived with an air of expectancy. The streets of Aeridor's capital were alive with a strange sort of energy, as if the kingdom itself held its breath for the evening's festivities. The grand castle loomed in the distance, its silhouette sharp against the ink-black sky, while lanterns lining the streets cast long, flickering shadows that seemed to whisper secrets in the wind.

Lyra stood before her mirror, the weight of her decision pressing down on her shoulders like a heavy cloak. She had known this evening would come, of course—her father had spoken of it in his letters, and Valerius had mentioned it briefly when they first met. But now, as the time for the ball drew near, it felt as though the weight of it had become something far greater than mere formality. Tonight, the court of Aeridor would be watching her, and the eyes of her enemies would be sharpest. She could almost feel the invisible threads of power

Chapter 5: The Masquerade Ball

weaving around her, connecting her to those who sought her favor—and those who sought to manipulate her.

The dress that had been chosen for her was unlike anything Lyra had ever worn. A gown of deep midnight blue, its fabric shimmering with the faintest touch of starlight, hugged her frame like liquid. It was elegant, flattering—but it wasn't her. The intricate lace at the bodice was woven with delicate golden thread, the design mimicking the patterns of stars and constellations. It was as if she were meant to be a part of something larger—a piece in a grand design. She wondered if the dress, like the kingdom itself, was trying to tell her who she was meant to be, or who others thought she should be.

She sighed, brushing a stray lock of hair from her face as she turned to the servant standing silently at the door. The woman's eyes were lowered, though Lyra could sense her curiosity just beneath the surface. She was no doubt eager to see the duchess's daughter make her debut in Aeridor's high court.

"Shall I fetch your mask, my lady?" the servant asked softly, her voice almost lost in the high, vaulted room.

Lyra nodded absently. "Yes, please."

When the servant returned with the mask, Lyra took it without hesitation. It was a beautiful creation—delicate filigree of gold and silver that clung to her face like a secret. A simple mask, one that covered only her eyes, allowing her to hide behind its ornate design. It felt like an armor, both a shield and a weapon, for who she would be in the ballroom tonight was not the same woman who had entered Aeridor's gates.

She was no longer simply the daughter of Duke Alaric—*Lyra of Solara*. Tonight, she was whoever she needed to be.

Tempting the Enemy's Daughter

The ballroom was as grand as any of the castles she had seen in Solara—perhaps more so. Towering windows framed the night sky, but the view was entirely obscured by layers of velvet curtains, leaving only the glow of a hundred candles to illuminate the room. The high vaulted ceilings seemed to stretch into infinity, and the marble floors gleamed beneath the rhythmic shuffle of dance.

Lyra entered the room with a calm, measured step, her heart beating in time with the soft murmur of courtly voices. Her mask shielded her identity, but it did little to lessen the weight of the eyes that turned her way. She could feel them— scrutinizing, judging, analyzing. They would never speak to her outright; that wasn't how these games were played. But in this court, the glances spoke louder than words.

The figures around her were dressed in a kaleidoscope of colors—rich silks, brocades, and velvets that made the room seem like a painting come to life. Lords and ladies mingled in clusters, their laughter soft but insistent. The nobles of Aeridor were careful with their expressions, and their words more so. This was a place where no one was ever entirely honest, and everything was cloaked in layers of carefully constructed facades.

"Lady Lyra, you look exquisite," came a voice from behind her. Lyra didn't need to turn to know who it was. The voice was deep, smooth, and far too self-assured to belong to anyone else but Lord Valerius.

She turned slowly, allowing her mask to hide the flicker of emotion that crossed her face. He was standing a few paces away, dressed in a formal black coat, its embroidered silver trim matching the ice-blue of his eyes. His dark hair was swept back, though a few strands had fallen over his brow, adding a

Chapter 5: The Masquerade Ball

casual charm to his otherwise composed appearance. He, too, wore a mask—black and simple, just enough to obscure the sharp line of his jaw and the intensity of his gaze.

"Thank you, Lord Valerius," she replied, her voice smooth but distant. "You, too, appear quite… distinguished this evening."

His smile was slight, but the gleam in his eyes suggested he had been waiting for her arrival. "I was beginning to think you might not come," he said, stepping a little closer. "But then, you wouldn't let the grand stage of Aeridor's court go unchallenged, would you?"

Lyra tilted her head slightly, studying him as he stood before her. He was close enough now that she could feel the heat of his presence, but his gaze was fixed, unyielding. She felt the strange pressure of his eyes on her, as though he were peering into her very soul.

"I've never been one to shy away from a challenge," she replied, her voice soft, yet sharp. "And I certainly wouldn't start now."

Valerius chuckled, his eyes still locked on hers. "Good. You understand the stakes, then. Tonight is not just a celebration. It's a test—a test for both of us. The game we've set in motion cannot be undone. Not now."

Lyra felt a sudden wave of unease ripple through her, but she kept her expression neutral. The weight of his words hung in the air, as though the masquerade itself had become something far more significant than a mere social affair. She had sensed the undercurrent of tension throughout the evening, but now it was undeniable—every delicate step, every graceful turn in the waltz, every shared glance between noble families was a move in a larger game. And the stakes were higher than a

Tempting the Enemy's Daughter

simple alliance between kingdoms.

"What do you mean by 'test,' Lord Valerius?" she asked, her voice more clipped than she intended.

His smile faltered, but only slightly. He leaned in a fraction closer, lowering his voice. "The ball isn't just a celebration of peace, Lady Lyra. It is a cover for something far more important. Tonight, we make our allegiances clear to those who are watching. And we must be careful with whom we align ourselves."

The words struck Lyra like a cold wind. She had suspected as much—the air in the castle had been thick with hidden meanings, with veiled gestures and whispered promises. But hearing it directly from him only confirmed what she had feared. Tonight, alliances would be formed, and power would shift in ways she could not yet understand.

Before she could respond, the music swelled, and a new partner appeared—a masked nobleman, his identity hidden behind a smooth black mask. He bowed low before her, extending a gloved hand. "Lady Lyra, may I have the honor of this dance?"

Lyra hesitated for only a moment before accepting the offer. Her instincts told her that to refuse would be to make a statement she wasn't ready to make.

As she placed her hand in his, she felt the subtle tension of the room rise. Every step she took, every movement she made, was being watched—by allies, by enemies, and by those who were both. The dance began, slow and elegant at first, with the music sweeping them across the polished floor. But beneath the graceful steps and delicate twirls, Lyra's mind raced.

Who was the masked nobleman, and why had he approached her so quickly? Was he simply another courtier eager to catch

Chapter 5: The Masquerade Ball

her attention—or was he part of something far larger, a part of the web of alliances Valerius had alluded to?

As the dance continued, she couldn't shake the feeling that the answers she sought were not just beyond the walls of Aeridor—but within them. And in this grand ballroom of masked faces and hidden intentions, she would have to uncover them quickly—or risk losing herself in the game entirely.

The music shifted, faster now, and the tempo quickened. Lyra's heart beat in time with it, and for the first time that evening, she let herself move with the rhythm, hiding behind her mask as she danced—each step carrying her further into a world where no one could be trusted, and every word, every glance, might be a lie.

The game had begun.

Top of Form

The dance seemed to stretch endlessly, the floor spinning beneath Lyra's feet as the masked nobleman led her effortlessly through the steps. She was acutely aware of the eyes watching her from every corner of the ballroom, but the more she focused on the rhythm of the waltz, the easier it became to shut them out. The music swept through the air, and her mind slipped into a trance-like state. Yet beneath the elegance of the dance, a subtle tension pulsed through her—a warning that the game she was now part of was far from simple.

The nobleman's gloved hand was cool, but firm as it guided her. His steps were confident, his grip never faltering, but there was an odd detachment in his touch, as though he were merely going through the motions, performing a role rather than enjoying the dance. His mask was smooth, his features concealed, but Lyra could tell there was something deliberate

Tempting the Enemy's Daughter

about the way he maneuvered, as though he were keenly aware of the significance of every step.

As they glided across the floor, her thoughts turned back to Valerius. His words about alliances and tests had unsettled her. Was he speaking of political alliances—or something more personal? His gaze had held a depth of meaning earlier, something that was both alluring and dangerous. He had made it clear that there were no innocents in this game.

When the dance came to an end, the masked nobleman gave a shallow bow and stepped away without a word, leaving Lyra to catch her breath. Her heart beat faster—not from the exertion, but from the realization that the night was only just beginning, and the stakes were higher than she had imagined.

She scanned the ballroom, her gaze naturally drifting to the far side of the room, where Lord Valerius stood, a figure of quiet command amidst the swirling guests. His mask still concealed his expression, but there was no mistaking the way people gravitated toward him. His presence seemed to fill the room, a subtle force that pulled people in without a word. A quiet power.

And then, as if sensing her eyes upon him, Valerius turned toward her. His gaze locked with hers across the distance, and in that instant, something unspoken passed between them. A silent acknowledgment of the invisible thread that connected them. Despite the distance, despite the sea of faces, the world around her seemed to narrow, focusing on him, the man who had been both a mystery and an enigma since her arrival.

She took a step toward him, only to be intercepted by another figure—a tall woman in a flowing red gown with intricate golden embroidery, her mask resembling the fierce face of a lion. Her eyes, sharp and calculating, fixed on Lyra

Chapter 5: The Masquerade Ball

with a glance that felt like a challenge.

"Lady Lyra," the woman said, her voice cool but not unfriendly. "How wonderful to see you here. I am Lady Isolde of House Raelan. I do hope you find Aeridor's court to your liking."

Lyra nodded politely, though she couldn't suppress the feeling that the woman was sizing her up, as if measuring her worth, searching for a crack in her composure. "It is certainly a grand spectacle," she replied smoothly, her voice soft but laced with subtle steel. "I imagine this is a night of great importance for the kingdom."

"Indeed," Lady Isolde agreed, her smile thin and sharp. "But it is not just for Aeridor, is it? No, tonight is about more than just revelry. It is about power. And power," she leaned in ever so slightly, her tone dropping to a near whisper, "is never without its price."

Lyra's brow furrowed slightly, but her smile never faltered. "Then I suppose I should prepare myself for whatever price may come."

Lady Isolde's smile widened, her eyes gleaming with an almost predatory satisfaction. "I do hope you are ready, Lady Lyra. But you must forgive me," she added, with a delicate wave of her hand. "I must speak with Lord Valerius. I will leave you to enjoy the evening."

Before Lyra could respond, Lady Isolde turned, gliding through the crowd with the ease of someone who had spent her entire life navigating the intricacies of court politics. She didn't look back, but Lyra had the distinct sense that the woman had placed her firmly in a category—one to be watched, perhaps, but certainly not to be trusted.

Lyra watched Lady Isolde approach Valerius, who greeted

Tempting the Enemy's Daughter

her with a measured smile. His eyes, however, flickered back to Lyra for the briefest of moments—just long enough for her to wonder if it was intentional, or if she was imagining things.

The tension in the room seemed to heighten as the music swelled once again, and the guests around her fell into their own private conversations and dances. Lyra had no illusions that the ball was anything other than a game of carefully crafted masks—both literal and metaphorical—and she was a player in this game whether she liked it or not.

Her gaze drifted back to the floor, where a number of dancers twirled in time with the music. In the midst of the grand spectacle, she realized there was a single, dangerous truth: alliances were being formed in this ballroom—alliances that were as fragile as glass, held together by fragile promises and the thinnest of veils.

She took a deep breath and steeled herself. Tonight, she would be watched, tested, perhaps even manipulated. But she would not be a pawn.

Her thoughts were interrupted by the soft touch of a hand at her elbow. She turned to find a courtier, a man of middle age with a thin, calculating smile and a mask of gold that glittered like a sunbeam. He bowed deeply before her, his eyes gleaming with the excitement of his own machinations.

"Lady Lyra," he said, his voice almost too smooth, "I am Baron Calean. A pleasure to make your acquaintance."

She studied him for a moment before replying with a polite nod. "The pleasure is mine, Baron Calean."

"I have heard much of your family," he continued, his words dipped in honey. "Your father has done great things for Solara. I imagine you have inherited some of his... talents."

Lyra couldn't help the flicker of amusement that crossed

Chapter 5: The Masquerade Ball

her face. "Talents?" she repeated. "I'm not sure I know what you mean."

Baron Calean leaned in a little closer, his eyes dark with unspoken promises. "The ability to navigate the ever-shifting tides of politics, of course. The art of making alliances... and breaking them." He gave a soft chuckle, as though sharing a private joke. "But I imagine you already understand that art better than most."

Lyra studied him, her gaze sharp. "And what, pray tell, do you believe that art to be worth, Baron?"

He smiled, his lips curling just enough to make her skin prickle. "Ah, a woman of substance. I like that. As for what it's worth... well, that remains to be seen, doesn't it? But I suspect, Lady Lyra, you may find that our paths—yours and mine—are not so different."

Her smile was cool, polite, but with an edge of warning. "We shall see," she said, her voice measured. "But I believe the evening calls for us to dance, Baron Calean. Perhaps another time for such discussions."

Without waiting for a response, she turned on her heel and made her way across the ballroom, her thoughts swirling. The web of intrigue in Aeridor was far more tangled than she had imagined, and every interaction seemed to weave her deeper into the threads of politics, power, and lies.

As she passed the dancers, she stole a glance at Valerius, still conversing with Lady Isolde. His face was inscrutable, but Lyra could feel the weight of his presence, even from across the room. He was the one pulling the strings, she realized—his influence was everywhere, even in the most subtle of exchanges.

The night was still young, but Lyra already understood one

undeniable truth: nothing in this court was what it seemed. And tonight, the dance had only just begun.

Seven

Chapter 6: Secrets and Lies

The masquerade ball stretched deep into the night, its energy slowly fading as the hours wore on. The guests drifted in and out of conversations, their voices softening, their movements growing less precise as the evening's revelry began to lose its sheen of grandeur. But for Lyra, the night was far from over. Beneath the layers of music and whispered words, the weight of her choices pressed harder with every passing moment.

She had danced, spoken, and smiled, playing her part. But beneath the glittering surface of Aeridor's court, she had felt the sting of something darker—something hidden.

As the final notes of the orchestra faded, the lights dimmed slightly, and many of the guests began to filter out into the more intimate corners of the castle. The ballroom, once a sea of swirling gowns and masked faces, now seemed more like a cavern, its high arches echoing with the soft murmur of low voices. Lyra had retreated to one of the palace's quieter alcoves, seeking a moment of reprieve. She was no longer certain whether the discomfort she felt was from the ball itself, or from the layers of deception that seemed to cling to everything here.

There was a tug in her chest, a growing unease that she couldn't quite shake. The meeting with Lord Valerius had been charged with an intensity that had unnerved her. His words, the ones left unsaid, haunted her still. It wasn't just about politics. Not only about alliances and broken pacts. There was something more to him—something he wasn't revealing. And it was that something that gnawed at her now.

As she stood near one of the grand windows, staring out into the darkened courtyard, the sound of footsteps behind her caught her attention. She turned, expecting to see yet another noble making their approach, but was instead met by the familiar figure of Dorian, the castle's head steward. His attire was more subdued than the colorful court garb, a simple black tunic, and his expression was one of barely concealed urgency.

"Lady Lyra," he said softly, bowing with practiced grace. "Forgive me for intruding. His Lordship—Lord Valerius—has requested your presence. He's... waiting for you in the study."

Lyra raised an eyebrow, surprise flashing in her eyes. "His Lordship?" she repeated, voice low, as if unsure of the meaning behind his words. She had been expecting a more public invitation—perhaps a dance or a casual exchange—but a private request, in a secluded part of the castle, was another thing entirely.

Dorian gave a slight, almost imperceptible nod. "He seems to believe that the evening has reached its... delicate stage, my lady. He is anxious to discuss something of great importance."

Chapter 6: Secrets and Lies

Lyra's mind raced, but she masked her concern with a composed smile. "Of course. Lead the way, Dorian."

The corridors of Aeridor Castle were as labyrinthine as the intrigues that played out within its walls. The high stone arches and thick tapestries muffled her steps as she followed Dorian through the dimly lit hallways, her thoughts swirling with possibilities. Why had Valerius summoned her in this manner? And what secrets had he kept from her so far?

The study, tucked away in a far corner of the castle, was a quiet room with shelves full of dusty tomes and scrolls. The walls were lined with dark wood, and a large desk dominated the center of the room, covered in maps and ancient texts. But it was the man sitting at the desk who drew her attention.

Valerius was leaning against the edge of the desk, his posture relaxed but his eyes sharp. The mask he wore earlier had been discarded, and the intensity of his gaze now seemed both familiar and foreign, as though it held pieces of a puzzle she hadn't yet figured out.

"Lady Lyra," he greeted, his voice low and smooth. "I hope you didn't find the ball too overwhelming."

She met his gaze with a cool, practiced composure, though her mind still swirled with questions. "It was... enlightening. But you did not call me here to discuss the evening's festivities, I suspect."

Valerius smiled, a flicker of something unreadable crossing his features. "No, though I hope you'll forgive my choice of venue. I thought it would be more private here. The walls of the castle have ears, and I would prefer not to be overheard."

Her curiosity piqued, Lyra took a step closer, her heels clicking softly against the stone floor. "I'm listening," she said, her voice steady. Despite the sudden change in their usual dynamic, her instincts told her this was more than a casual conversation.

Valerius gestured to a chair opposite the desk, motioning for her to sit. "Please," he said. "I know this may be... uncomfortable, but I need to speak candidly with you."

She took her seat, folding her hands neatly in her lap, watching him carefully. The light from the flickering fire cast shadows across his face, accentuating the sharpness of his features. There was something about him in this moment that felt more human—less the calculating lord, and more like a man weighed down by a difficult truth.

"I know I've been playing a game," he began, his voice more serious than she'd heard it before. "One I'm certain you've already noticed. This alliance... the courtship... it's all part of something larger than either of us."

Lyra's brow furrowed. "You speak as though you're trapped in this—like it's not of your choosing. But you and I both know the stakes. Your kingdom is on the brink of war with Solara, and mine is just as desperate for a resolution. We don't have the luxury of pretending that this is anything but what it is."

He looked at her with a pained expression, as if torn between his duty and his growing awareness of her scrutiny. "That's not what I meant." He pushed a hand through his dark hair, looking away for a moment. "What I meant was... there are things at play here, Lyra, things you don't know. Secrets that go far beyond the alliance between our kingdoms. Secrets I've been forced to keep, for both our sakes."

Lyra felt a flicker of unease, but she maintained her composure. "Secrets? I've never been one to trust in secrecy. You of

Chapter 6: Secrets and Lies

all people should know that."

He met her gaze again, his eyes flashing with an emotion she couldn't quite place. "You trust your father. But even he doesn't know everything. He doesn't know that the treaty, the pact we speak of—was never broken by human hands."

The words hung in the air, heavy with implication. Lyra's heart skipped a beat. "What do you mean? The treaty—the ancient pact—was shattered in a magical cataclysm. We both know that."

Valerius leaned forward slightly, his voice lowering even further. "Yes. But it wasn't an accident. It wasn't an act of nature. Someone... someone orchestrated it. And that someone is closer than you think."

Lyra's breath caught in her throat. The silence between them stretched taut, like a drawn bowstring. Her mind raced as she tried to make sense of his words. Someone within the court? A traitor? Or... someone more dangerous than that?

Before she could press him for more details, a sudden, sharp knock sounded at the door, interrupting the moment.

"Enter," Valerius said, his voice taut with something Lyra couldn't quite place.

The door creaked open, and the figure who stepped into the room sent a cold shiver down her spine. The woman's regal posture and confident air were unmistakable: it was Lady Isolde, her mask removed, revealing the sharp angles of her face and the calculating gleam in her eyes.

She smiled, but there was no warmth in it.

"I hope I'm not interrupting," she said smoothly, her voice like silk. "But it seems we have some... unfinished business to discuss, Lord Valerius."

Lyra's pulse quickened as the room seemed to close in

Tempting the Enemy's Daughter

around them. The pieces of the puzzle were starting to fall into place—but with each revelation, the picture became far more dangerous than she could have imagined.

And now, she realized, the game was changing.

The stakes were much higher than she had ever expected.

Lady Isolde's presence in the room was like a sudden storm, cold and inevitable. She stepped inside with the grace of a lioness, her eyes quickly darting from Lyra to Valerius, assessing the situation with a practiced glance. There was a certain energy about her, something calculated and dangerous that Lyra had felt from the moment they'd first met.

"I trust I'm not interrupting," Lady Isolde continued, her tone smooth but sharp, the words hanging in the air like a challenge. She took a step forward, the heels of her shoes clicking with an unnerving rhythm on the stone floor. The firelight in the room flickered, casting long shadows that danced across her face, giving her a slightly otherworldly air.

Valerius didn't answer immediately. His gaze, usually so composed, flickered just briefly—his frustration almost imperceptible but real. The moment stretched long between the three of them, the air thick with unspoken tension.

Lyra was the first to break the silence, her voice cool but laced with quiet defiance. "Lady Isolde," she said, turning her gaze to the woman who now stood between her and Valerius, "what brings you here at this hour?"

Isolde's lips curled into a smile, though it never reached her eyes. "I was simply looking for answers, Lady Lyra. After all, I've heard many rumors about the intentions of Aeridor's lord." She turned her gaze back to Valerius, her smile widening just enough to be unsettling. "But perhaps I've come at a convenient time—when matters are finally being addressed."

Chapter 6: Secrets and Lies

Lyra's brow furrowed, the sudden shift in dynamics prickling her senses. Isolde's words were deliberate, too pointed to be casual. It was as if she knew more than she was letting on—and Lyra didn't like the feeling of being out of the loop.

Valerius, seemingly unfazed by the intrusion, straightened his posture and gave Isolde a tight, controlled nod. "You're always welcome, Lady Isolde. But I don't believe we've concluded our conversation yet." His eyes flicked back to Lyra, a flash of something unreadable in his gaze, before he turned fully to Isolde. "If you have business with me, it would be best to speak plainly. There's no time to waste."

Isolde's gaze lingered on him for a heartbeat longer than necessary, but she nodded, giving the faintest incline of her head in acknowledgment. Then, without warning, she turned her attention back to Lyra, as if the tension between them didn't exist.

"I've heard many things about you, Lady Lyra," she said softly, her voice dripping with amusement. "Your father's daughter. The jewel of Solara, betrothed to the future of Aeridor. A dangerous combination. You are, without question, a woman of great value."

Lyra stiffened at the subtle implication, but kept her face neutral. "Flattery won't get you far, Lady Isolde. I am neither naive nor impressed by such words."

Isolde chuckled lightly, the sound colder than any laughter Lyra had heard before. "I see you are as sharp as they say. Very well. No need for pretense." She crossed her arms, surveying Lyra with an appraising look. "But the truth, my dear, is that you are here for far more than a diplomatic visit. You know that, don't you?"

Lyra's pulse quickened, but she kept her voice steady. "If

Tempting the Enemy's Daughter

you have something to say, Lady Isolde, then say it."

For a moment, Isolde didn't speak, instead letting the silence stretch long and uncomfortable. Then, finally, she spoke, her voice low and precise. "The treaty between Aeridor and Solara was never about peace, Lady Lyra. It was never about your father's grand idealism. It was about power—power that has long been controlled by forces you can't begin to comprehend."

Valerius's expression shifted, his jaw tightening ever so slightly, but he remained silent. He was watching, waiting, as if the conversation was unfolding in a way he had anticipated but not yet fully revealed.

"What are you talking about?" Lyra asked, her voice thin with rising suspicion. She stood from her seat, suddenly feeling as though she were in the midst of a web that was tightening around her with each passing moment.

Isolde turned her gaze back to Valerius, a look of understanding passing between them, one that only confirmed Lyra's worst fears. "The truth, Lady Lyra, is that the pact was never broken by the magic of two kingdoms at war. It was broken by something far older. Far more dangerous."

Lyra's heart skipped a beat. "What do you mean?" she pressed, taking a step toward them, her eyes now locked onto Valerius. "What are you hiding?"

Isolde tilted her head slightly, as if enjoying the dance of tension between them. "I believe Lord Valerius is the better one to answer that question, don't you, my lord?"

Valerius's expression was unreadable, his eyes darkened by some hidden burden. He sighed deeply, as though he knew the time had come to reveal the secret that had been eating away at him. "The ancient pact—your father's great legacy—was shattered not by the forces of war or magic, but by an event

Chapter 6: Secrets and Lies

that fractured the very fabric of reality itself."

Lyra's mind reeled, struggling to make sense of the implications. "Fractured reality? That's impossible," she muttered, shaking her head. "The treaty was shattered during the last great conflict. There's no way—"

Isolde stepped closer to her, cutting her off with a quick, sharp motion. "It was no accident, Lady Lyra. There were forces at work—forces beyond your understanding. The war itself, the conflict between our kingdoms, was just the catalyst. The true source of the fracture lies in a power that neither Solara nor Aeridor could ever control." She paused, letting the weight of her words sink in. "And someone—someone in this very castle—has been working to fix it. To repair the damage done to the fabric of time."

Lyra's mind raced, the pieces beginning to fall into place, but each connection only led to more questions. "Who?" she asked, her voice trembling with an urgency she couldn't hide.

Isolde's lips curled into a smile that was part sympathy, part cruelty. "I'm sure Lord Valerius has his suspicions. After all, he is the one who knows more than anyone else about the powers that manipulate events in the shadows."

Valerius looked at Lyra, his eyes dark and unreadable, his jaw clenched as if holding back something dangerous. His words came out in a whisper, but they hit her with the force of a storm.

"There are forces at play, Lyra," he said, his voice tight, "that neither of us can stop. The ancient pact wasn't broken by accident. And if we don't act quickly, what was once shattered will tear the very fabric of our worlds apart."

The room fell into an unsettling silence as the weight of his words hung heavily between them. For the first time, Lyra felt the full weight of the game she had stepped into—and the power, the danger, that now threatened not just the kingdoms of Solara and Aeridor, but something much greater.

She looked at Valerius, and for the first time, she wondered: Was he truly an ally? Or was he just another player in a game she could not yet understand?

And who, among them, was the true enemy?

The fire crackled in the hearth, casting flickering shadows that made the corners of the room seem to stretch and twist in unnatural shapes. Lyra stood motionless, her thoughts racing as she absorbed Valerius's words. The air in the room felt heavier, charged with a tension she hadn't anticipated—each breath she drew seemed to fill her chest with the weight of a growing uncertainty.

For the first time since arriving in Aeridor, Lyra questioned everything she thought she knew. She had come here to negotiate an alliance, to protect her kingdom, and perhaps to find a path through the maze of political intrigue that bound her life. But this—this was something altogether different.

Valerius was speaking of forces beyond her control, of a fracture in reality itself. The ancient pact, the one that had tied their kingdoms together for centuries, was not just a piece of diplomacy—it was a living thing, a force whose rupture threatened far more than the political stability of Aeridor and Solara. The weight of that revelation left her feeling strangely unmoored. And yet, somewhere deep inside, there was an undeniable thrill—a recognition that this was the true game, the one beneath all the layers of courtly appearances and power struggles.

Isolde's smile faded, her gaze moving between Lyra and Valerius with an unsettling calm. "So now you see," she said,

Chapter 6: Secrets and Lies

her voice smooth but laced with something dangerous. "The pact was never just about kings or kingdoms. It was about controlling the very fabric of reality itself. And someone is pulling the strings from the shadows, using the fracture as a means to change everything."

Lyra narrowed her eyes. "And you expect me to believe that someone in this very castle—someone among us—is working to repair it?"

Isolde's lips quirked in something between a smirk and a sneer. "Not just repair it. *Manipulate* it. The past, the present, the future—it's all in flux. And whoever controls that power controls everything."

A cold knot twisted in Lyra's stomach. "But why haven't we heard of this before? Why didn't my father—?"

"Your father's not in control here," Isolde interrupted sharply, her tone turning bitter. "None of us are. There are forces—more ancient than any kingdom—that work behind the scenes. Forces that have been in play long before your father's time. The true powers that govern the world are hidden from the eyes of kings. And the fracture you've heard of? It was no accident. It was orchestrated. Carefully. By someone who knew exactly what they were doing."

The room seemed to close in around Lyra. She glanced at Valerius, desperate for some clarity, but his face remained unreadable, his features set in an expression that was half frustration and half resignation.

"You know more than you're telling me," Lyra said, her voice tight. "Why are you withholding the truth?"

Valerius hesitated, then crossed the room to the desk. He placed his hands on the edge of it, bracing himself, as though the weight of the situation had become too much to bear. His eyes, usually so composed, betrayed a flicker of vulnerability. "Because the truth is… dangerous. If you knew everything, you would see how far-reaching this is. Not just for Solara or Aeridor, but for *everything*. Reality itself is bending—shifting. The balance of magic, time, and space is unraveling."

Lyra's heart pounded. "So… what does that mean for us? For *me*?"

Isolde leaned in slightly, her voice low and laced with something almost… possessive. "It means you are the key, Lady Lyra. The key to everything."

The words hung in the air, sinking into the space between them like a weight too heavy to lift. Lyra's mind reeled. Key to everything? She opened her mouth, but no words came out. She felt as though the ground beneath her feet was shifting, and she wasn't sure whether she was falling or simply standing in the midst of a storm.

Valerius spoke again, his voice steady but carrying an undercurrent of urgency. "The ancient pact—what your father has fought for—is tied to the very structure of time itself. Whoever controls the pact controls the timeline. And right now, the timeline is being rewritten. If we don't act soon, everything we know will cease to exist."

Lyra looked between the two of them, trying to piece together the shattered fragments of the conversation. A war over the future? Over time? She couldn't fathom it.

"How can I help?" she asked, her voice barely a whisper, as though even the act of asking would draw her into something from which there would be no escape.

Valerius shook his head, his eyes filled with regret. "I'm not sure you can, Lyra. We don't even know who we're fighting yet. The forces working to manipulate time are… beyond anything

Chapter 6: Secrets and Lies

we've ever encountered. There are spies—traitors—in both of our kingdoms. And worse, there are beings, entities from other realms, who wish to use the fracture to remake reality in their image."

The weight of his words hit her like a physical blow. Traitors? Entities from other realms? It was impossible. But the truth in his voice was undeniable.

Isolde, who had been quiet for a moment, finally spoke again, her voice soft but filled with venom. "The pact was more than just a treaty between kingdoms, Lyra. It was a binding agreement that kept time—and reality—intact. When your ancestors made the pact, they ensured that certain things would never change. But now, that balance has been disrupted, and it's only a matter of time before everything falls apart."

Lyra's mind spun. She wanted to argue, to dismiss everything they were telling her as absurd. But the pieces were starting to fit together—fitting in ways that made her feel both terrified and oddly empowered.

She took a deep breath. "And what about the one who broke the pact? Who orchestrated this?"

Valerius's jaw tightened. "That is the question. And the answer is something that neither of us can fully understand. Whoever it is has been playing this game for much longer than we've realized. And they've set things in motion in ways we can't stop—not without help."

Lyra's eyes narrowed. "Help from where?"

"From others," Isolde said, her tone sharp. "From people who understand what's at stake—people who know how to manipulate the energies that govern time and space. People who can help you understand the true purpose of the pact. But be warned, Lady Lyra—once you know the truth, there will be no going back. You'll be marked, just as we all are."

Marked? Lyra swallowed hard, her throat dry. It felt as if they were preparing her for something she couldn't fully grasp.

"And what does that mean for me?" Lyra's voice was steadier than she felt. "What do I have to do?"

Valerius's gaze softened for the briefest of moments, before it hardened again. "You need to choose, Lyra. You need to decide whether to help us… or to stand with your father and continue the war. Because the future—the real future—depends on the decisions we make now."

There it was. The final question. The one that would define everything to come. The future of both kingdoms, and perhaps reality itself, rested on a decision she wasn't ready to make.

But she knew one thing with certainty: this game, whatever it was, had only just begun. And she was already too deep to turn back.

The heavy silence lingered in the room, and as the final embers in the hearth flickered, Lyra's mind churned with a thousand thoughts. There was so much she didn't understand, so much more she needed to learn. But one thing was clear: the stakes were higher than anything she had ever imagined. And now, whether she was ready or not, she was part of something far larger than herself.

And in that moment, she knew there was no turning back.

Eight

Chapter 7: A Dangerous Game

The air in Aeridor Castle was thick with tension as the days passed. Lyra had never felt more like a pawn than she did now, trapped in a web of politics, alliances, and unseen forces. She found herself walking the halls of the castle with a new sense of wariness, ever aware of the eyes watching her, the whispers trailing in her wake. But it wasn't just the court that unnerved her; it was the looming presence of the game itself, a game she was now unwillingly a part of.

Her encounters with Valerius had become less frequent, though they were more intense when they did happen. She couldn't escape the weight of his words, the implication that the future—*her* future—was tied to decisions she had yet to fully understand. The fractured timeline, the manipulation of reality, the ancient pact—it all seemed too vast, too complex to comprehend in its entirety. But she could feel it in her bones: whatever this game was, it was about to shift into something

Tempting the Enemy's Daughter

far darker.

Valerius had suggested they meet again, though in a place far less public than before. The castle's library was a grand, labyrinthine space, lined with towering shelves of ancient texts, scrolls, and maps. The faint smell of old paper and wax candles hung in the air, giving the room an atmosphere of timelessness. But there, in the heart of the library, amidst the quietude of centuries-old knowledge, a new battle was unfolding—a battle of strategy, not war.

The chessboard in front of them was set with an almost eerie precision. Black and white pieces were arranged, each carefully positioned as though the game had been ongoing for days. Lyra sat across from Valerius, her hands resting on her lap, though her fingers twitched with the impulse to move a piece. They'd already played once before, but it felt as though this match was far more than a simple game.

"You know the rules, Lady Lyra," Valerius said, his voice low, the flickering candlelight casting shadows on his face. His posture was casual, but his eyes were sharp, assessing her every move. "Each piece you move has consequences. There are no small victories in this game."

Lyra raised an eyebrow. "And what do you hope to achieve with this... game? Am I supposed to learn something from this?"

Valerius met her gaze steadily, his fingers moving over a knight, shifting it one square forward. "Perhaps. Or perhaps it's just a way to sharpen your mind, to get used to the consequences of your decisions. We've already begun playing the game, Lyra. Whether we like it or not, every move we make has far-reaching effects."

She leaned forward slightly, her eyes narrowing as she

Chapter 7: A Dangerous Game

studied the board. A sense of unease settled in her chest. "And what happens if I make a mistake?"

"The same as in any game," Valerius replied. "You lose."

Her heart skipped a beat, but she kept her voice steady. "Lose what, exactly?"

He paused, then allowed his lips to curl into a small, knowing smile. "The game is bigger than you think. Each piece represents something—an action, a choice, a life. You lose a piece, you lose something precious. A battle lost can change the course of everything."

Lyra shifted uneasily in her chair, the weight of his words pressing down on her. Every piece on the board was a potential risk, each move made with the knowledge that it could irrevocably alter the course of events. But what choice did she have? Every conversation, every glance exchanged with the people in Aeridor had begun to feel like a calculated move in a larger game—one in which the stakes were higher than she could ever have imagined.

"I didn't come here to play games, Valerius," she said, her voice quiet but firm. "I came here to understand why this is happening. Why *I* am being dragged into it."

He didn't answer immediately, but his eyes softened, just the faintest trace of something more vulnerable flickering in them. Then, slowly, he slid his queen into a new position on the board, trapping Lyra's knight in a calculated move.

"Because you are the key," he said, his voice tinged with an edge of regret. "The ancient pact binds you to this game. Your bloodline… your father's legacy… it's all tied to the fracture. The game isn't just about kingdoms. It's about time, about reality itself. Whoever controls the flow of time controls everything. And you, Lady Lyra, are a pivotal piece."

Tempting the Enemy's Daughter

Lyra's pulse quickened at the thought. Her father's legacy. Her bloodline. *Her* role in all of this. Was she merely a pawn to be sacrificed in a larger game? Or could she control her own fate?

With a quiet curse, she moved her knight, trying to wrest control from Valerius's calculated attack. But as soon as she made the move, she realized it was a mistake. Valerius had already anticipated it.

"You're too hasty," Valerius observed, his voice cool. "You can't rush through this game, Lyra. Every choice must be measured. Every consequence considered. We're not just playing for power. We're playing for survival."

She clenched her jaw. "I'm not a fool, Valerius. I understand that."

But as he captured her knight with a quiet, almost effortless move, she couldn't help but feel like she was losing—losing her grasp on the very game she thought she was in control of. Her mind raced, trying to calculate her next move, but the feeling of being trapped only grew stronger. What was Valerius's true aim? Was he truly trying to teach her? Or was he testing her, seeing how she would react to the pressure?

"There's more at stake here than just the kingdoms, Lyra," he continued, his voice lowering as he leaned forward slightly, his eyes intent on her. "If we don't act soon, everything could collapse—the past, the present, the future. The fracture in time is already shifting. Someone is trying to manipulate it. And we can't let them succeed. That's why we play."

Her heart raced as the weight of his words settled in. The pressure was mounting, and it wasn't just the board between them that was at stake—it was the very fabric of reality.

The game wasn't just a metaphor.

Chapter 7: A Dangerous Game

It was a warning.

Lyra's eyes narrowed, her mind working through the possibilities. The question was no longer *if* she would play. It was *how* she would play—and who she could trust. The choices she made now would ripple through time, and the consequences would be felt far beyond this castle.

Valerius's next move sent a jolt through her. His queen had moved to the center of the board, placing her king in check.

He was closing in.

"You're cornering me," Lyra said, her voice quiet, but there was an edge to it now. "But you won't win, Valerius."

He smiled, almost imperceptibly, as he surveyed the board. "That remains to be seen."

As she stared down at the pieces on the board, Lyra realized something unsettling: she wasn't just playing against Valerius. She was playing against *fate* itself.

And the game was far from over.

Lyra's fingers hovered over her next move, the weight of the game pressing heavily on her mind. She glanced at Valerius, whose eyes never left the board. His brow was furrowed in concentration, and his lips were set in that faintly amused, ever-so-certain smile that made her wonder just how much he truly understood about the forces at play.

Her knight was gone. Her bishop was trapped in a corner. And now, her king was in check, threatened by his queen—one move away from being cornered entirely.

Lyra clenched her jaw, refusing to let him see how close he was to winning. It wasn't just about this game, not anymore. It was about proving to herself that she wasn't a mere pawn in this larger game they were all playing. She couldn't afford to lose—*not* to him.

Tempting the Enemy's Daughter

"You're playing too fast," Valerius murmured, his voice so low it almost felt like a breath against her skin. "You're letting your emotions control your strategy, Lady Lyra. In this game, there is no room for haste. Every move, every choice, must be made with precision. A single mistake can change everything."

Lyra's pulse quickened, but she forced herself to stay focused. She needed to think. *Think clearly*. There had to be a way out of this. If she could outmaneuver him here, in this small, controlled space, perhaps it would give her the confidence to face the greater challenges awaiting her.

"You're right," she said, her voice sharp as she slid her hand across the board, moving her rook to a defensive position. "But every move is a risk, isn't it, Valerius? No matter how careful you are, at some point, you have to take a leap of faith."

Valerius's eyes glinted as he observed her move. It wasn't quite a mistake, but it wasn't an optimal defense either. For a moment, he remained silent, his gaze never leaving her, almost as if he were studying her. Then, with a slight nod, he returned his attention to the board, and in one swift motion, slid his queen across the table, seizing the advantage.

"Faith, Lady Lyra?" His lips curled in that faintly amused smile. "In games like these, faith doesn't have a place. There is only strategy. The moment you place your trust in something outside of yourself, you lose the game."

Her eyes flicked to the board. Her king was now trapped in the corner, with no way to move. The game was over.

She didn't show it, but inside, a rush of frustration surged through her veins. She'd made a mistake. She'd let her emotions cloud her judgment, and now the game was lost.

But she wasn't ready to admit defeat—not yet.

"Checkmate," Valerius said, his voice quiet but final.

Chapter 7: A Dangerous Game

Lyra's gaze hardened, but she couldn't bring herself to argue. She had lost. The game, the battle, everything. It stung more than she was willing to admit, but she held her ground. "So it seems," she said, her tone measured.

He watched her for a long moment, as though weighing her reaction. Then, unexpectedly, he leaned back in his chair, a thoughtful expression crossing his face. "You've got the spirit of a true player, Lyra. But your recklessness is your undoing. A leader cannot afford to be impulsive. Not when the stakes are this high."

Her heart pounded. "What's the point of all this, Valerius? Why play these games? You say it's about survival, but every move you make... every word you say feels like a test. What am I supposed to learn from this?"

He met her gaze with a steady intensity. "You're supposed to learn that every move you make has consequences. Not just for you, but for everyone around you. It's the same in the kingdoms. Every decision you make, whether you want to admit it or not, ripples outward. In war, in peace, and in matters of fate."

She bit her lip, the words hanging heavy between them. "And what happens when the game is over? What happens to the ones who lose?" Her voice softened slightly. "What happens to me?"

Valerius was silent for a moment, his eyes betraying nothing. For a second, he looked like a different man—a leader, burdened by something far heavier than any political game. Then, with a slow, almost reluctant movement, he reached for the pieces, beginning to reset the board.

"Those who lose," he said quietly, "don't just lose the game. They lose everything they've ever known."

The weight of his words sank into her, the finality in his voice striking her with the force of a blow. She was no longer simply playing a game. She was part of something far bigger, something with consequences that stretched across the very fabric of existence itself. And she couldn't afford to make another mistake.

Valerius's fingers moved deftly, arranging the pieces with the precision of a master. "You may not understand it now, but you will. You'll learn what this game is really about, and you'll learn quickly. You'll need to. Because time—*our* time—is running out."

A cold shiver ran down her spine. She could feel it—the tightening grip of the game she was trapped in. There was no way to escape. Not anymore.

"I don't know if I'm ready for this," Lyra admitted, her voice a little quieter than she intended. She glanced at the board, then back at him. "But if this game is as important as you say, then I have no choice but to play it."

Valerius's eyes softened, just for a moment, before he spoke again. "None of us are truly ready for what's to come. But the time for hesitation is over. The game has already begun, Lyra. And we must move forward, no matter the cost."

Lyra's heart raced, but she nodded, her resolve firming. She may have lost this round, but she would not lose the war. She would learn how to play this game, no matter the risks.

And she would not let Valerius—or anyone else—determine her fate.

As Valerius set the pieces back into their starting positions, Lyra steeled herself for the next move. The game wasn't over. It was just beginning.

Chapter 7: A Dangerous Game

Outside the library, the wind howled through the castle's ancient towers, echoing through the corridors like a warning. The world was shifting, and every passing moment brought them closer to a future neither of them could predict.

But one thing was certain: the game was far from finished, and the stakes had never been higher.

The pieces were set again. The game was about to continue. Lyra stared at the chessboard in front of her, the smooth ivory squares almost mocking her as she pondered her next move. The weight of Valerius's words pressed on her chest, suffocating her like a thick fog.

"Every move has consequences," she repeated softly to herself, her mind racing. "Every move could alter everything."

She wasn't playing just for her own survival anymore. Every piece on the board represented something far more important—an entire kingdom, a fragile peace, or the delicate strands of time itself. The game was bigger than she had ever imagined, and she had already made her first mistake.

Her eyes flicked back to Valerius. He was studying her carefully, his posture relaxed but his eyes sharp with intent. The tension in the air was thick, as though every second of silence was another piece of a larger puzzle being laid into place.

She had to focus. The future, her future, was no longer something she could take for granted. She was a part of something far beyond her control, and every choice she made could have consequences far worse than a lost game of chess.

"So, what now?" Lyra asked, her voice steady but her mind churning. "We reset the board, and now we continue?"

Valerius's lips curled slightly, a faint, approving smile tugging at the corners of his mouth. "Yes, now we continue.

But remember: no one resets the game. You don't get to take back your decisions in the real world. It's not like chess, Lyra. You can't just move the pieces and pretend it never happened."

Lyra swallowed hard. He was right. She couldn't undo the choices she had already made—the people she had already met, the alliances she had already begun to form. And, more than anything, she couldn't undo the delicate balance she had just stepped into, a balance that could collapse with a single wrong step.

"Then what's the point of all this?" Lyra asked, gesturing at the chessboard. "Why make me play?"

"To teach you patience. To teach you discipline," Valerius said softly, his eyes never leaving hers. "But also to show you how the smallest actions can ripple outward. The world, like this game, is full of pieces that seem insignificant, but when you pull the right strings, you can move mountains."

He pushed his queen forward again, a calculated move that forced her to respond.

"Don't get too comfortable," Lyra muttered, her eyes narrowing as she prepared her defense. She wasn't about to lose again—not like this. Not after everything she had learned.

"I'm not," Valerius said, his tone turning more serious. He leaned forward, his fingers brushing the edges of the board. "This isn't just about winning. It's about control. About knowing when to make your move and when to wait."

Lyra set her jaw, moving a pawn to protect her queen. It was a small move, almost insignificant, but in this game, it felt like the only thing she could do. There was something about Valerius's calm, assured demeanor that made her feel as if the stakes were higher than ever. This was more than just a lesson in chess. It was a lesson in survival.

Chapter 7: A Dangerous Game

"I've been thinking," she said, trying to break the silence, her voice steady as she moved a piece. "You said the game isn't about power, but you've also made it clear that we're fighting for something much bigger than that. What is it, Valerius? What exactly are we fighting for?"

He didn't answer right away. Instead, he continued to move his pieces methodically, each move calculated, almost mechanical. Then, finally, his gaze lifted to meet hers.

"We're fighting for *the future*, Lyra. The future of time itself."

The words hit her like a blow. For a moment, she forgot about the game altogether. The future of *time*? What did that even mean?

"I don't understand," she said, her voice shaky despite herself. "You speak in riddles, Valerius. What does that mean? The future of time? You're talking like we're trying to fix the past, or control the future, or—"

"No," he cut her off, his voice sharp now, the calm facade slipping for a fraction of a second. "We're not fixing anything. We're trying to *survive* it. The fracture in time—it's not a crack that can be mended by simple magic or diplomacy. It's a tear in the very fabric of reality. And someone is using it to rewrite history itself."

Lyra sat back in her chair, her thoughts suddenly spinning. "Rewriting history? Who—who would do such a thing?"

"Someone who understands the true power of the fracture," Valerius said, his eyes darkening. "Someone who knows how to manipulate time—not just the past or the future, but the very *structure* of it."

His words hung in the air, heavy with implication. Lyra's stomach twisted as she tried to comprehend what he was telling her. This wasn't just about kingdoms or wars. It was about something much darker—something that could tear apart everything they knew.

"And you think that whoever is doing this, whoever controls the fracture... they're controlling the game?" she asked quietly, a sense of dread creeping into her chest.

Valerius nodded slowly, his gaze never leaving hers. "Yes. And whoever controls the fracture controls *everything*. The future. The past. And the power to change both. If they succeed, reality itself will be rewritten. And kingdoms like Aeridor and Solara will be nothing but pawns in a much larger game."

The chill that ran through her spine was more than just the weight of his words. It was the realization that she wasn't just a player in this game—she was *essential* to it. She was the daughter of the Duke of Solara, the key to an ancient pact that bound her people to Aeridor in ways she had never truly understood. And now, with the stakes higher than ever, she was part of something much larger—a battle that could decide the very fabric of existence.

"You've been training me," Lyra said slowly, her fingers tracing the edge of the board. "For something. What is it?"

Valerius's expression softened, but there was an edge of sadness in his gaze. "You're being prepared to fight. To make decisions when the time comes. The time is coming sooner than we realize. And when it does, you'll have to choose—who you stand with, and who you're willing to sacrifice."

The weight of his words settled over her like a blanket of cold dread. She wasn't just playing a game anymore. She was in a war for the very future of time, a war against forces far more powerful than she could understand. And in the end, there might be no winning.

Chapter 7: A Dangerous Game

"Then I'll play my part," Lyra said, her voice firm, the last vestiges of hesitation falling away.

Valerius studied her, his expression unreadable, before nodding slowly. "I knew you would. The game has already begun, Lady Lyra. And now, we must see it through."

The pieces on the board gleamed in the candlelight, each move carrying the weight of a future yet to be decided.

And for the first time, Lyra understood: she was no longer just a player in a game. She was the one who could decide whether the game would end in victory or destruction.

The game was truly afoot.

Nine

Chapter 8: Betrayals and Alliances

The evening had fallen over Aeridor Castle like a dark cloak, heavy with secrets. The winding corridors were empty now, the silence broken only by the occasional echo of footsteps and the distant crackling of the hearths. The grand hallways, lined with tapestries depicting the kingdom's storied past, now felt suffocating. Every corner, every shadow, seemed to conceal something more than just the weight of history. It felt as if something—someone—was lurking, waiting for the right moment to strike.

Lyra stood at the window of her chambers, staring out at the vast expanse of the Aeridor countryside. The moon was high in the sky, its light silver and ethereal against the darkened world. The land stretched out before her—lush forests, rocky hills, and distant mountains that marked the border between Aeridor and Solara. In the distance, the glow of Aeridor's capital flickered like a dying star.

Chapter 8: Betrayals and Alliances

It all seemed so far removed from the tension that simmered within the castle walls.

Her thoughts were a whirlwind. After the game of chess with Valerius, after the cryptic warnings about the fracture in time, Lyra couldn't shake the feeling that she was being pulled in too many directions. There was the alliance between her father, Duke Alaric, and Lord Valerius. There was the fragile peace between their kingdoms. And there was *her*—trapped in the heart of a game that she didn't fully understand, playing a role she had never chosen.

But now, more than ever, it was clear: no matter how hard she tried to avoid it, she was caught in the web of political intrigue, and perhaps even something far darker. And the worst part was, she couldn't trust anyone—not even Valerius.

A soft knock on the door interrupted her thoughts. Her heart skipped in her chest, and she turned quickly, almost hoping it was someone who would offer her a break from the isolation, someone who would reassure her that she wasn't as alone as she felt.

"Enter," she called, her voice steady but betraying a hint of the unease she had been trying to suppress.

The door creaked open, and a shadow stepped into the room—a figure clad in the dark, elegant robes of Aeridor's court. It was Rian, a young noble who had served as one of Valerius's trusted advisors. He was the one who had accompanied her the day she arrived at the castle, and though his demeanor was polite and professional, there was something in his eyes—something that made Lyra uncomfortable. She had never fully trusted him, and the way he looked at her, with his quiet intensity, only heightened that sense of wariness.

"My lady," he said with a respectful bow, though his smile

didn't reach his eyes. "A message has arrived for you."

Lyra raised an eyebrow. "A message? Who from?"

Rian's gaze flickered briefly to the closed door behind him, his posture stiffening. "It's... private. I was instructed to deliver it directly to you."

The hairs on the back of her neck stood on end. There was something too formal about his tone, too rehearsed. She had the distinct feeling that Rian wasn't simply a messenger. He was playing a part, and whatever that part was, it was far more important than he was letting on.

Without saying a word, Rian stepped forward, producing a small, sealed envelope from within his robes. The wax seal bore no insignia she recognized, only a strange, intricate design—a symbol that looked almost ancient.

Lyra took the envelope from him, her fingers brushing against his, a shiver running through her at the contact. The moment felt oddly intimate, the air between them thick with unspoken tension.

"Thank you," she said, keeping her voice neutral, though she could feel the weight of Rian's gaze on her as she broke the seal.

He hesitated, his lips tightening, but then he gave her another small bow. "If you need anything, my lady, I'll be just outside." And with that, he turned and left without another word.

Lyra glanced down at the letter, her heart racing. There was no indication of who had sent it, but something about the way it had been delivered made her feel like a part of something far more dangerous than she could comprehend. The cryptic seal, the fact that it had come through Rian—someone so closely tied to Valerius's court—suggested that this wasn't just

Chapter 8: Betrayals and Alliances

a simple communication. It was part of the game.

She unfolded the letter, her fingers trembling slightly as she read the carefully scripted message inside:

"Trust no one, not even Valerius. The balance of power has already shifted, and you are the key. Be wary of those who claim to be allies—some have their own agenda. If you want to survive, you must act quickly. The fracture is more than just a rift in time. It's a doorway. Find it before they do. Only then can you stop what is coming."

The letter was unsigned, but the words were clear, their meaning chilling. The fracture wasn't just a metaphor, nor was it simply a rift in time. It was something tangible—a doorway that could change everything. But what *was* coming? And who was she supposed to trust?

Her stomach turned. She'd been warned. *Don't trust anyone.* That included Valerius. But how could she not? He was the one who had shared the most with her—who had explained the stakes, the power of the fracture, the dangerous forces at play.

And yet... what if that was all part of the game? What if Valerius was playing a role, just as she was? What if his warnings were just another manipulation?

A knock at the door broke her reverie, and this time, it was a familiar, welcome sound.

"Lyra?" Valerius's voice, deep and commanding, called from the other side.

Her heart skipped in her chest. She quickly shoved the letter into a drawer and locked it. "Come in," she called, trying to sound unaffected.

The door opened, and Valerius entered, his presence filling the room like a storm. His eyes immediately locked onto her, searching her face for any signs of distress. His gaze flickered briefly to the desk where she had hidden the letter, but he didn't mention it.

"I've been meaning to speak with you," he said, his voice low but urgent. "There are things happening that we can't afford to ignore. We have to move swiftly. The situation is growing dire. There's been a shift—an unexpected one. We need to prepare."

Lyra's chest tightened. *Another shift?* The words from the letter echoed in her mind, and a surge of doubt flooded through her.

"Prepare for what?" she asked carefully, keeping her expression neutral.

Valerius stepped closer, his eyes never leaving hers. "There are forces at work within Aeridor that I can't fully trust. You've already seen some of them—Rian, for example." His voice dropped even lower, almost to a whisper. "I don't know how deep his loyalty runs, but I have reason to believe he's been working with someone… *someone* from Solara. And if he is, it changes everything."

Lyra's heart skipped a beat. *Rian?* Working with Solara? The very man who had delivered the mysterious letter? Her mind raced. This was more than just political maneuvering. This was treachery. A betrayal that threatened everything.

Valerius's face was set, grim. "There are spies in this castle. We need to find them before they make their move."

Lyra swallowed hard, the weight of his words sinking in. The game was growing more dangerous with every passing day. And now, she was trapped in a web of alliances and betrayals, unsure who to trust.

The only thing she knew for certain was this: The time for

Chapter 8: Betrayals and Alliances

hesitation was over.

Outside, the wind picked up, howling through the castle's towers. Lyra stood at the window once again, her heart pounding. The storm had only just begun.

Lyra's mind spun, her thoughts as tumultuous as the storm howling outside the castle walls. Rian, a spy for Solara? Valerius's warning clung to her like a second skin, the weight of his words growing heavier with each passing moment. She had always known that the political games between Aeridor and Solara were fraught with dangers, but this—the revelation of betrayal within the very walls of the castle—was far worse than she had ever imagined.

Her gaze darted to the window, where the flickering light of the distant capital illuminated the night like a dying ember. *They're closer than we think*, she thought bitterly. *I'm surrounded by them, playing a game I don't understand.*

"What should we do?" Lyra asked, her voice barely above a whisper, her gaze fixed on Valerius. Her heart drummed in her chest, but she forced herself to stay calm, to focus on the immediate danger.

Valerius studied her intently, his expression unreadable. For a moment, the mask of the confident, almost untouchable lord slipped just slightly, and she saw something else—an edge of frustration. He was as trapped as she was. There was nowhere to turn, no ally they could trust entirely.

"We need to confront him," Valerius said quietly, his voice cold but sharp, like the steel edge of a blade. "Rian may be the pawn, but he's playing a part in something much larger. We need answers."

Lyra's mind raced. Confronting Rian—how would they

Tempting the Enemy's Daughter

even approach that? And if Rian truly was working for Solara, if he was a spy, what would it mean for the fragile alliance between their two kingdoms? She had no choice but to trust Valerius in this—he had navigated these waters far longer than she had—but something about this felt *off*. It was as if they were both being manipulated by unseen hands, their every move carefully orchestrated by forces they couldn't yet see.

But she couldn't back down now. Not after everything. Not after the letter she'd received.

She turned to face him, meeting his intense gaze. "Then we confront him," she said firmly, her voice steadier than she felt. "But we do it carefully. If Rian's working with Solara, we can't afford to make mistakes. We need leverage."

Valerius nodded slowly, his lips pressing into a thin line. "I agree. We need to make him think we're on his side, at least for now. Get close to him, learn what he knows, and *then* we strike."

For the first time, the weight of their shared predicament settled in her chest. She wasn't just playing for survival anymore; she was playing to protect everything—her kingdom, her family, and the fragile peace between their two realms.

"Where do we start?" Lyra asked, already steeling herself for whatever came next. She would have to keep her wits sharp, her instincts sharper. This game was unlike anything she had ever imagined, and each move could be her last.

Valerius stepped forward, his gaze never leaving hers. "We start by gaining his trust. Make him believe you're still with him, still loyal to the kingdom of Aeridor." His voice softened just slightly. "And Lyra… whatever you do, do not let your guard down. I don't care how well he plays the part. Trust is a luxury we cannot afford."

Chapter 8: Betrayals and Alliances

Her breath caught in her throat. She knew he was right. She had learned enough in the last few days to understand that alliances were fluid, loyalty was fleeting, and anyone, even the most trusted advisors, could turn at a moment's notice.

"I won't," she said, her voice a low whisper.

That evening, the corridors of Aeridor Castle felt darker than usual. The servants had long since gone to their quarters, and the distant echoes of footsteps grew more muted, swallowed by the thick stone walls. Lyra moved quickly, her steps quiet and deliberate as she made her way to the small study where Rian had last been seen. She had already prepared herself for the confrontation, rehearsing the conversation in her mind.

The dim light of a single candle flickered inside the study as she approached the door. She paused, her hand hovering over the handle. The letter Valerius had warned her about still weighed heavily on her mind. Who had sent it? And what was its true meaning? The more she thought about it, the more she realized that *Rian* could very well be the key to everything. He knew more than he was letting on, and she intended to find out what.

She opened the door and stepped inside, the room smelling faintly of ink and parchment. There, seated at a table, was Rian. He looked up at her arrival, his expression a mask of politeness.

"My lady," he greeted her smoothly, rising to his feet with a practiced bow. "I hope I didn't disturb you."

Lyra closed the door quietly behind her, her eyes scanning the dimly lit room. There was a desk stacked with papers, and a map of the kingdom sprawled across the far wall. It looked innocent enough—no signs of secret communications or clandestine dealings. But she had learned that appearances could be deceiving.

"No, not at all," she replied, keeping her voice casual, even as the tension in her chest coiled tighter. She moved forward, lowering herself into a chair opposite him, but kept her posture poised, her gaze steady.

She watched him closely, waiting for a hint of something—a slip of the tongue, a nervous gesture—that would betray him.

For a long moment, the silence stretched between them. Rian seemed unbothered, his hands folded calmly on the table, his posture relaxed. His eyes never wavered from hers.

Lyra finally broke the silence. "I wanted to thank you," she said softly, her voice laced with calculated sweetness. "For delivering that letter earlier. It was most... unexpected."

Rian raised an eyebrow, a flash of something—amusement?—in his expression. "Of course, my lady. I do my best to serve."

"Serve," Lyra repeated thoughtfully, leaning slightly forward in her chair. "That's what we all do, isn't it? Serve the kingdom. Serve our lord, our families. We serve the greater good."

Rian's eyes glinted with a sharpness that didn't escape her notice. His lips parted, but he remained silent, his gaze assessing her.

Lyra's heart pounded in her chest, but she kept her voice steady. "Tell me, Rian, who *do* you serve? Who do you really serve?"

At the question, his face stiffened ever so slightly, a flicker of discomfort crossing his features. For the briefest moment, she saw the mask crack. But then, just as quickly, it was gone, replaced with that same disarming smile.

"I serve Lord Valerius, of course. I've sworn my loyalty to Aeridor." His voice was smooth, but there was something

Chapter 8: Betrayals and Alliances

almost *too* practiced in his tone.

Lyra leaned back in her chair, the weight of his words hanging between them. She wasn't sure how much he knew—or how much he was trying to hide—but she could sense something was off.

"I see," she said slowly, her voice even. "And yet, some allegiances are more... complicated than they first appear."

The faintest twitch of his eye, the briefest tightening of his jaw—she had caught him. Lyra's pulse quickened.

She leaned in closer, her gaze piercing. "There are those who serve more than just a lord, aren't there, Rian? Some serve an idea. Some serve a kingdom... and some serve something far more dangerous."

Rian's lips pressed together, his eyes narrowing slightly, but he said nothing. The silence stretched on, thick and heavy.

Lyra smiled, her eyes glinting with quiet triumph. The game had truly begun.

And in this game, she wasn't going to be the one who lost.

The wind outside howled again, but inside the study, the room felt still—too still. As the seconds ticked by, Lyra felt the walls of deception close in, the weight of the lies pressing down upon them both. It was only a matter of time before one of them would crack.

The question was: who would it be?

The silence stretched between them, thick and heavy, as if the very air in the room had thickened with the weight of unspoken truths. Lyra held Rian's gaze, her expression steady, though her heart pounded beneath the surface. She had never been one for games of bluff, but in this moment, she felt as though she were playing her hand in the dark, uncertain of

Tempting the Enemy's Daughter

whether she held the better cards.

Rian's eyes flickered for the briefest moment—a subtle shift, a tightening of his jaw that betrayed just enough to send a ripple of triumph through her. She had struck a chord. But whether that chord was the beginning of unraveling him or the prelude to her own undoing, she couldn't yet tell.

He leaned forward slowly, his gaze narrowing as he studied her, trying to gauge the depth of her knowledge, or perhaps testing how far she would push. His lips curled into a half-smile, but it lacked warmth.

"I see you're more perceptive than I gave you credit for, my lady," Rian said quietly, his voice calm but layered with something dangerous beneath the surface. "But be careful where you tread. Some questions are better left unasked."

Lyra's pulse quickened at his words, but she didn't let it show. She wasn't here to back down, not now, not when she was so close. She leaned in a little closer, her eyes narrowing in return.

"What are you hiding, Rian?" she asked, her voice low, almost a whisper. "And what does it have to do with Solara?"

For a split second, a flicker of something—fear?—passed across his face, too fast to catch. But it was there, a brief crack in his composed demeanor. Lyra's heart skipped a beat. *This is it.*

He straightened suddenly, his lips forming a thin line. "You're treading on dangerous ground, Lady Lyra. You have no idea what you're involving yourself in."

Her eyes never wavered. "Then tell me. What is it that I don't know?"

Rian's expression shifted—no longer a mask of politeness but a mask of cold calculation. The air between them grew

Chapter 8: Betrayals and Alliances

heavier, the room darker, as if their words alone were enough to dim the light in the study.

"Do you think this is all coincidence?" he asked, his voice low and edged with something like contempt. "The tension between our kingdoms? The pact your father made with Lord Valerius? You think it's just a matter of diplomacy?"

Lyra's breath caught in her throat. He was revealing more than she expected. And yet, she couldn't show weakness now, couldn't let him see how deeply his words were affecting her.

"I think it's more than that," she said, her voice even, though her mind raced. "I think there's something you're not telling me. Something that goes deeper than just politics."

Rian's eyes darkened. He was no longer pretending to be the loyal servant of Aeridor's court. He was something else now—someone with his own agenda, his own interests, and Lyra had just stumbled onto them.

"You should have stayed out of it, Lyra," he said softly, almost regretfully. "But now that you've gotten this far, there's no turning back."

Before Lyra could respond, Rian suddenly stood, moving with a speed and grace that startled her. His hand reached into his coat, pulling out a small object—a pendant, carved with the same intricate symbol she had seen earlier on the mysterious letter. The same symbol that had haunted her since the moment she first laid eyes on it.

Her breath caught. "Where did you get that?" she demanded, her voice sharp, her instincts screaming that she had crossed a threshold. The pendant was far too familiar.

Rian didn't answer right away. Instead, he let the pendant hang in the air between them, catching the light from the candle on the table. His eyes met hers, hard and unyielding.

"It's not about what you *know*, Lady Lyra," he said quietly. "It's about what you're willing to accept."

There was a weight in his words—an implication that left a cold chill in her bones.

Lyra stood suddenly, her chair scraping loudly against the stone floor. She was shaking, her pulse racing, as the realization began to sink in. This wasn't just about spies or political maneuvering. This was something much darker, something *older*. A dangerous game was being played, and she was already in it, tangled in threads she could not see.

Rian stepped forward, his eyes glinting with something predatory. "You may think you're in control, Lady Lyra, but you're not. Not yet. There's still much to be revealed, and when the time comes, you'll understand."

"What do you mean?" she asked, her voice tight, every instinct screaming at her to back away.

"The fracture is just the beginning," Rian said, his voice colder now, each word like a carefully laid stone. "It's not just a rift in time. It's a rift in reality itself. And there are those who will stop at nothing to exploit it."

Lyra's breath hitched. Her eyes narrowed, trying to make sense of his cryptic words. "Exploit it? What are you talking about?"

Rian's smile faded, replaced by an expression of grim determination. "You'll see soon enough. The alliances between your father and Lord Valerius—they're not as they seem. The pact was never meant to last. It's just a means to an end."

Lyra could feel her world tilting. The ground beneath her feet felt less sure. Every instinct in her screamed to leave, to get out of the room and distance herself from this man, from this

Chapter 8: Betrayals and Alliances

madness. But there was something in Rian's eyes—something that made her feel that she had stumbled onto the very core of the problem. The fracture, the betrayal, the hidden forces at work—it all tied together in ways that were still beyond her comprehension.

"Who else is involved?" she asked, her voice barely above a whisper, the weight of her own words suffocating her.

Rian paused for a long moment, his gaze flickering with something unreadable. Then, almost reluctantly, he spoke.

"You've met them already," he said softly, his voice barely more than a murmur. "Some are closer than you think. Some are sitting right beside you. But you'll never see them until it's too late."

Lyra felt a chill run down her spine. The words didn't make sense, but the implications—those were clear. Someone close to her, someone she trusted, was part of this web of betrayal. And she had no idea who it was.

Suddenly, the door to the study swung open with a loud crash, and both Lyra and Rian turned toward it, startled. Standing in the doorway, silhouetted by the flickering light from the hallway, was Lord Valerius.

He stepped into the room, his eyes sweeping over them both, his expression hard, unreadable. Lyra's heart skipped in her chest, her pulse thundering in her ears. She hadn't expected him to come—certainly not this soon.

"Rian," Valerius's voice was low and commanding, a blade sheathed in velvet. "You've overstayed your welcome."

Lyra's breath caught in her throat. She knew what this meant—she had seen the tension in Valerius's eyes earlier, heard the warnings in his voice. And now, she understood. Valerius had known all along. Rian was a threat, a piece in a game much larger than either of them could yet fully comprehend.

But she also realized, with a chill that settled deep in her bones, that Rian had just delivered a message far more dangerous than she had anticipated.

The web of deception was tightening around her.

And the game was far from over.

Lyra stood frozen, her heart racing as Valerius strode into the room, the heavy silence amplifying the tension. His gaze flickered briefly to Rian, but it was clear that his attention was primarily on her. The air in the study grew thick, charged with the weight of unspoken things. She had thought she understood the stakes of the game she was playing, but now the realization struck her like a blow to the chest: she was standing on the edge of a cliff, and the fall would be far worse than she could have ever imagined.

Valerius's eyes never left hers, and for a moment, Lyra felt as though he could see straight through her, as if he could read the swirling maelstrom of confusion and suspicion that churned in her mind.

"What did he tell you?" Valerius's voice was calm, but there was an edge to it, a sharpness that set her nerves on edge. His words were not a question, but a command—an unspoken challenge.

Lyra's throat tightened. She wasn't ready for this confrontation—not yet. She hadn't fully grasped the meaning of what Rian had said, but she knew that revealing everything she had learned would only make her more vulnerable. Valerius already suspected something was wrong. To show weakness now would put her at a disadvantage she couldn't afford.

Chapter 8: Betrayals and Alliances

"He was just..." She faltered for a second, weighing her words carefully, her mind whirling. "He was just speaking in riddles, Valerius. Nothing that matters."

A flicker of doubt passed through Valerius's eyes, but it vanished almost as quickly as it came. He stepped farther into the room, closing the distance between them with a slow, deliberate pace. His presence was magnetic, the aura of power and control he exuded suffocating, yet oddly comforting. Lyra tried to steady herself, but the tension in the room felt as though it were pressing against her chest.

"Nothing that matters," Valerius repeated, his voice deceptively soft. "Do you truly believe that?"

Lyra's gaze flicked to Rian, who stood silent in the corner of the room, his arms folded across his chest, watching the interaction with an unreadable expression. For a moment, she considered the possibility that Valerius already knew everything—that he had orchestrated this confrontation from the beginning. He was a master manipulator, after all, and she had seen enough to know that he played a far more dangerous game than anyone else in the room.

She swallowed hard, then forced herself to meet Valerius's gaze. "It's just words, Valerius. Nothing more. Rian has a tendency to speak in cryptic nonsense. You know that."

The lie tasted bitter on her tongue, but she pressed on, praying that it would be enough.

Valerius stopped in front of her, his piercing eyes never leaving hers. "You know," he said quietly, "I have seen many things in my time. People are rarely what they seem. And you, Lady Lyra, are no exception. But this..." He waved a hand between them, a subtle motion that suggested the web of tension that had formed in this room. "This is something else entirely."

He didn't wait for her response. Instead, he turned his head slightly, signaling to Rian without so much as a word. The unspoken command was clear.

"You've heard enough," Valerius said coldly, his eyes now focused entirely on Rian.

Rian didn't flinch at the command. He stood tall, his jaw clenched tight, his eyes flashing with a mix of irritation and begrudging respect. There was something calculating in his expression as he took a step forward, his hands still clasped behind his back.

"I've said all I needed to say," Rian replied, his voice almost too calm. "It's not my place to tell her what she isn't ready to understand."

For a moment, the two men exchanged a silent, almost imperceptible glance. Lyra could feel the tension between them, like two pieces of a puzzle that were slowly fitting together, revealing the contours of a far larger picture—one that she wasn't yet ready to see.

Valerius nodded once, a sharp, curt movement, and Rian gave a small bow before turning to leave the room.

"Wait," Lyra called out before she could stop herself. Her pulse quickened, her mind racing. She couldn't let him leave yet, couldn't let him disappear into the shadows before she had answers. "What is the fracture? What does it mean?"

Rian paused in the doorway, his back still to her. "You'll find out soon enough," he said cryptically, his voice carrying a note of finality. "Just remember, Lady Lyra: time is not always what it seems. And trust is a far more dangerous thing than you realize."

With that, he was gone, his footsteps fading into the

Chapter 8: Betrayals and Alliances

corridor.

For a long moment, Lyra stood motionless, her breath shallow as she processed what had just transpired. She felt more isolated than ever—trapped in a world of shadows and half-truths, surrounded by people whose true intentions were still hidden beneath layers of deceit.

Valerius, who had been silent since Rian's departure, turned to her slowly, his expression unreadable. He stepped closer to where she stood, but this time, there was no warmth in his gaze. No trace of the almost familiar intensity she had seen earlier. Instead, there was a coldness to him, a formality that set her on edge.

"You have to understand, Lyra," he said quietly, his voice low but commanding, "this is no longer just a political struggle. It's something far darker. Something that has been brewing for years."

Lyra's stomach churned at the weight in his words. She didn't know whether to trust him or not. Did she even know who he was anymore? She had seen so many sides of him, and each one felt like another carefully constructed mask.

"Darker?" she repeated, trying to keep her voice steady. "What do you mean? What's really going on, Valerius?"

He didn't answer immediately. Instead, he regarded her with a look that was both intense and calculating, as though weighing her every word.

"The fractures in the alliance," he began slowly, "they are not mere political failures. They're the result of something far older. Something that predates even the pact between Aeridor and Solara."

Lyra took a step back, her mind racing. "What do you mean 'older'? The pact between our kingdoms—"

"Was a lie," he interjected, his tone biting. "The pact was never meant to hold. It was a shield. A way to keep us from facing the truth of what happened generations ago."

Lyra's chest tightened. This was worse than she had imagined. The magnitude of his words was slowly beginning to sink in, but she couldn't grasp it completely. She needed to know more.

"Generations ago?" she echoed. "What are you talking about? What happened?"

Valerius's gaze flickered toward the door through which Rian had left. His jaw clenched, and for a moment, there was something vulnerable in his expression—something that made her wonder if, despite his aloofness, despite his coldness, he too was caught in something much bigger than he could control.

"The fractures, Lyra. The fractures in time, in reality itself. They've been there for as long as anyone can remember, but only now are they beginning to show themselves."

Lyra's breath caught in her throat. "What does this have to do with me? With the two kingdoms?"

"It has everything to do with you," Valerius said softly, his voice lowering. "You are part of something that goes beyond either Aeridor or Solara. You're at the center of something far greater than anyone has realized. Something... ancient."

His words hung in the air like a storm waiting to break.

Lyra felt a chill settle over her, as though the world around her had shifted just slightly, revealing the shadows that had always been there, just beyond the edge of her vision.

The game had taken a darker turn. And now, there was no going back.

Ten

Chapter 9: The Web of Deception

Lyra's mind spun as she left the study behind, her heart heavy with the weight of Valerius's words. There were no simple answers to be found here—only more questions, more shadows, more webs of lies and betrayal. She had come to Aeridor believing that her mission was one of diplomacy, a straightforward assignment meant to ease the tension between her father's kingdom and the enigmatic Lord Valerius. But now, she saw the truth: she had walked into a labyrinth, and every path seemed to lead her deeper into the darkness.

She barely registered the passage of time as she made her way down the long hallways of the castle. Her footsteps echoed in the empty corridors, but there was no one in sight. The day had grown late, and the castle, once alive with the bustle of servants and nobles, now seemed abandoned, as though even the walls were holding their breath.

Her thoughts were tangled in the words Rian had spoken:

"The fracture is just the beginning." What did he mean by that? And why had Valerius seemed so… evasive? He had known more than he had let on, but what could it all mean? The fracture in time, the ancient pact—was this all just the product of old wounds that had never fully healed, or was there something far more sinister at play?

A figure suddenly stepped into her path, pulling her out of her reverie. It was Eamon, one of Valerius's closest advisors, a man whose loyalty was well known—but in this web of deception, how could she trust anyone?

"Lady Lyra," he said smoothly, his voice low and respectful. "I trust you are well?"

Lyra didn't immediately answer. She studied him for a long moment, assessing him as best she could. Eamon was tall, his face chiseled and fair, his manner always composed. He had been at Valerius's side for years, but she had never quite been able to shake the feeling that there was more to him than met the eye. She had often wondered if his calm, measured demeanor was the mask of a man with far more dangerous ambitions.

"I am well," she replied cautiously, her voice steady. "But I am… troubled."

Eamon's brows furrowed in polite concern. "Troubled? Might I inquire why, my lady?"

Lyra hesitated. She had learned to guard her thoughts carefully in Aeridor, especially when it came to those closest to Lord Valerius. But Eamon's presence here, at this moment, felt too much like an invitation to continue the conversation. He was a man who prided himself on being in the know, on understanding the intricacies of the court. He might be able to offer her some answers—if he could be trusted.

Chapter 9: The Web of Deception

"I've learned... troubling things today," she said slowly, testing her words. "There are forces at work that I don't fully understand. And I'm not sure who I can trust anymore."

Eamon's eyes glinted for a moment, his lips curling into a small, knowing smile. "Trust," he repeated softly, as though savoring the word. "That is always the most dangerous element of any alliance. But I suspect you've already discovered that, Lady Lyra."

She stared at him, the pit of her stomach sinking. "You know something," she said, a hint of accusation in her voice. "About the fracture. About the lies."

Eamon's expression shifted, the faintest trace of something like amusement—or was it resignation?—crossing his features. "Not lies, my lady. Deceptions, yes. But not lies. There are things far more dangerous than simple truths."

Lyra's breath caught. She had expected nothing less, but the implications were staggering. "What do you mean?"

Before Eamon could respond, the sound of approaching footsteps echoed down the corridor. Lyra turned, her heart skipping a beat. She recognized the gait immediately—heavy, purposeful. Lord Valerius was coming toward them. His presence was unmistakable, a force unto itself.

Eamon straightened instantly, his face smoothing into a mask of professional indifference. "Lord Valerius," he greeted him smoothly, bowing slightly. "A pleasure as always."

Valerius's gaze flicked briefly over Eamon before turning to Lyra. There was something unreadable in his eyes, a quiet intensity that sent a shiver down her spine. He said nothing for a moment, simply studying her, as though trying to gauge her very soul.

"Lady Lyra," he said finally, his voice low and edged with an

Tempting the Enemy's Daughter

emotion she couldn't name. "I see you've been speaking with my advisor."

Lyra inclined her head, her own expression carefully neutral. "We were discussing matters of mutual interest."

"Ah." Valerius's lips curled slightly, though the smile did not reach his eyes. "Such matters are... delicate. And not all can be shared so freely."

Eamon's gaze flickered to Valerius, but the lord paid him no mind, his attention fully focused on Lyra. For a moment, there was an uncomfortable stillness between them, as though the air had thickened, pressing in around them.

Lyra felt the weight of his scrutiny, but she refused to look away. "I'm trying to understand," she said, her voice firm. "What's really happening here, Valerius? What is the fracture, and why is it affecting everything?"

Valerius was silent for a long moment. His gaze never wavered, and Lyra's pulse quickened under the intensity of his stare. Finally, he spoke, his voice carrying a low, almost ominous tone.

"Do you truly want to know, Lady Lyra?" His words were measured, as though he were choosing them carefully. "Because once you understand, you will see that nothing can ever be the same. The fracture is not just a tear in time. It is a rupture in the very fabric of reality itself."

Lyra's breath caught in her throat. She had heard rumors—whispers of something ancient, something powerful, something that had broken the balance of the world long before her time. But hearing it from Valerius's lips, hearing the gravity of it, made the weight of those words feel far heavier than anything she had imagined.

"You speak as if it is already too late," she said, her voice

Chapter 9: The Web of Deception

barely above a whisper.

Valerius met her gaze squarely, his expression unwavering. "In some ways, it is. But there are those among us who still believe the fracture can be healed—if we act quickly enough."

"And who are these people?" Lyra asked, though she already knew the answer.

Valerius did not reply at once. His lips thinned, and for a brief moment, he seemed lost in thought. Then, almost reluctantly, he spoke.

"The ancient factions—the ones that still remember the old ways. They are watching, waiting. And they are not all on the side of Solara or Aeridor."

Lyra blinked, her mind racing. "You're saying there are others? More players involved in this?"

"Yes," Valerius said quietly, his voice lowering. "Some have been in the shadows for centuries. Some of them may be closer than you realize."

The words hung in the air, chilling in their implication. Lyra felt a sudden tightness in her chest. There were people—forces—at work behind the scenes, manipulating things in ways she couldn't fully understand. And it was clear now: the stakes had never been just about a broken alliance or political maneuvering. There was something far larger, far darker, at play.

"What do we do?" she asked, her voice strained, a sense of urgency building within her. "How do we stop this?"

Valerius stepped closer, his voice dropping to a whisper. "We find the truth. We uncover the ones who are manipulating time and reality itself. And we make them pay for what they've done."

IIis words sent a chill through her, and for the first time,

Tempting the Enemy's Daughter

Lyra realized just how dangerous the game she was playing had become. This was no longer about alliances or betrayals. This was about something far more ancient—and far more powerful—than she could have ever imagined.

The web of deception had been spun long before she arrived, and now, she was caught in its tangled threads. The only question that remained was whether she would be able to escape—or if the web would pull her under.

As she turned to leave the corridor, the weight of Valerius's gaze pressed on her back. She didn't know what was waiting for her in the shadows, but one thing was certain: nothing would ever be the same again.

Lyra's mind raced as she made her way down the dimly lit corridor, her steps echoing in the stillness. The castle had grown quieter since the day had begun, the only sounds now the distant rustle of servants and the creak of the old stone walls settling. But to Lyra, it felt like the world had been hollowed out, leaving only the weight of her thoughts and the ominous shadow of the secrets she had uncovered.

The conversation with Valerius had left her shaken. There was more to the fracture, to the web of deception, than she had initially realized. What was once a matter of political negotiation was now something far more dangerous—and far more personal. Every step she took in Aeridor felt like it led her further into the heart of a conspiracy, a conspiracy that threatened not only the fragile peace between Solara and Aeridor, but the very fabric of reality itself.

She had to know more. She had to understand how far this web of deceit stretched, and who was truly pulling the strings behind the scenes. The more she learned, the more the pieces seemed to fall into place, but there was something missing—a

Chapter 9: The Web of Deception

vital part of the puzzle that was still eluding her.

As she reached the end of the corridor, she noticed a shadow move at the edge of her vision. She froze, every muscle tensing. For a moment, she thought it was just her nerves playing tricks on her. But when she turned the corner, her suspicions were confirmed. There, standing in the shadows near a carved stone pillar, was a figure—a figure she had not expected to see again so soon.

Rian.

He didn't move when she spotted him, his face half-hidden in the dark, but she could feel his eyes on her—intense, calculating.

Lyra didn't hesitate. She walked toward him, her steps firm despite the unease that crept through her. The last time they had spoken, the words had been cryptic, the tension between them palpable. She had left that conversation with more questions than answers, but now, there was no escaping the feeling that Rian held the key to everything.

He spoke before she could say anything, his voice low and careful. "You're moving too quickly, Lady Lyra."

Her breath caught in her throat. "Moving too quickly?" she echoed, raising an eyebrow. "What do you mean?"

Rian stepped out of the shadows, his eyes flashing with something between caution and concern. "You've learned some things—things that were never meant for you to understand yet."

"And you think I should ignore them?" Lyra countered, frustration edging her tone. "I'm not in the habit of pretending I don't see what's in front of me. I can't ignore the truth just because it's inconvenient."

Rian studied her for a moment, then nodded, as though he

had expected this response. "The truth is a dangerous thing. Not all truths are meant to be known." He hesitated, then added, "There are people who want you to know the truth, but there are also those who will kill to keep you from it."

Lyra's heart skipped a beat. "Who?" she asked, her voice suddenly tight with the urgency of the question. "Who is it that wants me dead for knowing the truth?"

Rian didn't answer immediately. Instead, he stepped closer, his voice dropping to a whisper. "Not just you, Lady Lyra. They want all of us dead. Aeridor. Solara. The kingdoms, the people. All of us. What's coming… what's already here… it's bigger than any of us."

Her pulse quickened at his words. "What's coming?" she asked, but even as she spoke, a horrible realization dawned on her. She had known, deep down, that this was never going to be just a war between kingdoms. There was something far more sinister at play.

Rian's expression darkened. "The fracture is more than a rift in time. It's a tear in the fabric of reality itself. It's the result of ancient magics—things that were locked away, forgotten, hidden for a reason. There are those who want to control it, to use it to reshape the world. And there are others who would rather see everything burn than allow it to be used."

"Who are these people?" Lyra demanded, feeling the cold weight of his words settling in her chest.

Rian glanced around, checking for any sign of movement before speaking again. "There's a faction within Aeridor—a secret group of powerful individuals. Some are close to Valerius. Some even hold sway in Solara. They've been manipulating events for centuries, waiting for the right moment to seize control."

Chapter 9: The Web of Deception

Lyra felt her stomach churn. Valerius had warned her that there were others—factions at play, lurking in the shadows. But to hear it from Rian, to know that some of these people were so close to the heart of the two kingdoms... it sent a chill through her.

"So, all of this—the fractured alliance, the tension between our kingdoms—it's just the surface, isn't it?" Lyra asked, her voice strained with the weight of the realization. "It's all part of a much bigger game."

Rian nodded slowly. "Exactly. The war between Aeridor and Solara is just the distraction. The fracture is the real game. And the people behind it... they've been orchestrating everything from the start."

Lyra's mind raced. If Rian was telling the truth, it meant that the ancient pact between the kingdoms had been built on a foundation of lies. The political maneuvering, the alliances, the betrayals—they were all part of something far more dangerous. And she, unwittingly, had been dragged into the middle of it.

"What do we do?" Lyra asked, her voice barely above a whisper.

Rian's eyes softened, the hardness in his gaze giving way to something almost vulnerable. "We have to find the source of the fracture, Lady Lyra. We need to understand it completely before they do. If we don't..." His voice trailed off, and for a moment, the weight of his words hung between them like a sword poised to fall.

"And if we do find it?" she asked. "What happens then?"

Rian didn't answer right away. Instead, he studied her face, as though searching for something—an understanding, perhaps, or a willingness to accept what would come next.

"If we find it," he said finally, "we can stop them. But it won't be easy. The forces at play here are ancient. Powerful. And they won't hesitate to destroy anyone who stands in their way."

Lyra felt a surge of determination rise within her. She had never shied away from a fight, and this was no different. The stakes were higher than she could have ever imagined, but there was no turning back now.

"I'm ready," she said, her voice firm.

Rian gave her a long look, then nodded. "Very well. But you must be careful, Lady Lyra. The web is far more complex than it seems. The more you uncover, the deeper you will go—and the more dangerous it will become."

He turned to leave, but then paused, looking back at her. "I'll be in touch. And be careful who you trust. Some people are not who they seem."

With that, he melted back into the shadows, leaving Lyra alone with her thoughts once more.

As she stood there, her heart pounding, Lyra realized that the game had only just begun. And this time, the stakes were higher than her life—or even the lives of the people she loved. The very fabric of reality itself was at risk.

And she was right in the center of it all.

Lyra stood frozen in the corridor, the weight of Rian's cryptic words pressing heavily on her chest. The shadows seemed to close in around her, as though the walls themselves were tightening their grip. She had learned many things in her life, but this… this was a different kind of game. This was no longer about mere politics or alliances. There were forces at work, ancient forces, and she was just one pawn on a vast chessboard.

Chapter 9: The Web of Deception

She felt a sudden rush of cold air sweep through the corridor, the faintest echo of movement nearby, and her heart skipped. She was not alone.

Turning sharply, she saw a figure standing a few paces behind her—tall, silent, and unmistakable.

Valerius.

For a moment, the two of them simply stared at each other, the tension thick enough to slice with a knife. He was still wearing the dark cloak he had donned earlier, the hood pulled low over his brow. But there was nothing casual about his appearance now. He stood with the weight of command, the unspoken authority of someone who had seen far more than he ever let on.

Lyra swallowed hard. Despite everything that had happened—everything she had learned—she still couldn't deny the power he held over her. The strange mix of attraction and suspicion that simmered between them had become more complicated, more volatile.

"I've been looking for you," Valerius said, his voice calm but laced with something else—something she couldn't quite decipher.

Her pulse quickened, though she kept her voice steady. "Have you?"

Valerius took a step closer, his eyes never leaving hers. "I trust our conversation earlier with Eamon went well?" His tone was deceptively casual, but there was an edge to it, a knowing that made her skin prickle.

Lyra clenched her jaw, unwilling to let him see how Rian's words had affected her. "It went… informative. Though I'm not certain I know everything I should yet."

He studied her for a long moment, his gaze piercing. It

felt as though he were reading every thought, every flicker of emotion that crossed her face. But then his lips curled into a small, inscrutable smile.

"You're cleverer than most give you credit for," he said softly, as if the compliment was an afterthought. "That could be both your greatest strength and your most dangerous flaw."

Lyra's eyes narrowed. "I've never been one to shy away from danger."

Valerius nodded, his smile lingering. "I know. But this is different. This isn't a danger that can be fought with swords or political maneuvering." He stepped closer, his presence almost overwhelming. "You're swimming in a river of deceit, Lady Lyra. The current is swift, and it doesn't care who drowns."

She stood her ground, though the metaphor hung heavily in the air. Her instincts screamed at her to step back, to regain some semblance of control over the conversation, but she didn't. Instead, she faced him head-on, her voice steady, though it betrayed the flicker of uncertainty she couldn't suppress. "And what do you suggest I do? Turn back and pretend none of this is happening?"

For a moment, Valerius didn't answer. He seemed to weigh her words, his eyes shifting between her face and the shadows around them. Then, as if making a decision, he sighed.

"No," he said quietly, "I don't expect you to turn back. But I do expect you to understand the gravity of what you're dealing with here." His voice dropped lower, the intensity in it unmistakable. "I don't know if you fully grasp how much you've already learned—or how much you've already put in motion."

Lyra tilted her head, feeling the familiar tension tightening in her chest. "You seem to think I'm unaware of the stakes,"

Chapter 9: The Web of Deception

she said, each word measured. "But if you think I'll back down now, you're mistaken. I've seen enough to know that the web is much larger than either of us expected."

Valerius's gaze sharpened at her words, and for a brief moment, the mask of politeness slipped, revealing something darker beneath. "I never said I thought you would back down," he said softly, his voice laced with an almost imperceptible challenge. "But I wonder if you truly understand the full scope of what's at play here. If you do, then you'll realize just how fragile everything is—how close we are to losing it all."

He paused, letting the weight of his words settle between them before taking another step closer, his eyes flickering to the side. Lyra could feel the intensity rising, the air thick with tension.

"I think you've been told part of the truth, Lady Lyra," he continued, his voice dropping to a murmur. "But not all of it. There are still things hidden from you—things you cannot yet see."

Her breath caught in her throat. She knew there was more he wasn't saying, more that had been kept from her. But what? And why?

Before she could speak, Valerius's gaze flicked over her shoulder, and his expression tightened, his stance shifting. It was subtle, but Lyra caught the change—he had sensed something before she had.

"Someone is watching," he muttered under his breath, barely loud enough for her to hear.

Her heart skipped, and her instincts screamed. She spun around, scanning the hallway for any sign of movement. The shadows in the corner seemed to shift, but when she looked closely, there was nothing there. No hidden figures, no telltale

Tempting the Enemy's Daughter

signs of someone lurking in the dark.

Valerius didn't wait for her to ask. He motioned for her to follow him, stepping quickly into a nearby alcove, half-hidden behind a tapestry that hung from the wall. Lyra hesitated for only a moment before she followed, her pulse racing.

When they were safely out of view, Valerius turned to her, his face taut with urgency. "There are eyes everywhere, Lyra," he whispered. "I don't know who you've been speaking to, but someone is following your every move."

Lyra's chest tightened. "You think it's Rian, don't you?"

Valerius's gaze shifted briefly, his lips tight. "It could be. Or it could be someone else entirely. Someone who has been feeding information to Solara—and to Aeridor's enemies. The web is tangled, but not in ways you or I can control."

She felt a sudden pang of fear at his words. The thought of someone in her inner circle betraying her, using her as a pawn in a game she couldn't even begin to comprehend, made her stomach churn.

"What should we do?" she asked, her voice low and urgent.

Valerius's eyes met hers, a flicker of something dark passing between them. "We find out who's pulling the strings before they find out that you know too much. And we make sure they can't use you—or anyone else—against us."

Lyra nodded, the weight of his words settling in. She had always known there was a cost to this game. But she hadn't anticipated just how high that cost would be.

Her mind raced. The pieces were finally starting to come together, but there were too many unknowns—too many layers of deception that she had yet to uncover. And as much as she hated to admit it, she needed Valerius's knowledge, his reach, his ability to navigate the shadowed halls of power.

Chapter 9: The Web of Deception

"I won't back down," she said firmly, meeting his gaze with resolve.

Valerius's lips curled into a half-smile, though it held no warmth. "I never thought you would."

For a moment, the two of them stood there, the silence stretching between them as the weight of their decisions settled upon them both.

The web was tightening. And no one, not even the most powerful among them, was certain how it would end.

Eleven

Chapter 10: A Daring Escape

The moon hung high in the sky, casting pale light over the stone walls of Aeridor Castle. Inside, the castle was still, save for the soft murmurs of distant servants finishing their evening tasks. But in the heart of the fortress, in the quiet corridors and secret chambers, a sense of urgency pulsed through the air.

Lyra moved swiftly through the shadows, her footsteps light and measured. Her breath came in quiet, controlled bursts, and her mind raced with the enormity of what she was about to do. The decision had been made. She could not stay here—not under the watchful eyes of those who would use her as a pawn in their dangerous game.

The revelations she'd uncovered over the past days—Rian's warnings, Valerius's veiled threats, the web of deceit that bound the two kingdoms—had made it clear that staying in Aeridor was no longer an option. And yet, leaving would not

Chapter 10: A Daring Escape

be easy. There were too many eyes watching her. Too many forces pulling at her from every direction.

She had no choice but to escape.

The corridors of the castle twisted and turned like a labyrinth, the stone walls seeming to close in around her. Every step she took felt both calculated and dangerous, as though the very ground beneath her feet was conspiring against her. But she had been here long enough to know the castle's secrets, to understand the hidden passages and forgotten ways that led to freedom—or to ruin.

She passed by a narrow alcove where a torch flickered faintly, the orange glow casting long shadows across the floor. Pausing, she checked the small leather pouch tied to her belt. Inside was a key—a key that had once belonged to her father's most trusted advisor, a man she had learned to trust herself. He had slipped it to her in secret, the same night she had learned that there were traitors among the Solarian court.

The key was to a hidden door, one that led out of the castle and into a series of tunnels buried beneath the foundation. She had never used it before, but she had heard enough whispers to know that the passage was a lifeline—a way out when all else failed.

Lyra glanced down both ends of the hallway, ensuring no one was in sight. The shadows were thick and comforting in their silence, but she knew it wouldn't last. Soon, someone would notice her absence, and then the chase would begin. She couldn't afford to be caught. Not now. Not after everything she had learned.

With a quick, silent motion, she pressed the key into a stone alcove beneath a tapestry. A soft click echoed through the corridor, and a section of the wall groaned as it shifted, revealing a narrow passageway beyond. Lyra's heart raced, but she didn't hesitate. She slipped inside, her movements swift and practiced.

The tunnel was cold and narrow, the air stale from years of disuse. Her boots echoed faintly as she made her way deeper into the darkness. The walls seemed to close in on her, and she fought the creeping sense of claustrophobia that threatened to overwhelm her. She needed to focus. She couldn't afford to lose her nerve now.

The passage twisted and turned, leading her deeper beneath the castle. She had memorized every step of the way, every hidden alcove and side passage. It was an old escape route, one that had once been used by kings and nobles in times of peril. The route had been abandoned long ago, but its existence remained a secret known only to a select few.

As she walked, Lyra's thoughts raced. Where would she go once she escaped the castle? What would she do next? There were too many unknowns, too many pieces of the puzzle still missing. But one thing was clear: she could no longer remain in Aeridor, caught between forces she couldn't control.

There was a city to the north—an ancient, forgotten place known only in stories, a place whispered about in the darkest corners of the world. Some said it was a haven for outcasts and fugitives, a place where the broken could find sanctuary. Others claimed it was a myth, a city lost to time and the ravages of war. But Lyra had heard enough rumors to believe there was some truth to them. If she could make it there, she might find the answers she sought—answers about the fracture, about the forces manipulating both Aeridor and Solara.

She had no other choice.

The passage ahead of her narrowed even further, forcing

Chapter 10: A Daring Escape

her to crouch low as she continued forward. She was almost there—almost to the end.

Suddenly, a sound echoed through the tunnel—a faint scraping, like boots dragging across stone. Lyra froze, her heart skipping a beat. Had someone discovered her escape? Or was it simply the echoes of the castle itself?

She held her breath, straining to listen.

The sound grew louder. Someone was coming.

Her hand instinctively went to the small dagger she kept hidden at her side. She couldn't afford to be caught—not now. Not when she was so close to freedom.

Lyra quickly turned into a side passage, her body flattening against the cold stone wall. She pressed herself into the shadows, her breath shallow and quiet, every sense heightened.

The footsteps grew louder, and then she saw a shadow emerge in the dim light—a figure, cloaked in dark robes, moving swiftly down the passage.

It was a guard. One of the castle's watchmen.

Her pulse quickened. He was almost on top of her. She didn't have much time.

Her mind raced, calculating her options. She couldn't fight him—not here, not now. But if she waited too long, he would pass too close, and her presence would be discovered.

Just as the guard's footsteps reached the intersection, Lyra took a deep breath and slipped forward, her movements swift and fluid. She darted across the passage, her back pressed to the stone wall, avoiding the guard's line of sight by mere inches.

She held her breath as she watched him pass. The guard's heavy steps grew fainter as he continued down the main tunnel, unaware of the intruder just a few feet away.

With a relieved sigh, Lyra stepped back into the main passage, her heart hammering in her chest. She hadn't been spotted, but she knew it was only a matter of time before someone realized she was gone.

The exit was ahead. She could feel the cool night air creeping through the cracks in the stone as she neared the end of the tunnel.

But as she approached the final bend, the faintest sound reached her ears. A rustling. A soft, deliberate movement in the dark.

Lyra stopped dead in her tracks.

Her heart pounded. She wasn't alone.

Someone was waiting at the exit. Someone who knew she would come this way.

Her fingers tightened around the hilt of her dagger.

There would be no escape without a fight.

The air in the tunnel grew colder, and a tight knot of dread formed in Lyra's stomach. Whoever waited at the exit knew the path as well as she did. They had anticipated her every move. She hadn't heard them approach, but they were there now—silent and waiting, like a predator lurking in the shadows.

Her hand tightened around the dagger at her side, the cold metal comforting against her palm. She wasn't about to let herself be caught, not now, not when she was so close. But she had to be careful. The guard she had nearly passed moments ago wasn't the only one in the castle. There could be more ahead. More who knew the tunnels.

Forcing her mind to focus, Lyra took a slow, steady breath. She couldn't afford to panic. Panic would get her caught.

There was a soft scraping sound again, followed by a barely

Chapter 10: A Daring Escape

audible shift in the air. The presence ahead was getting closer, edging closer to the exit. Whoever it was was trying to move quietly, but Lyra's heightened senses—sharpened by years of court intrigue and political games—told her the figure wasn't as subtle as they thought.

She took one more breath, steadying herself. The tunnel opened up ahead into a small, cramped chamber that led to the exit. She could see the faint outline of the heavy, rusted iron door in the distance—her freedom just beyond it.

Taking a calculated risk, she pressed her back against the tunnel's stone wall, trying to make herself as invisible as possible in the shadows. The dark cloak she wore helped conceal her presence, but her breathing still felt too loud in the thick silence of the passage. She had to remain completely still.

The footsteps grew closer. Then they stopped.

She froze, barely able to hear the soft shuffle of cloth against stone as the figure moved within a few feet of her hiding place. The silence stretched unbearably long. She could almost feel the presence, like the chill of an unseen hand resting on her shoulder. Lyra's pulse thrummed in her ears, her entire body coiled tight, prepared to spring into action.

And then, a voice—low and unmistakable—cut through the tension like a blade.

"You're not as quiet as you think, Lady Lyra."

Lyra's breath caught in her throat.

Rian.

The air seemed to freeze, her body instinctively tense with both recognition and a sudden rush of frustration. He had been waiting for her. Waiting, knowing exactly where she would go. The realization that she had walked straight into his trap struck her like a physical blow. But even as her mind raced, part of her couldn't help but feel a certain bitterness at the knowledge.

"I should have known you'd be here," she said, her voice cool despite the knot of anxiety tightening in her chest. She stepped forward from the shadows, dagger still in hand, her eyes narrowing at the figure now standing before her.

Rian's face was partially obscured by the hood of his cloak, but his eyes glinted with an unsettling familiarity—like a predator watching its prey, patient and calculating.

"You think you can run from this?" His tone was soft but firm, and the words hung in the air, charged with meaning. "You can't escape this, Lyra. Not now, not like this."

Lyra's hand gripped the dagger tighter, but she didn't move. "Why are you doing this?" she demanded, her voice steadier now. "You've been helping me. Or have you been manipulating me this entire time?"

Rian's expression was unreadable as he stepped closer, his pace slow and deliberate. "I'm doing this because you still don't understand the stakes," he said softly, almost regretfully. "The fracture is a danger to both kingdoms, yes. But what's worse than that is who's trying to control it. It's not just about Aeridor and Solara. It's much, much larger than that."

Lyra didn't lower the dagger. "What are you saying?"

Rian's lips twitched, almost as if he were about to smile. "I'm saying that if you leave now, you're playing into their hands. The ones pulling the strings don't care about kingdoms. They care about power. And you, Lyra, are a part of that power."

The cold dread that had been lingering in the pit of her stomach intensified. She stepped back a pace, suddenly unsure of everything she thought she knew. "What do you want from

Chapter 10: A Daring Escape

me?"

Rian's gaze softened, but only for a moment. "I want you to understand that the game you're in now is far too dangerous for you to be playing alone. I came to stop you from making a mistake, Lyra. But I can't make you stay. I can't protect you if you keep running."

Lyra's mind swirled with conflicting thoughts. Every instinct told her to flee, to push forward and escape into the night. But something about Rian's words held her in place, his presence like an immovable force in the dark.

"You're asking me to trust you again," she said, her voice quiet but filled with disbelief. "After everything that's happened, after everything you've shown me, you think I can just… trust you?"

He took another step forward, his eyes never leaving hers. "I've never asked you to trust me, Lyra. I've asked you to understand. And I'm asking you now to make a choice: stay here and keep running, or trust me long enough to help you stop what's coming."

The sound of approaching footsteps—quick, purposeful—echoed down the passageway, cutting through the tense silence between them. Lyra's heart raced, and she could feel the heat of the moment slipping from her control. The danger was growing closer, and if she stayed here much longer, she'd be trapped.

She glanced back toward the exit, but the figure standing before her was the one she had to face first.

"I'm not going back," she said, the words sharp and resolute. "I won't let them control me."

Rian's gaze darkened, but he nodded, as though he had expected this answer. "Then you leave me no choice," he murmured.

Before Lyra could react, Rian's hand darted out, gripping her wrist with surprising strength. The motion was so fast, so deliberate, that she barely had time to draw a breath before he twisted her arm, disarming her with a practiced flick of his wrist. Her dagger clattered to the stone floor.

"Don't make this harder than it has to be," he warned, his voice low, his grip firm but not cruel.

Lyra tried to yank her arm free, but his hand tightened. Her pulse thundered in her ears, the pressure of his hold a stark reminder of just how little control she had over the situation. She had no choice but to meet his gaze—cold, calculating, but with a hint of something she couldn't quite place.

"I'm not going back with you," she said, defiance in her tone.

Rian's eyes narrowed. "Then you leave me no choice," he repeated softly. "You're not running alone, Lyra. Not anymore."

The sound of footsteps grew louder. She could feel the presence of others closing in, shadows converging on her from all sides. The realization hit her like a cold wave.

She had walked straight into a trap.

And now, there was nowhere to run.

Rian's grip tightened around her wrist, and for a moment, the cold steel of his fingers felt like the last remaining tether to the life she had known. Her pulse hammered in her temples, the weight of her predicament sinking in with brutal clarity. There were no more choices to be made—no more clever political maneuvering or secret passages to hide in. She was caught, and in a way, it felt like the walls were closing in on her from all sides.

But even as she stood there, trapped in the shadowed tunnel,

Chapter 10: A Daring Escape

something deep inside Lyra hardened. She wasn't about to let anyone—least of all Rian—dictate her future. Not anymore.

Her free hand shot out, fingers wrapping around the hilt of the dagger that had fallen to the stone floor, just within reach. The guard would be upon them soon, but for now, Rian had left her one final opportunity to regain control.

She twisted her body sharply, pulling against his hold with all her strength. His hand slipped slightly, and in that brief moment of vulnerability, Lyra lunged, grabbing the dagger with a swift motion. Her heart pounded, but her focus was absolute. She spun around, bringing the blade up to his throat in a single, smooth motion.

Rian froze, his dark eyes widening in surprise, but there was no fear in them—only that familiar, calculating calm. He didn't move an inch.

"Let go of me," Lyra demanded, her voice sharp with barely contained fury. The blade trembled slightly in her grip, but she held it steady, her breath shallow and quick. "Now."

For a long moment, there was no response. The flickering light from the tunnel entrance cast long shadows across his face, but in the dimness, she saw the faintest hint of a smile play at the edges of his lips. It wasn't a smile of victory, nor one of amusement—it was something darker, something far more dangerous.

"I told you," he said softly, his voice barely above a whisper, "you can't run, Lyra. Not from me, and certainly not from the consequences of your actions."

Her pulse raced, the weight of his words pressing in on her. She knew he was right. There was no escaping the tangled web of alliances, betrayals, and half-truths she had become entangled in. But she wasn't about to give up now—not after

Tempting the Enemy's Daughter

everything she had sacrificed to get this far.

She tightened her grip on the dagger, feeling its cold weight as if it were the only thing holding her together. "Let me go," she repeated, her voice low but unyielding. "Or I will make you."

The smile finally faded from his lips, replaced by a flicker of something more guarded. He looked down at the blade pressed against his throat, then back at her, assessing, calculating.

"Do you really think you can kill me, Lyra?" His voice was still calm, but there was an underlying tension now, a thread of something dangerous beneath the surface. "You've spent too long in your father's world, believing that strength is what matters. But you're out of your depth here. This game is much bigger than you think."

Lyra's eyes narrowed. She had heard these words before—from Valerius, from others who sought to undermine her, to make her question her place in the world. But no matter how many times she heard it, she wasn't about to back down. Not now. Not after everything she had learned.

"I've learned more than enough," she said, her grip tightening on the dagger. "And I will not let anyone—least of all you—control me. Now, let go."

Rian's gaze softened, just for a fraction of a second. He let out a slow breath, his expression shifting from one of quiet menace to something almost pitying.

"Lyra," he said, his voice now tinged with something that almost sounded like regret, "you don't have to do this. You don't have to fight me."

Her resolve faltered, just briefly, as his words seemed to carry a weight of sincerity that cut through the tension.

Chapter 10: A Daring Escape

For a fleeting moment, she wondered if perhaps she had misunderstood him. Could Rian really be trying to help her? Was this just another manipulation—another carefully spun lie to pull her back into the web?

But before she could think further, the sound of approaching footsteps reached her ears. It was the unmistakable clatter of armor—several guards were closing in fast, their heavy boots echoing in the narrow tunnel.

Lyra's mind raced. She had mere moments before they would be upon her, and if she didn't act now, she would be trapped in the castle once again, with no way out.

Without warning, she drove the dagger forward—just enough to make a point, just enough to draw blood, but not enough to truly hurt him.

Rian gasped in surprise, his hands instinctively pulling back. But he didn't cry out or try to retaliate. Instead, he stepped back slowly, his eyes meeting hers with an unreadable expression.

"You'll regret this," he murmured quietly, his voice now colder than before. "You'll regret not listening to me."

Lyra didn't wait to see what he would do next. The guards were almost upon them, and she couldn't afford to stay any longer. She spun on her heel, the dagger still clenched tightly in her hand, and sprinted toward the tunnel exit.

Rian's voice echoed behind her, full of quiet menace. "You can't outrun what's coming, Lyra!"

She didn't look back. The sound of her feet pounding against the stone floor was the only noise in the stillness as she raced toward the narrow iron door, now just a few feet ahead.

With one final, desperate push, she reached the door. She

grabbed the cold handle, twisting it with force, but it didn't budge. Her heart stuttered in her chest. The lock was old, and the door was rusted shut.

Lyra's breath came in short, frantic gasps, her hands trembling as she fumbled with the lock. The footsteps behind her were louder now, closer. She could hear the clatter of armor and the harsh breathing of soldiers who had caught her scent. Time was running out.

She pulled with all her strength, her breath ragged, sweat beading on her brow.

And then—finally—a loud *click*. The door swung open just as the first guard rounded the corner.

Without a second thought, Lyra slipped through the opening, throwing the door shut behind her. She didn't look back. There was no time.

The cold night air hit her like a slap to the face, but it was welcome. She could hear the guards shouting behind her, their voices muffled through the thick stone, but the world outside the castle was wide open. There was a narrow path ahead, leading into the dark wilderness beyond.

She ran, her lungs burning, her legs moving faster than she thought possible. The world blurred around her, the fear and adrenaline fueling every step. She wasn't sure where she was going or how far she could go, but for the first time in days, she felt like she was free.

But even as she pushed forward, the haunting words Rian had whispered followed her like a shadow.

You'll regret this.

And deep down, in the cold pit of her stomach, Lyra couldn't shake the feeling that he was right.

Twelve

Chapter 11: Running from the Past

The wind was sharp, biting into her skin as Lyra raced through the dense forest, her boots crunching against the frosty underbrush. The cold air stung her lungs, but it was nothing compared to the burning knot of fear and uncertainty that twisted in her chest. Behind her, the castle loomed like a dark shadow in the distance, a place she had hoped to leave behind forever. Yet, the weight of her escape clung to her like a shroud, reminding her that she had not yet outrun the dangers that followed her.

Her mind was a whirlwind of thoughts. Rian's words echoed in her ears, his voice soft and cold, filled with warnings that gnawed at her resolve. *You'll regret this.* His words weren't just empty threats. They felt like a promise—a promise that whatever lay ahead, it would be far worse than anything she could leave behind in Aeridor.

But she couldn't go back. Not now.

Tempting the Enemy's Daughter

She had made her choice.

Her escape had been messy, frantic, and full of the chaos of the moment. The guards' shouts had faded into the night behind her, but she knew they wouldn't give up the hunt so easily. Aeridor's reach was long, and her flight would not go unnoticed. She was a daughter of the Solarian Duke, an enemy of Aeridor, and her disappearance would send ripples through both kingdoms. The game was no longer about politics or power—it had become personal. The walls had come down, and she was running from everything: her family, her past, and the truth she had been unwilling to face.

Her breath came in ragged gasps, the sting of the night air sharp in her lungs as she pushed herself harder. The landscape around her shifted, from dense trees to a clearing, where the snow lay untouched, a silent witness to her flight. She paused for a moment, her chest heaving as she surveyed her surroundings. There was no sign of pursuit—at least, not yet—but that didn't mean she was safe. She couldn't afford to stop for long.

She had heard stories. Rumors whispered in hushed voices in the dark corners of the castle, of a place beyond the kingdom—a city hidden from the world, lost in legend and time. Some said it was a refuge for those who had nowhere else to go. Others claimed it was a myth, a place born from the desperation of those who sought to escape the burdens of their past.

But Lyra had no choice. Her only hope was to find that city. A place where she could disappear, where no one could reach her—or, perhaps, more importantly, where she could learn the truth of the ancient pact that had torn her world apart.

Her thoughts drifted back to the fractured relationship

Chapter 11: Running from the Past

between Solara and Aeridor, to the shattered promises, and to the promises of power that neither kingdom had ever truly kept. The fracturing of the pact was more than just a political maneuver. It was something older, something darker—a magical event that had irrevocably torn the fabric of their worlds. She needed to know what had happened. Why had the pact been broken? And who—if anyone—was behind it?

Who can I trust now? The question lingered in her mind, taunting her.

Rian had been right about one thing: she was out of her depth. The lines between ally and enemy were no longer clear. Every move, every decision felt like it could be the last one. She had been manipulated for too long, and now, with no one left to turn to, she was alone.

But she would not give up. She couldn't.

As the trees thinned ahead, Lyra spotted a narrow path winding through the snow. It was barely visible, obscured by a thin layer of frost, but it was there, leading away from the open field and deeper into the unknown. This was the direction she had been told to follow—the last piece of a trail that would lead her to sanctuary.

She took a deep breath, and with a final glance over her shoulder, she began to walk down the path. Her pace slowed, but her senses remained sharp. The forest was eerily silent, the only sounds the crunch of her boots in the snow and the distant calls of night birds.

The journey was long, and with each passing hour, the weight of her escape pressed heavier on her shoulders. She had no map, no clear sense of where she was going. The path seemed to stretch on endlessly, winding through the dense woods, then rising into a series of rocky hills that cut through the landscape like jagged teeth.

By the time the first light of dawn crept over the horizon, Lyra's legs ached, and her body was drained from the cold and exertion. She had not stopped to rest, too afraid that if she did, she might not be able to keep going. But the sun was rising now, and the dim gray light of morning brought with it a flicker of hope. If she could just make it through the hills, she might be close to her destination. She had to be.

But as the hours dragged on, that flicker of hope began to feel like a distant dream, slipping further and further from her grasp. The path twisted and turned, and she found herself no longer sure if she was heading in the right direction. Her breath came in ragged gasps as the wind picked up, biting at her exposed skin. Snowflakes began to swirl around her, turning the landscape into a swirling blur of white.

Lyra paused, her body trembling from exhaustion. She could feel the sharp sting of the cold creeping into her bones, her fingers numb from the chill. She couldn't stop now—she had come too far—but the path ahead seemed to vanish into the swirling snowstorm that had descended so suddenly.

Is this how it ends? Her mind whispered, but she refused to entertain the thought.

She couldn't afford to lose her resolve. She had to push forward. She had to survive.

A sound broke through the storm—low, like the crack of branches underfoot. Lyra's heart skipped in her chest. It was too soon for the storm to have covered up her tracks. She had been moving cautiously, but this was different. The sound was deliberate. It was someone—or something—following her.

Panic rose in her chest as she spun toward the noise, her

Chapter 11: Running from the Past

hand instinctively reaching for the dagger at her side. But the snow whipped around her, making it impossible to see anything clearly. The storm was intensifying, turning the world into a blur of white. Her breath came faster, panic beginning to claw at her throat.

And then, through the storm, a shape appeared.

A figure, tall and cloaked in dark furs, moving swiftly and deliberately through the snow.

Lyra's heart hammered in her chest as she took a step back, every instinct screaming at her to run. But before she could turn, the figure spoke—its voice low, but unmistakable.

"Lyra."

Her breath caught in her throat.

She knew that voice.

Slowly, she lifted her eyes to meet the figure's gaze, even as a thousand questions spiraled through her mind. And in the midst of the snowstorm, her heart skipped a beat as she realized who had found her.

It was Rian.

And he was no longer alone.

Lyra froze. The cold wind bit at her exposed skin, but it was the sight of Rian standing before her that made the air feel like ice. She had thought, in the chaotic moments of her escape, that she had outrun him—escaped his reach, maybe even outrun the shadow of everything he represented. But now, there he was, his dark cloak billowing in the storm, his presence unmistakable and undeniable.

For a moment, neither of them moved.

Her heart thudded against her ribcage, each beat laced with panic, frustration, and something else—something colder, deeper. It wasn't just that he had found her. It was the

Tempting the Enemy's Daughter

undeniable truth that she had been running from him, from the choices she had made, and now there was nowhere left to go. *Nowhere.*

"You," she finally said, her voice sharper than she had intended, but the tremor of her own fear was unmistakable. "What are you doing here?"

Rian's face was partially obscured by the heavy hood of his cloak, but the shadows only seemed to deepen the intensity of his eyes. His gaze locked onto hers, and for a moment, there was no malice in it—just the kind of calculating calm she had learned to expect from him, mixed with something else: a hint of regret, perhaps? Or maybe it was just the storm, twisting her perception.

"I'm here to make sure you don't make things worse," he said quietly, his voice cutting through the howling wind. There was no anger in his tone, only quiet determination. "You shouldn't be out here alone."

Lyra's pulse quickened. *Shouldn't be out here alone?* She couldn't tell if he was trying to protect her or control her. She had already escaped once, had made her decision to leave him and everything he represented behind. She wasn't about to allow him to dictate her choices again.

"You don't get to decide what's best for me," she snapped, taking a cautious step backward. "Not anymore."

Rian didn't move. His stance was calm, as though he expected her to react this way. As though he had anticipated her defiance. "I never wanted to control you," he replied evenly, his voice calm but heavy with something Lyra couldn't quite place. "But I can't let you make a mistake that could cost you everything."

Her heart hammered in her chest. *Everything.*

Chapter 11: Running from the Past

Her escape, her freedom, her choices—were they really hers to make, or were they already controlled by forces far beyond her understanding? Lyra clenched her fists at her sides, fighting the overwhelming urge to either flee or strike out. But this wasn't the time for either. The weight of the moment settled heavily on her shoulders.

"Don't try to make this about me," she said through gritted teeth, her voice low but fierce. "This is about the kingdoms, about *you* and what you want. I'm not part of your plan anymore, Rian. I'm not some pawn you can move around a chessboard."

Rian's eyes softened, but only for the briefest of moments. His lips parted, as though to respond, but the storm around them grew fiercer, cutting off his words. The wind howled louder, a torrent of snow swirling around them, the air thick and biting. They were far from the shelter of the castle now, deep in the wilderness where the cold could kill. It was a silence between them, a space filled with unspoken words, heavy with the things neither of them was willing to say.

Finally, Rian took a step forward, his movements deliberate, calm. "We don't have time for this," he said, his voice now urgent, his tone shifting to one of pragmatism. "You need to come with me. It's not safe here, Lyra. They're already looking for you. We can't keep running like this."

Lyra felt a flicker of something in her chest, something that made her hesitate. She knew he wasn't wrong. She had spent so many hours running—running from her father's expectations, running from the consequences of her decisions, and now running from Rian. But was it truly a run for freedom, or was it just a flight from responsibility? Could she keep avoiding the truth?

Tempting the Enemy's Daughter

"You don't know what they'll do to me if they catch me," she said, voice low, her breath coming out in clouds of mist. The wind was so fierce now that she could barely hear her own words over the storm's roar. "They'll use me as a pawn. Or worse."

Rian's face hardened, and for the first time since they had met, there was a flicker of something dangerous in his eyes. "I know exactly what they'll do," he said. "That's why you can't be out here alone. The men you're running from aren't just soldiers, Lyra—they're spies. Masters of manipulation. You'll never outrun them."

Her chest tightened. She had heard rumors, whispers of betrayal, spies embedded within both kingdoms—agents who worked in the shadows, twisting the truth to suit their masters. But hearing Rian speak so plainly about it made everything feel far more real. The line between enemy and ally had blurred long ago, but this… this was something different.

"You're wrong," she snapped. "You don't know me. You don't know what I'm capable of." The words came out sharper than she intended, a quick reflex born of her growing frustration. She was tired—tired of running, tired of being manipulated, tired of having to fight for every scrap of freedom she could find.

Rian said nothing, only studying her with those unreadable eyes of his. His next words came with an undeniable weight, like the shift of the earth beneath their feet.

"Then prove me wrong. Come with me, Lyra. There's still time. You're not the only one being hunted. Your father's enemies are coming for you, too. And you're not going to outrun them, not on your own."

The finality of his words hit her like a blow. Her stomach

Chapter 11: Running from the Past

twisted. *Her father's enemies.* What did he mean? And why was he so certain that her father would be as much of a threat to her now as the people she had fled from?

In that moment, she realized something that sent a chill through her entire being. No matter how far she ran, no matter how much she tried to fight or escape, she couldn't outrun the past. It was always going to catch up with her.

The choice had never been hers, not truly.

Rian's words hung in the air, heavy with implications. The storm swirled around them, the wind biting harder now, and yet she felt an odd stillness descend upon her.

Lyra looked away, her gaze drifting to the horizon, to the endless expanse of snow and wilderness that stretched far beyond the trees. There was no answer she could give him— no words to undo what had already been done. And no way to escape the tangled web of betrayal and lies that had drawn her in.

"I don't know if I can trust you," she finally whispered, her voice almost lost in the wind.

Rian's response was quiet, but filled with an eerie certainty. "You don't have to trust me, Lyra. You just have to trust that what's coming is worse than anything either of us has faced before."

A cold shiver ran down her spine. The storm around them seemed to intensify, and for a long moment, neither of them spoke. Lyra knew this was no longer about survival alone. It was about choosing sides—and maybe, just maybe, realizing that the world they lived in was more fractured and complicated than she had ever known.

With a final, resigned glance at Rian, Lyra turned away from the path she had been following.

Tempting the Enemy's Daughter

She had no choice but to follow him now.

The wind howled around them, cutting through the trees like a living thing. Lyra's breath came out in short bursts, visible in the frigid air, as she reluctantly turned away from the path she had been following. Her mind screamed to turn back—to run in the opposite direction, away from Rian, away from the uncertainty that followed him like a dark cloud. But her body betrayed her; the storm was relentless, and she was too exhausted, too cold, too lost in the turmoil of her own thoughts.

Rian had found her. That alone told her that her plan, her escape, had already been compromised. She was no longer free to move as she pleased. The weight of that realization settled heavily on her chest.

"Come on," Rian urged, his voice cutting through the storm as he motioned for her to follow. "We need to get to shelter before this gets worse."

Lyra hesitated, casting a final glance over her shoulder at the desolate, snow-covered path she had been following. The hidden city she had sought—the one spoken of in whispers and half-forgotten tales—seemed like a distant dream now, slipping further from her reach with every passing moment.

She didn't know if she could trust Rian. She didn't know if she could trust anyone anymore. But the storm would kill her if she stayed out here long enough. And no matter how much she loathed admitting it, she couldn't face another night alone in the wilderness, hunted by enemies she barely understood.

With a resigned sigh, Lyra nodded. "Lead the way."

Rian didn't waste a second. He turned and started down the narrow trail, cutting through the dense woods, his movements sure and practiced. Lyra followed closely behind, struggling

Chapter 11: Running from the Past

to keep up. The wind bit at her face, the snow swirling around her in a maddening blur. But Rian moved with a sense of purpose, a steadiness that she had come to recognize, even though she hated admitting it.

For hours, they trudged through the snow, the forest growing darker as the sun began to set behind a thick veil of clouds. The temperature dropped further, and Lyra's limbs grew stiff from the cold. She felt as if she were walking in a dream—her mind half-fogged by exhaustion, her body fighting to keep moving. The pounding of her heart was the only sound she could hear besides the storm.

Finally, they reached a clearing. In the distance, Lyra could make out the outline of a structure—a small, weather-worn cabin nestled against the foot of a hill, its chimney sending a thin stream of smoke into the sky.

Rian motioned toward it. "There. We can rest there for the night."

They reached the cabin just as the last light of day was swallowed by the storm. Rian pushed the door open with ease, as if he had been here before, and stepped inside, ushering Lyra in after him. The warmth hit her immediately—the air inside was thick with the smell of wood smoke and something earthy. She breathed it in gratefully, feeling her muscles relax for the first time in what seemed like forever.

The cabin was small and rustic, with a stone hearth at the far end and a single table in the center of the room. A few shelves lined the walls, stacked with dried herbs, candles, and old books. It was a place of quiet solitude, far removed from the concerns of both kingdoms.

Rian went to the hearth and stoked the fire, adding a few more logs. As the flames crackled to life, Lyra took a seat by

Tempting the Enemy's Daughter

the small wooden table, her mind still racing.

Rian didn't speak at first. Instead, he moved around the cabin, securing the door, checking the small window, and casting a few wary glances outside as if expecting someone—or something—to follow them. It wasn't until he was finally settled on the opposite side of the table that he met her eyes.

"Are you going to ask me where we are?" he said, his voice low.

Lyra narrowed her eyes at him. "I already know where we are. We're in the middle of nowhere."

Rian's lips twitched into a half-smile, but the expression didn't quite reach his eyes. "I thought you would've figured it out by now. This is where we've been running from, all this time."

The words hit her like a blow to the chest. Her stomach twisted. "What do you mean?"

"You're not the only one with a past to run from," Rian said quietly, his gaze darkening. "This cabin isn't just a place of refuge. It's a place where things... *happen.* Things I can't explain yet."

Lyra's brow furrowed. There was something in his voice—a shadow of regret, something unspoken—that made her pause. She didn't want to feel sympathy for him. Not after everything. Not after he had been the one to drag her into this tangled mess of politics, betrayal, and family loyalty. But still, something about the way he said it made her wonder if, maybe, he was trying to warn her about something bigger than the two of them.

"You've been here before?" she asked, her voice softer now, despite herself.

Rian nodded. "A long time ago. I didn't think I'd be back

Chapter 11: Running from the Past

here. But we don't have much time." His gaze lingered on her, an odd intensity in his eyes. "I wasn't lying when I said you're not safe. And neither am I. You don't know who's watching. They're already trying to track us."

Lyra's heart skipped a beat. "Who?"

"The ones who want the same thing you do," Rian said, his voice hardening. "The truth. They're the ones who control the hidden city, the ones who know what really happened when the pact was broken. They'll do anything to keep it buried, to keep the power where it is."

Lyra leaned forward, her interest piqued despite herself. "The hidden city…?"

Rian's eyes were sharp. "Yes. But that's not the only thing they control. They're also the ones who have been pulling the strings between Aeridor and Solara. They're the ones who've been manipulating us all."

Her blood ran cold as the implications hit her. She had been so focused on the immediate danger, on outrunning her father's enemies, on surviving. But this—this was bigger. Much bigger. The betrayal, the alliances, everything—it all pointed to something far more sinister.

Lyra felt a flicker of fear—a coldness that made her blood feel like ice. "And you think… what? That if we go after the truth, we'll just walk away unscathed?"

Rian didn't answer immediately. He stood up, walking toward the window and peering out into the growing storm. The cabin was silent except for the crackling fire.

"We don't have a choice," he finally said, his voice quieter than before. "If we don't uncover the truth now, it's all going to fall apart. Both kingdoms will burn, and we'll be the ones left standing in the ashes. The people who broke the pact… they're still out there. And they won't stop until they get what they want."

Lyra's pulse quickened. She had been running from one thing to another, trying to outpace the consequences of her own decisions. But now, with Rian's words hanging in the air, the weight of what they were truly facing felt like an anchor pulling her down.

"What happens if we don't stop them?" she asked, her voice barely a whisper.

Rian turned to face her, his eyes dark with resolve. "Then everything we know will cease to exist."

Lyra swallowed hard. The storm outside raged on, but inside, she could only feel the growing pressure of the storm that had just begun to gather around them.

The game had changed. And there was no turning back.

Thirteen

Chapter 12: Finding Sanctuary

The fire crackled low in the hearth, its light casting flickering shadows across the small, rustic cabin. The warmth that had welcomed them in felt almost too comforting, a stark contrast to the cold chaos of the world outside. Lyra sat at the table, her hands wrapped around a mug of something hot, though she couldn't bring herself to drink it. The swirling thoughts in her mind consumed her, each one pushing the last further into the depths of confusion.

Rian had been right about one thing: there was no going back. The truth they were chasing wasn't a simple matter of politics or diplomacy. It was something far deeper. The broken pact between Aeridor and Solara, the hidden city, the secretive powers lurking in the shadows—everything was tied together in a web of manipulation and betrayal far older than either kingdom. Lyra felt like she was standing on the edge of a precipice, one step away from being consumed by the storm.

She stared into the fire, her gaze unfocused, lost in the quiet crackling of the flames.

Rian had disappeared into the back of the cabin some time ago, presumably to check the cabin's meager provisions or to plan their next move. Lyra knew better than to ask him questions now. He had a way of keeping his thoughts hidden, revealing only what he deemed necessary. If anything, he was more a puzzle than a person.

But there was something in the way he'd spoken earlier, in the urgency of his tone, that gnawed at her. *The hidden city,* he'd said. *The ones who control it.*

The city she had once dreamed of finding—the city that was supposed to be a place of sanctuary—was no sanctuary at all. It was a place of power, a place of control. And Rian was right: it was no longer just about escaping her father's influence. She had to understand the bigger picture, the reason the ancient pact had been broken in the first place. If she didn't, she would be left with nothing but the rubble of a kingdom destroyed by its own secrets.

A soft creak from the back of the cabin drew her out of her reverie. She glanced up as Rian reappeared, a small bundle of dried herbs in one hand, a leather satchel slung over his shoulder.

"Pack your things," he said, his voice low and urgent. "We're moving out."

Lyra blinked, surprised by the sudden shift. She had expected them to rest, to gather their strength before continuing their journey. But the look in Rian's eyes told her there was no time for rest. His urgency was palpable, and the tension in his jaw suggested something more than just the storm outside.

"What's happening?" she asked, rising from her seat. "Are

Chapter 12: Finding Sanctuary

we under attack?"

Rian shook his head, his eyes scanning the room as if listening for something beyond the sound of the wind. "Not yet. But they're close. Whoever's tracking us has found our trail."

Lyra's heart skipped a beat. Her pulse quickened, her thoughts racing. "How long do we have?"

"Maybe an hour. Maybe less. We'll be safer on the move."

Lyra grabbed her cloak and hastily stuffed a few essential items into her own satchel: water, some provisions, and a dagger she'd taken from the cabin's meager stash. Her mind was still reeling from the conversation they'd just had. There was no time to process it. No time to ask questions or second-guess their next move. The moment was slipping away, and she had to act.

As she fastened the straps of her pack, she couldn't help but feel the weight of her decision press down on her. What was she running toward? What was the endgame? Rian had spoken cryptically about the truth, about the hidden city, and the manipulation that had shaped the kingdoms' fates. But did she truly understand what she was up against?

"I'll be ready in a minute," she said, her voice tight with the uncertainty she couldn't shake. She could feel Rian's eyes on her, could sense the patience in his silence. He wasn't judging her; he was waiting for her to decide. And in a way, the gravity of that waiting was more unnerving than anything else.

Without a word, Rian moved toward the door, his movements smooth, efficient, as if he had long ago accepted that their lives were never going to follow a simple path. Lyra couldn't help but admire that about him—how he moved through the world, how he dealt with the chaos.

Tempting the Enemy's Daughter

But even admiration couldn't shake the sense of dread creeping through her chest. The world they had entered, this dangerous, shadow-filled world, wasn't something she could control. Not anymore. The threads were already too tangled, and the consequences of pulling one would unravel everything she had once known.

Minutes later, they were standing outside the cabin, the storm still raging. The snow whipped around them, obscuring the landscape, reducing everything to a blur of white and grey. It was a disorienting sight, as though the very world had been wiped clean, leaving nothing but the bitter cold and the weight of their decisions.

Rian took the lead, moving with the same practiced ease that had marked his earlier movements. They passed through the dense forest in silence, only the crunch of snow beneath their boots breaking the otherwise quiet air. The storm was growing fiercer, the wind howling through the trees as if the world itself were protesting their departure.

They walked for hours, the landscape shifting around them, the forest giving way to rocky cliffs and barren hills. Lyra kept her eyes fixed on Rian's back, her mind spinning with questions that she didn't dare ask. Why was he so sure they could outrun their pursuers? Was there really a sanctuary ahead, or was this just another stop in their flight from the inevitable?

Finally, when the cold had begun to gnaw at her bones and her legs had started to tremble with fatigue, Rian stopped. He turned to face her, his expression grim but resolute.

"We're close," he said, his voice low. "It's just up ahead. But you need to keep your guard up. There's no telling who else might be watching."

Chapter 12: Finding Sanctuary

Lyra nodded, her heart thumping in her chest. She felt a surge of hope, mixed with wariness. Could this place, wherever it was, truly offer them the safety they so desperately needed? Or was it just another illusion—a temporary respite before the storm caught up with them?

As they moved forward, the trees began to thin, and the path began to slope upward. Soon, the wind had died down to a muted whisper, and the snow seemed to settle into an unnatural stillness. Lyra looked up, startled to see a faint glow ahead, like a distant fire burning in the heart of the mountain. It was a soft, steady light, different from the cold, harsh glow of the storm.

"What is that?" she asked, her voice barely above a whisper.

Rian glanced back at her, his eyes gleaming with an intensity that made her pulse quicken. "It's the city," he said simply.

Her breath caught in her throat. "The hidden city?"

Rian nodded, his expression unreadable. "It's not what you think. But it's the only place we can go now. The only place left that can help us."

Lyra swallowed hard, her thoughts spinning as they moved forward together, stepping into the unknown. The weight of the moment pressed down on her chest as they drew closer to the city's warm, glowing lights, a sanctuary that promised both safety and a new set of dangers.

And as they crossed the threshold into that strange place, Lyra had no idea what would await them—only that there would be no going back from this point onward. The path ahead was uncertain, and yet it was the only one they could walk.

For better or worse, they had entered the heart of the storm.
Top of Form

Tempting the Enemy's Daughter

The faint, ethereal glow from the hidden city grew stronger with each step. Lyra could feel the air shift around her as they ascended the last stretch of rocky terrain. The wind, once howling and bitter, had fallen silent, and the snow now clung to the ground in an unnatural stillness. The world seemed to hold its breath as if it were waiting for them to cross the threshold into something that had been long forgotten by time.

Rian moved ahead, his silhouette cutting through the dimming light. Lyra followed closely, her heart pounding in her chest, her thoughts a swirling storm. Everything she thought she understood about the world—about loyalty, power, and the pact between her kingdom and Solara—seemed to be unraveling. Rian had hinted at the truth, but there was still so much left unsaid.

They reached the summit of the hill, where the last of the trees gave way to a breathtaking view. Below them, nestled between the folds of the mountain range, lay a city unlike anything Lyra had ever seen. It was not a city of grand stone buildings or towering spires, like the ones she had grown up with in Aeridor. No, this was something far older, far more enigmatic.

The city appeared to be carved into the very mountain itself, its structures winding and flowing like a river of stone. There were no straight edges or geometric patterns—everything seemed to blend into the landscape, as if the city had grown organically from the earth. Buildings that resembled natural rock formations stood side by side with ornate structures made of materials that glowed faintly with an inner light. There was an energy here—something primal, ancient, and undeniably alive.

Chapter 12: Finding Sanctuary

"What is this place?" Lyra whispered, her voice a mix of awe and confusion.

"This," Rian said quietly, "is Nymira. The hidden city. It's been here for centuries, hidden from the world. Few know of it, and fewer still have ever set foot here."

Lyra felt her pulse quicken. "Nymira…" She repeated the name, feeling its weight settle in her chest. It was more than just a name. It was a place of secrets, of power. And she had just stepped into its heart.

Rian turned to her, his expression darkening. "I wasn't kidding when I said it's not what you think. The people here… they don't care about kingdoms, or alliances. They care about something much older. Something that neither Aeridor nor Solara could ever understand."

The uncertainty in his tone sent a shiver down her spine. She had followed Rian, trusted him, but now that they were here, something about this place felt… wrong. It was beautiful, yes, but it was also unsettling in ways that Lyra couldn't yet articulate. The very air seemed thick with a power she couldn't place, as if the city itself were breathing, waiting for them.

Rian led her down the narrow path that wound toward the heart of Nymira, where the glow was brightest. The buildings grew taller as they descended, their structures like great living things, twisting and growing from the very stone and earth around them. Every corner seemed to hide another secret, another layer of this enigmatic city.

Eventually, they arrived at the base of a massive structure, a great spiraling tower that reached up into the clouds. The architecture was unlike anything Lyra had seen before—curved walls, shimmering surfaces that seemed to pulse with light, and carvings of symbols she didn't recognize. It was both beautiful and terrifying, as if it were alive, and every part of it was infused with an ancient magic that hummed just beneath the surface.

"This is where we'll find answers," Rian said, his voice steady but low.

Lyra nodded, though she couldn't shake the sense that the answers they would find here might not be the ones she wanted to hear.

As they approached the entrance, two figures stepped forward out of the shadows—tall, cloaked, and silent. They were the first people Lyra had seen since entering the city, and they looked every bit as out of place as she felt. Their eyes gleamed from beneath their hoods, strange and knowing.

"State your purpose," one of them said, his voice like gravel, deep and commanding.

Rian didn't flinch. "We've come for the truth. We need to speak with the Elders."

The figure's gaze flickered over Lyra, and for a moment, she felt the weight of their scrutiny, as if they were searching for something deeper than her outward appearance. But then the figure nodded once and stepped aside, allowing them to pass.

"Follow me," the other figure instructed, his voice softer but no less authoritative.

Lyra's heart raced as they entered the tower, the walls now closing in on them, the air growing thicker with each step. It wasn't just the architecture that felt oppressive—it was the overwhelming sense of ancient knowledge and power that seemed to pulse through the very stones of the tower. Every step they took felt like it was drawing them deeper into a web of fate, and Lyra couldn't tell if she was walking toward salvation or destruction.

Chapter 12: Finding Sanctuary

The corridor was long, stretching far beyond what seemed physically possible, the walls decorated with symbols and carvings she couldn't read. The deeper they went, the more the light seemed to dim, and the temperature dropped. The air was cool, but the unease in her stomach was far colder than any chill.

Finally, they arrived at a large chamber, its ceiling soaring high above them, too high for Lyra to make out the details. The room was lit by strange, flickering lights that seemed to emanate from the very walls, casting long shadows across the floor. In the center of the room, seated upon thrones of smooth stone, were the Elders of Nymira—three figures, their faces hidden in the shadows of their hoods. Their presence was palpable, their energy almost suffocating.

Rian stepped forward, his shoulders stiff with purpose. "We need your help," he said, his voice commanding.

The Elders remained silent for a long moment, their eyes—or at least Lyra assumed they were their eyes—focused on her. The silence was thick, heavy with unspoken thoughts and intentions.

Finally, one of the Elders spoke, her voice like a soft breeze, ancient and otherworldly. "You have come far, child of Solara. But you are not yet ready for the truths you seek."

Lyra's heart skipped a beat. "What do you mean? We've been running from the truth for so long. I need to understand—everything."

The Elder's gaze softened slightly, though the weight of her words still lingered. "The truth is not a simple thing. It is a force, a current that runs through time itself. To understand it is to risk unraveling the very fabric of what holds this world together. Are you willing to face the cost?"

Tempting the Enemy's Daughter

Lyra felt a lump form in her throat, her instincts telling her to run, to turn away before she was dragged deeper into this dark, dangerous place. But the truth called to her—like a flame flickering in the distance, drawing her in.

"I'm willing," she said, her voice stronger than she felt. "I have to know. My kingdom… my people… everything is falling apart. If I don't understand what happened, if I don't know what caused the breaking of the pact, it will all be for nothing."

The Elder leaned forward, her voice dropping to a whisper. "Very well. But know this: the truth you seek will not free you. It will bind you to a fate far darker than you can imagine."

Lyra swallowed hard, but there was no turning back now. She had crossed the threshold of Nymira. And whatever truths lay hidden here, whatever consequences awaited her, she was ready to face them.

The Elder raised a hand, and with a soft motion, the room seemed to shift, the air vibrating with energy. "Then let us begin."

And in that moment, Lyra knew that the path ahead would be one she could never return from.

The air in the chamber grew heavy, charged with an unseen energy, as though the very walls were attuned to the Elder's words. Lyra's heart hammered in her chest, the sense of impending revelation pressing down on her like a tangible force. Her eyes flicked toward Rian, but he was already stepping back, his expression unreadable. He had brought her here, and now, it seemed, he was leaving the rest to the ancient beings seated before them.

The Elder who had spoken lifted a hand, and the light in the room dimmed, the shadows stretching unnaturally across

Chapter 12: Finding Sanctuary

the stone floor. Lyra felt a strange pull—her body seemed to grow heavier, as if the truth they were about to impart might physically drag her down into the depths of some forbidden place.

"You are not yet ready for what you seek," the Elder repeated softly, her voice a blend of gentleness and steel. "But you will be. In time."

Lyra opened her mouth to protest, to demand answers, but the words lodged in her throat. Something about the Elder's presence made her feel as though speaking would be futile. The atmosphere around her was thick with centuries of knowledge, centuries of untold stories, and the weight of history itself. Here, in this ancient place, words felt too small, too insignificant.

Instead, Lyra's eyes drifted to the other two Elders, who remained eerily silent. The first Elder—the one who had spoken—glanced toward them, as if confirming a silent agreement. Slowly, she raised her arms, and the air seemed to ripple. A low hum began to fill the room, a sound that made Lyra's ears buzz, as if the fabric of reality itself were being stretched.

"To understand the past," the Elder said, her voice now reverberating with power, "you must first understand the threads of time that bind us. You must see the fracture that began long before the pact was ever broken."

A deep, resonating tone filled the room, and before Lyra could react, a vision materialized before her eyes—a cascade of images, as if the very walls of the chamber had become a portal into the past.

The images were fleeting at first, flashes of landscapes she did not recognize—vast forests, sprawling plains, and cities made of stone that felt older than anything she had ever seen. Then, there were faces. Faces of people, not unlike herself, yet ancient—carved with lines of wisdom and burden.

The vision flickered again, and Lyra gasped. In an instant, she saw the moment when the pact was first forged, the two kingdoms of Aeridor and Solara coming together under the banner of a shared destiny. There was magic in the air, palpable and raw, flowing like a river between the two rulers—the King of Aeridor and the Duke of Solara, both bound by an oath that would unite their peoples for generations.

But then the vision shifted, darkened.

Lyra's breath caught in her throat as the images morphed into something darker—terrifying. She saw the first cracks appear in the world, a rift opening in the sky, tearing apart the fabric of reality itself. The magic that had once flowed so freely now seemed twisted, distorted, a black storm of energy that tore through the kingdoms like a ravenous beast.

And standing at the center of it all, a figure—neither man nor woman, neither human nor creature—wielding that power with cruel precision. The entity, an extradimensional force, seemed to be feeding off the rift, growing stronger as the world around it fractured.

The vision shifted again, this time showing the aftermath: a broken kingdom, the cities of Aeridor and Solara in ruins, their once-glorious capitals reduced to rubble.

The city of Nymira was not untouched by the storm. Lyra saw it, a once-sacred place that had been a sanctuary, now consumed by the same darkness. The people of Nymira, the Elders included, had attempted to protect the city, but the rift was too powerful, too far-reaching. The sanctuary that had once offered refuge had become a prison, a place cut off from

Chapter 12: Finding Sanctuary

the rest of the world by the fractured reality.

And in the center of it all, a single truth echoed in Lyra's mind:

The pact was not broken by human hands. It was destroyed by a force beyond our control.

The vision snapped back into darkness, leaving Lyra breathless and shaken. She staggered, her legs weak beneath her as if the weight of what she had seen had physically drained her. Her hand clutched at the nearest pillar for support, her breath coming in shallow gasps.

The Elder's voice broke the silence, calm and unwavering.

"The force you saw," the Elder said softly, "was not a natural thing. It is an entity that exists outside of our world, beyond time itself. It seeks to rewrite reality to its will. The breaking of the pact was not a betrayal by your people or by Solara, Lady Lyra. It was the work of an entity that fed on the chaos between your kingdoms—one that sought to break the very structure of time and space."

Lyra's mind spun. She was still reeling from the vision, the raw power of it, the sense of something ancient and malevolent looming over everything she had ever known. Her eyes darted from one Elder to the next, her voice finally breaking free of the tight knot in her throat.

"What is this entity?" she demanded. "How do we stop it?"

The Elder who had been silent until now raised a hand. Her voice was low, carrying the weight of centuries. "Stopping it is not so simple. It is a force beyond comprehension. A force that twists time itself to suit its purpose. And it is already too late to restore what was lost. What remains now is the struggle to keep what is left intact."

Lyra clenched her fists, her determination sharpening. "But

the kingdoms... my people... are they just to be destroyed by this thing? Is there no way to fix the damage that's been done?"

The Elder looked at her, eyes unreadable from beneath her hood. "The path to restoring balance lies within the fragments of time—fragments scattered across the world. But the journey will not be easy. Those who seek to alter reality risk losing themselves in the process. And those who attempt to control the past... often find that the past does not wish to be controlled."

The words sent a chill down Lyra's spine. The implications were clear, even if they weren't fully revealed. The ancient city, its people, and the pact that had once bound the kingdoms together were all part of a much larger tapestry—a tapestry that was now coming apart at the seams. To fix it, to make things right, Lyra would have to face forces beyond even her understanding. She would need to trust in allies who might not be who they appeared to be.

Rian, standing in the shadows behind her, caught her eye. There was no judgment in his gaze, only a quiet understanding. Whatever truth lay ahead, they would face it together.

The Elder who had spoken last stepped forward, her gaze lingering on Lyra as if searching for something within her.

"There is still hope, Lady Lyra," she said softly. "But it lies in your hands. The future of your kingdom, and of the world itself, rests on the choices you make now."

Lyra inhaled sharply, the weight of the responsibility settling over her like a cloak she could not shed. She wasn't sure she was ready. She wasn't sure anyone could ever be ready for the challenges ahead.

But she knew one thing: the answers were here, in the heart

Chapter 12: Finding Sanctuary

of Nymira, in the ancient magic that had shaped the world and in the hands of those who guarded its secrets.

And no matter the cost, she would see this through. The future of her kingdom—perhaps even of time itself—depended on it.

With a final, resolute glance at the Elder, Lyra stepped forward.

"I'm ready."

And in that moment, she understood—whatever came next, she had crossed the threshold. There would be no turning back.

Fourteen

Chapter 13: Unlikely Allies

The air in the chamber crackled with energy as Lyra stood at the threshold of the Elders' secrets, her resolve hardening like steel forged in fire. She had made her choice—there was no going back now. The truth was a path she had to follow, no matter how perilous or fraught with darkness.

The Elder who had spoken last—her voice like a breeze against the weight of time—motioned for Lyra to follow her. The others remained seated, silent but attentive, their eyes ever-watchful.

Rian, standing beside her, stepped forward, his gaze unwavering. "Where are we going?" he asked, his voice low, filled with a curiosity that bordered on suspicion.

"To the Nexus," the Elder replied, her voice soft but heavy with meaning. "There, you will meet those who understand the true nature of what is happening, and perhaps they can offer the guidance you seek."

Chapter 13: Unlikely Allies

Lyra's brow furrowed at the mention of the Nexus. "What is the Nexus?" she asked, unable to hide the confusion in her voice. She had heard whispers of such places in stories and old legends, but none of them had ever seemed real—until now.

The Elder's lips parted slightly in a small, almost imperceptible smile, though her eyes remained serious. "The Nexus is a place where all paths converge. It is a place of knowledge, hidden in the folds of time and space. And there, you will meet allies—some familiar, some new, but all crucial to what lies ahead."

Rian glanced at Lyra, his expression unreadable. "Allies?" he murmured, as if tasting the word. "I've heard of the Nexus, but never in the context of… allies."

The Elder nodded solemnly. "Not all who reside in the Nexus are of this world, Rian. Some are from the past, others from the future. And a few, perhaps, exist beyond time altogether."

Lyra's heart skipped a beat. *Beyond time?* The thought was unsettling, but she couldn't afford to dwell on it now. Not when the fate of both Aeridor and Solara—and perhaps the entire world—hung in the balance.

The Elder raised her hand again, and the stone beneath their feet seemed to vibrate with ancient power. A doorway—unseen moments ago—manifested before them. It was not a door of wood or iron, but an ethereal rift, a shimmering tear in the fabric of space itself. The edges glowed faintly, as though stitched together with threads of light and shadow. It beckoned them forward.

"This is the passage to the Nexus," the Elder explained. "Beyond this doorway lies a realm where reality is fluid. Time does not move in a straight line here. You will need to trust what you see… and even more, trust those you meet. Many will try to lead you astray. But there are those among them who mean to help."

Lyra swallowed hard, the weight of her decision pressing down on her chest. She glanced at Rian, whose eyes were narrowed with suspicion. But beneath his cautious exterior, there was something else—something akin to hope. He might not have understood it fully, but he was with her, as he had been from the beginning.

"Let's go," Lyra said, her voice firm.

With a final look back at the Elders—who watched in silence, their faces unreadable—Lyra stepped through the shimmering doorway. Rian followed closely behind her, and in the instant they crossed the threshold, the world around them seemed to fold in on itself.

Everything spun, colors and shapes blurring together as they were swept away by the force of the Nexus. There was no sense of direction—no sense of time or space. All that existed was the sensation of endless movement, as if they were both floating and falling at once.

Then, with a sudden jolt, everything came to a standstill.

Lyra blinked rapidly, her senses returning as she steadied herself. She found herself standing in an expansive, circular chamber—a place that seemed to stretch far beyond what the eye could see. The walls were composed of shifting patterns, like light and shadow in constant flux. It was as if the room itself was alive, breathing with an energy she couldn't comprehend.

At the center of the room stood a vast, intricately carved pedestal. Upon it, a glowing orb pulsed softly, casting an eerie

Chapter 13: Unlikely Allies

light across the chamber. It felt both alien and familiar—a reminder that nothing in the Nexus was ever what it seemed.

Standing in the shadows, along the edges of the chamber, were figures. Several of them were cloaked, their features hidden, but others were visible—figures Lyra instantly recognized, though she had not seen them in years.

"Lyra."

The voice was low, smooth, and unmistakable. It belonged to a man she had hoped to never see again.

From the shadows stepped Duke Alaric, her father.

The shock that ran through her was instantaneous, freezing her in place. For a moment, she couldn't breathe, couldn't move. *What was he doing here?*

Her father was dressed in the same resplendent silks of Solara, his dark hair braided back, his piercing gaze fixed firmly on her. There was no warmth in his eyes, only the cold, calculating intensity she had grown up with.

"Father?" Lyra said, her voice trembling despite herself.

Alaric's lips curled into the smallest of smiles. "I see you've made it this far, my daughter. I always knew you had the potential to understand what is truly at stake."

Lyra's heart raced, her thoughts spinning. "What are you doing here, Father?" she asked, stepping back instinctively, as though distancing herself from him might somehow make sense of the situation.

Alaric chuckled softly. "I should be the one asking you that, Lyra. You have come to the Nexus, a place beyond your understanding, seeking answers you are not ready to hear. Yet here you are, standing beside your... *ally*," he said, his gaze shifting to Rian, who stood a few paces behind Lyra.

Rian's face darkened, his hand instinctively going to the

Tempting the Enemy's Daughter

hilt of his blade. "What do you mean by that?" he demanded, stepping forward.

Alaric raised a hand to stop him. "Peace, young man. You misunderstand. I am not here to fight. I am here because I, too, seek something from the Nexus. Something… that only those who truly understand the nature of time can grasp."

Lyra's mind was racing. *Her father?* Here, of all places, in the heart of the Nexus, with all its secrets and hidden power?

"I don't understand," Lyra said, her voice strained. "How could you be here? The Elders… they said this place was hidden. That only a few could ever reach it."

Alaric's smile deepened, though there was no warmth in it. "The Nexus is not simply a place. It is a doorway to many things—paths not just through time, but through potential realities. I did not come here by chance, Lyra. I have known of this place for many years, and I have sought it out. I've long known that the fate of our world rests on the power contained within it."

Lyra's eyes narrowed. "What are you talking about?" she demanded.

Alaric's voice dropped to a whisper, but his words hit like a blade to the chest. "The true enemy is not the entity that broke the pact. It is the very fabric of time itself. The timelines are unraveling. What you seek to mend, I intend to control."

Lyra felt a chill grip her heart. "What are you saying, Father?"

Alaric's eyes glinted with something that could only be described as a mixture of ambition and cold resolve. "You're not the only one with a stake in this, Lyra. I intend to reshape the past, present, and future to my will. And I will use whatever it takes to get what I want."

Behind him, the cloaked figures stirred, and Lyra's gaze

Chapter 13: Unlikely Allies

darted around the room, realizing for the first time that she was not just in the presence of her father. She was surrounded by others, people whose allegiances were as unclear as their motives.

The Nexus had never seemed so dangerous. And her father—her very own father—was no ally at all.

Lyra felt a shiver of dread run down her spine. Whatever was happening here, whatever forces were at play in this strange, timeless place, the stakes had just risen higher than she could have ever imagined.

Top of Form

Lyra's heart raced as she tried to process the truth that had just been laid bare before her. Her father, Duke Alaric, the very man she had believed to be a steadfast protector of Solara's legacy, was now revealing himself as a player in a much larger game—one that spanned across time itself. And from the look in his eyes, Lyra knew that this was no idle ambition. He was prepared to bend the future to his will, no matter the cost.

Her breath caught in her throat as she stared at him, unable to fathom the depths of his betrayal.

"You intend to *control* time?" Lyra's voice trembled, but she forced herself to stand tall. "You would destroy everything just to remake it in your image?"

Alaric's smile tightened, his gaze unreadable. "No, my dear. I don't intend to destroy anything. I intend to preserve Solara, Aeridor—everything we've built—and ensure its survival for eternity. The rift, the fractures in time, they threaten everything. But the Nexus…" He gestured to the shimmering room around them. "The Nexus offers us a way to stabilize reality. It offers us a way to control the flow of time itself."

A cold shiver ran through Lyra. "By rewriting history?" she

spat, her fists clenching at her sides. "You would erase the very fabric of what makes us who we are, just to ensure your own power?"

"Not just power," he countered, his voice quiet but intense. "Survival. There is a much greater danger at play here than you understand. And you, Lyra, are in the way."

Before she could respond, a low voice interrupted, one that held a surprising hint of familiarity.

"You're not the only one who has come for the Nexus, Alaric."

Lyra whipped her head around to see Rian step forward, his hand still near his blade. His eyes met Alaric's with a mixture of disdain and warning.

Rian's words hung in the air like a weight. Lyra didn't have to look closely to see the tension in his posture. It was as if he, too, had understood something in that moment that Lyra had missed. Rian wasn't here just to guide her; he had his own reasons for being part of this strange, twisting journey.

Alaric's expression flickered, but it was gone as quickly as it appeared. "Ah, Rian. The man from Aeridor," he said, his voice dripping with a mock politeness. "I should have known you were involved. A piece on the board I hadn't expected, but still… a piece, nonetheless."

Rian didn't flinch, his eyes cold and unwavering. "I'm no piece to be moved around, Alaric. And neither is Lyra."

The tension between them crackled like static, and for a moment, Lyra felt the weight of a decision pressing on her shoulders. What was Rian's true role in all of this? He had been a loyal ally, no doubt—but had he been hiding something from her? And if he knew her father so well, how deeply did their histories intertwine?

Chapter 13: Unlikely Allies

Before she could voice her thoughts, a third voice cut through the stillness of the Nexus, deep and commanding, one that made the hairs on the back of Lyra's neck rise.

"Enough."

From the shadows at the far end of the chamber, a tall figure emerged, cloaked in silver and black, his face hidden by a mask of intricate design. He moved with a fluid grace, almost like he wasn't quite part of this world, and yet somehow—he was. Lyra's breath caught in her throat as the stranger stepped into the light, revealing his striking features: sharp cheekbones, dark eyes that shimmered with intelligence, and an air of ancient power that sent an involuntary chill through her.

"Who is this?" Lyra whispered, though she knew the answer before Rian spoke.

"This is Seraphis," Rian said in a low voice. "One of the last of the Timewalkers."

Lyra's mind reeled. *Timewalkers?* The very name felt like a myth—like something out of a legend she'd heard as a child. Timewalkers were said to be those who could navigate through the currents of time itself, bending the fabric of reality to their will. But they were supposed to be gone—destroyed in the wars that had once raged across Aeridor and Solara.

"Timewalkers are but whispers in history, forgotten by most," Seraphis spoke in a voice that carried across the room like a deep echo. "But I am still here. And I was not the only one who survived."

Lyra's eyes narrowed. "You..." She faltered, unsure of how to address him. "What do you want from the Nexus?"

Seraphis' mask shifted slightly, as though he were smiling beneath it. "I seek what we all seek—control over the unfolding of time. A chance to undo the chaos, to bring balance. But," he added, turning his gaze to Alaric, "not at the expense of history. Unlike you, Duke Alaric, I do not wish to rewrite it to suit my personal desires."

Alaric's face darkened, his posture stiffening. "You think you can stop me? Stop the restoration of order?"

Seraphis' voice was calm, unbothered. "I don't think. I *know*." He stepped closer to Lyra, his presence both overwhelming and reassuring at the same time. "Your father speaks of 'restoring' the timeline, Lyra. But what he truly wants is to control it. He cannot be trusted. And his efforts will not save Solara, Aeridor, or anyone else."

Lyra's mind swirled with the weight of his words. Her father, whom she had once seen as a protector of her kingdom, was now revealed as something else entirely—a man who would go to any lengths to control not just the present, but the past and future, too. And Seraphis? This Timewalker, this ancient figure from the forgotten past, had aligned himself against her father. But who could she trust?

Before she could ask another question, the masked figure looked toward Rian, a knowing look passing between them.

"You were right to bring her here, Rian," Seraphis said, his voice lowering with a hint of approval. "But there is more at stake than you realize. This isn't just about time or kingdoms— it's about the very fabric of existence. We cannot allow anyone to control it."

Lyra's mind spun. *Rian knew Seraphis?* They were allies. *But in what way?*

She turned to Rian, her gaze locking onto his. "You knew about all of this. You knew what my father was planning, didn't you?"

Rian's face remained unreadable, though his eyes softened

Chapter 13: Unlikely Allies

as they met hers. "I didn't know everything, Lyra. But I knew your father's ambition. And I knew I couldn't let him control time. Not the way he wants."

Lyra shook her head, trying to process the weight of their conversation. The past few days had been a blur—betrayals, secrets, alliances—and now, her own father stood as one of the greatest threats to the world. There was no going back from this.

Seraphis's voice broke through her thoughts. "You must choose, Lady Lyra. There are no more safe roads. No more easy answers. You have come this far, and now the final choice lies with you."

Her heart pounded in her chest. *Choose?* She had been making choices ever since she left Solara, but none of them had been this heavy. She had always thought of herself as loyal—first to her father, then to the idea of peace between the kingdoms. But now, peace seemed an illusion. Her father was a threat. And Seraphis? He was a stranger, his motives unclear, yet he spoke with a conviction that she couldn't ignore.

"I need time," Lyra said, her voice hoarse. "To think. To understand."

Seraphis nodded slowly. "You have until the rift collapses further. After that, time may no longer be a luxury."

Rian placed a hand on her shoulder, offering her silent support. But in that moment, she felt more alone than ever.

Time was running out. And the decisions she made now would shape the fate of everyone, even those she loved.

Lyra knew that whatever path she chose, the consequences would be far-reaching.

The weight of Seraphis's words hung in the air like a storm cloud, pressing in on Lyra. She wanted to scream, to demand

Tempting the Enemy's Daughter

answers to the questions that spun through her mind like the twisting currents of the Nexus itself. But instead, she stood there, silent, her heart a battleground between duty and her own burgeoning sense of something much larger than the petty politics she had grown up with.

Rian's hand on her shoulder was a steady presence, a reminder that, for all the uncertainty swirling around them, she was not alone.

She turned to face him, her voice barely a whisper. "What do we do now?"

Rian didn't answer right away, his gaze flickering from her to the mysterious figures gathered in the room. His jaw tightened, and for the first time since they'd entered the Nexus, Lyra saw a flicker of hesitation in his eyes.

"I don't know," he said quietly, as if the words themselves were a struggle. "But I do know this: We can't trust your father. And we can't let him control the timeline. Not like he plans to. We have to stop him, Lyra."

Her eyes widened. "Stop him? But how? He's... he's my father. How do you expect me to just—"

"*Your father* is not the man you think he is," Seraphis interjected sharply, his voice like the crack of thunder. "He is consumed by his own need for control. He wants to remake the world, but not for the betterment of anyone but himself."

Lyra flinched at the venom in Seraphis's tone, but she couldn't deny the truth in his words. Alaric had been playing a dangerous game, and Lyra was only beginning to understand the scope of it. Her father had always been a master of manipulation, but this—this was different. Time itself was at stake.

She swallowed hard. "Then... what do you want from me?"

Chapter 13: Unlikely Allies

Lyra asked Seraphis, her voice barely audible, as if she feared the answer would tip the balance of her very soul.

Seraphis regarded her with an unreadable expression, and for a moment, she wondered if he could see the conflict raging within her. The silver mask he wore seemed to glow faintly, adding an eerie air to his presence. It was as if he were not fully present in the world, but rather a being from somewhere outside of time, a glimpse into the future—or perhaps the past.

"You have a choice, Lady Lyra," Seraphis said. "One that will shape the fate of all realms."

"Another choice?" Lyra couldn't hide the bitterness in her voice. "I'm getting tired of choices, Seraphis. Every time I think I know what to do, the ground shifts beneath me."

"Then stop thinking about what you *want* to do, and focus on what you *must* do," Seraphis replied, his tone firm, as if he had dealt with indecision before. "Your father has already made his choice. He has decided that the world must bend to his vision. But you—" He paused, looking directly into her eyes. "—you still have the power to choose a different path."

Lyra's chest tightened. She glanced at Rian, who was watching her with an expression she could not read. His loyalty to her was unwavering, she knew that. But even he had his own motivations, his own secrets. She wasn't sure where his true allegiance lay anymore, and it made her question everything.

"What does that mean?" Lyra asked. "If I choose not to help him... what happens to Solara, to Aeridor, to everything?"

Seraphis's mask gleamed in the shifting light of the Nexus, and for a moment, it seemed to take on an otherworldly glow. "What happens next is not for any of us to decide. But you must stop him from manipulating the rift. If he succeeds in controlling time, everything—*everything*—will be lost."

A sharp pang of uncertainty pierced Lyra's heart. *Is it really that dire?* Her mind flashed back to her father's words, the fervor with which he spoke about controlling time, of *saving* everything that was dear to him. He had always insisted that his actions were in the interest of protecting Solara and its legacy. *Was that truly a lie?*

"What if there's another way?" Lyra asked, her voice trembling despite her best efforts. "What if the rift is the key to healing everything—without destroying the future? Without rewriting history?"

Seraphis shook his head slowly. "There is no healing here, not as your father would imagine. The rift has caused a fracture in the very fabric of reality. If your father succeeds, he will rewrite everything, but not in the way he thinks. He will unravel the balance of existence itself, and the world as you know it will cease to be."

"Then what do you suggest?" Lyra demanded, her anger flaring. "Just trust you? Another stranger from beyond the veil of time who *claims* to have all the answers?"

A flicker of something akin to sadness passed across Seraphis's face. "I don't expect you to trust me, Lady Lyra. Trust is a luxury in times like these. But I ask you to listen." He turned away from her and walked slowly toward the pedestal, the orb glowing faintly in the center of the room. "The Nexus offers power. It offers answers. But you cannot wield it alone. If you are to undo the damage done by the rift, you must form alliances. Allies who may not be who they seem. People who, in another life, may have been your enemies. The future is not set, but the choices you make will determine whether or not we can stop this catastrophe."

Chapter 13: Unlikely Allies

"Who do you mean?" Rian asked, his voice full of suspicion.

Seraphis paused, as if choosing his words carefully. "The hidden city. The people there have knowledge that can help you, though their motives are unclear. But they, too, understand the gravity of what is happening."

Lyra felt a ripple of disbelief. *The hidden city?* She had heard of such a place in hushed whispers—a city that existed outside the known realms, where time, space, and magic all intertwined. A city so secretive, even the greatest of scholars could find no trace of it in the histories of Aeridor and Solara.

"You expect me to seek their help?" Lyra's voice was incredulous. "And you think they will help me? Us?"

Seraphis didn't look at her as he responded. "They will help you. Or they will watch you fail."

Rian's eyes hardened, his stance defensive. "And you? Where do you stand in all of this, Seraphis? Are you merely guiding us, or do you have your own agenda?"

Seraphis turned toward him, his face unreadable behind the mask. "I am neither your enemy nor your ally, Rian. I am a witness to the unfolding of time. My role is not to intervene, but to offer counsel to those who are brave enough to choose the right path. I have seen too much to ignore the danger that looms, and I will do what is necessary to protect the timeline. You can decide if you want to stand with me or against me. But the choice is yours."

Lyra felt the weight of the room pressing in on her. The alliances were shifting, the world was changing, and she was caught at the center of it all. Her father had made his move, and now she had to make hers. But how could she choose between the man she had once called family and the people who might hold the key to saving not just her kingdom, but reality itself?

"We need to go to the hidden city," Lyra said, more to herself than to anyone else. "But I don't know if I can trust *them*."

"Then you must trust your instincts," Seraphis replied, his voice softer now, as though he understood the weight of her decision. "The Nexus will guide you, as long as you are true to your path."

Lyra looked at Rian, who nodded in silent agreement.

"We'll go," she said, her voice steady despite the turmoil inside her. "But we must be cautious. Everyone here has a reason for being involved, and no one is without a hidden agenda."

Seraphis gave a slow, deliberate nod. "Exactly. Trust only what you know to be true, Lady Lyra. And above all, remember: time is a weapon, and your choices will determine whether you wield it… or it destroys you."

With that, the chamber seemed to shift once again, the air heavy with anticipation as they prepared to step further into the unknown. The path ahead was uncertain, fraught with dangers, but Lyra had no choice but to continue. For the fate of two kingdoms—and perhaps all of existence—rested in her hands.

Fifteen

Chapter 14: The Truth Unveiled

The air in the Nexus chamber had grown thick with tension. Lyra's mind raced, her thoughts swirling like the swirling energies that seemed to pulse through the very walls. She could feel the weight of Seraphis's words pressing down on her chest, a constant reminder of the delicate balance that now hung in the balance. Her father's manipulation of time, his ambition to control the rift—it was all tied together, more intricately than she had ever imagined.

And yet, despite everything, there was still so much she didn't understand.

The masked figure, Seraphis, had given them a new course of action: seek the hidden city, find the answers there, and stop her father before it was too late. But the more she thought about it, the less sure she felt about the path she had to walk. Trusting Seraphis was one thing, but trusting the people of the hidden city was another.

Her eyes flickered to Rian, who stood a few paces behind her, still processing everything that had transpired. He had agreed with Seraphis's plan without hesitation. That meant something—though whether it was something to be trusted was another matter.

But there was one question Lyra couldn't shake, a question that burned at her heart.

"Why?" she whispered, barely able to hear her own voice over the heavy silence of the chamber. She turned slowly to Seraphis, who had moved closer to the central pedestal, studying the shifting orb with quiet intensity. "Why did the rift happen? What was the true cause of the fracture? What shattered it? I don't understand. If it was something outside of us, something beyond our control... then why are we being held accountable?"

Seraphis's gaze lifted from the orb, his silver mask reflecting the flickering light from the Nexus. "The rift was not caused by any one individual or kingdom," he said, his voice soft, yet carrying the weight of ancient knowledge. "It was caused by a catastrophic magical event—an event that fractured not only the boundaries of time but of reality itself."

Lyra's breath hitched. "Reality itself?"

Seraphis gave a slow nod. "Yes. You see, the ancient pact between Aeridor and Solara was not just a political alliance. It was much more than that. The pact held together not only the kingdoms but also the fabric of reality. Over time, the pact weakened, as it was bound by forces that neither kingdom fully understood. Your father's ancestors—along with Solara's—created the bond to prevent a greater force from tearing everything apart. But the bond was never meant to last forever. And when it finally broke..."

Chapter 14: The Truth Unveiled

Lyra's mind reeled as she processed the enormity of his words. Her father had always spoken of the importance of the pact, but she had never been told of its true nature—of its power. Of how it had been holding together the very balance of the world.

Seraphis continued, his tone measured, as though he was carefully choosing each word. "The fracture caused a ripple effect through time. The rift you now see is not just a tear in the fabric of the present, but a distortion that stretches backward and forward, unraveling the timeline. If left unchecked, it will consume everything."

"But why now?" Lyra's voice faltered, as if she were afraid to hear the answer. "Why is the rift tearing apart now? What changed?"

Seraphis hesitated for a moment, his masked face unreadable. Then he spoke in a lower, more urgent tone. "Your father, Duke Alaric, did not *break* the pact, not directly. But he uncovered something—something buried deep in the annals of history—that could manipulate the rift. He discovered the existence of the Nexus long ago, and he began to study it in secret, believing it to be the key to not only saving Solara but controlling time itself."

Lyra felt the ground beneath her feet shift as the pieces began to fall into place. "My father… he's been using the rift to try and control time?"

"Yes." Seraphis's voice was like ice, sharp and unforgiving. "And he has come dangerously close to unlocking its true potential. The rift is not just a tear. It is an anchor, an intersection between different timelines, and your father has been trying to manipulate it, thinking that by controlling it, he could stabilize the future—his future."

Tempting the Enemy's Daughter

Lyra's heart pounded in her chest as the realization hit her. *Her father wasn't just trying to fix the world—he was trying to control it. He was trying to reshape everything to fit his vision.* And in doing so, he was playing with forces that no one, not even Seraphis, fully understood.

"But that's madness," she whispered. "If he controls time... then everything will be different. There will be no past, no future—only what he wants."

"Exactly," Seraphis replied. "And therein lies the danger. Time is not a thing to be controlled. It is a force, a current that cannot be bent without consequence. And your father believes he can master it. He believes that by controlling time, he can preserve Solara, protect his legacy, and ensure the survival of his kingdom. But what he doesn't understand—what no one understands—is that in trying to control time, he will break it beyond repair."

Lyra's mind spun. She had grown up listening to her father's vision, his endless speeches about the importance of Solara, about the glory of the kingdom and its future. She had always believed in it, too. But now, in the cold light of Seraphis's words, it all seemed like a fragile illusion, a dream that was being crushed under the weight of her father's ambition.

"What will happen if he succeeds?" Lyra asked, her voice barely above a whisper.

Seraphis's mask gleamed in the dim light. "The timeline will fracture irreparably. The past will bleed into the future, and the present will cease to exist as we know it. Kingdoms will fall, histories will be rewritten, and the very concept of time will cease to be linear. There will be no stability. No order."

Lyra's thoughts raced as she considered the implications of his words. *Could her father truly destroy everything?* Could

Chapter 14: The Truth Unveiled

he undo everything she had ever known, all for the sake of preserving a kingdom that had already begun to crumble under the weight of its own legacy?

She looked up at Rian, her eyes desperate for answers. "What do we do? How do we stop him?"

Rian's expression was grim, his jaw set in determination. "We go to the hidden city. We learn the truth about the Nexus and its true power. Only then will we be able to stop your father."

"But how?" Lyra asked, her voice trembling. "How can we fight him? He's already set everything in motion."

Seraphis spoke, his tone even but full of a strange urgency. "We must find the Heart of the Nexus. It is the only way to restore balance. The Heart is the key to both undoing the damage your father has done and preventing the rift from consuming all of existence."

"The Heart?" Lyra repeated, her voice barely a breath. "What is it?"

"It is an artifact," Seraphis explained. "A relic from the time before the kingdoms were even formed. It was hidden away, locked in a place beyond time, a place that exists outside of the normal flow of the timeline. If we can find it, we can stabilize the rift. But we will need to act quickly, before your father unlocks the full power of the Nexus."

Lyra's heart raced as she processed the enormity of the task before her. The Heart of the Nexus—an artifact of unimaginable power, hidden away in a place that defied the laws of time itself. It sounded like something out of a legend, a story told around campfires to children. But this was no fairy tale. This was reality.

And reality, Lyra knew, was far more dangerous.

Tempting the Enemy's Daughter

"Where is it?" Lyra asked, her voice steady despite the fear that gripped her chest.

Seraphis turned, his silver mask glinting in the light. "The location is hidden, scattered across multiple points in time. The only way to find it is to follow the clues embedded in the timeline itself. And to do that, we will need to trust those who are willing to fight alongside us."

Lyra's mind raced as the weight of her father's actions pressed on her. She was no longer just the daughter of the Duke of Solara. She was the key to stopping the destruction of everything—and the choices she made from this point on would determine the fate of all kingdoms, all lives, and all of reality itself.

The clock was ticking.

And Lyra had no time to waste.

The weight of Seraphis's revelation felt like a physical blow. Lyra stood still, her breath shallow, her mind reeling. The truth of the rift—of the ancient pact between Solara and Aeridor—was far darker than anything she had imagined. Her father's obsession with control had led him down a path so dangerous, so destructive, that it threatened not just his kingdom, but the very fabric of time itself.

The Heart of the Nexus.

The words echoed in her mind. If it was the only thing that could stabilize the rift, then it was her only hope. But the reality of what she had to do was clear: to stop her father, to prevent the complete unraveling of the world, Lyra would have to find this artifact—a relic of unimaginable power—and race against time itself.

Her heart raced as she glanced at Rian. His face was set in grim determination, but there was something in his eyes that

Chapter 14: The Truth Unveiled

made her pause—a flicker of doubt, perhaps, or something more. She couldn't place it, but it unsettled her nonetheless.

Seraphis seemed to sense the shift in the air, the growing uncertainty between them. His voice, when he spoke again, was calm but carried a quiet urgency. "We are out of time. Your father's manipulation of the rift is progressing more quickly than you realize. Every moment we delay gives him more control over the fabric of reality. If we don't act soon, it may be too late to reverse the damage."

Lyra's fists clenched. "I know. But how can we even begin to find the Heart? If it's hidden across multiple points in time, how can we track it down?"

Seraphis stepped forward, his movements fluid and precise, as though each step was deliberate, calculated. "The Nexus will show us the way," he said simply, as if it were an obvious answer. "It holds the key to unlocking the path. But we must enter its depths and understand its true nature—before your father does."

Rian stepped forward, his expression serious. "And the hidden city? You mentioned them before. How do they fit into all of this? Can they help us?"

Seraphis's eyes flickered, but his expression remained impassive. "The inhabitants of the hidden city understand the Nexus in ways that even I do not. They are the guardians of ancient knowledge, protectors of the flow of time. They possess the maps and clues needed to navigate the fractured timelines. But they will not help us without first understanding our motives. They are cautious, distrustful of outsiders, and we will have to earn their trust."

Lyra felt a sinking sensation in her chest. Every step forward seemed to take her deeper into a web of uncertainty, of alliances that were as fragile as the timelines themselves.

"What if we can't earn their trust?" she asked, the question hanging heavily in the air. "What if they refuse to help us?"

Seraphis tilted his head slightly, as if considering her question for the first time. "Then we will have no choice but to take matters into our own hands. But I trust that if we show them the gravity of the situation, if we demonstrate that your father's actions threaten the existence of their city as much as it threatens ours, they will come around. They have no love for those who seek to alter the course of history."

Rian's voice cut through the silence. "So we'll go to the hidden city, find the Heart of the Nexus, and hope the inhabitants there will help us—if they don't turn on us first. That's the plan?"

Seraphis turned his sharp gaze toward Rian, and for the first time, a flicker of something like respect crossed his face. "It's a risky plan, yes. But it is the only plan we have. The rift is tearing at the very foundation of the timeline. We must act quickly, or everything—*everyone*—will be lost."

The finality in his tone settled over Lyra like a shroud, heavy and unyielding. She took a deep breath, trying to center herself in the midst of the storm that was gathering around them. She had no illusions about what lay ahead. The journey to the hidden city was fraught with danger, not just from her father's spies, but from the unknown forces that controlled the Nexus and its inhabitants.

Rian stepped closer, his eyes locking with hers. "Lyra, you don't have to do this alone," he said softly, his voice steady but laced with an undercurrent of concern. "We'll face this together. Whatever comes next, we'll face it together."

For a moment, Lyra allowed herself to meet his gaze, to feel

Chapter 14: The Truth Unveiled

the warmth of his support. She had always been alone in her struggle against her father's machinations, her own sense of duty binding her to a legacy that no longer felt like her own. But now, standing on the precipice of something far greater than herself, she realized that she couldn't—*wouldn't*—do this alone.

She nodded, a silent promise forming in her chest. "Together."

Seraphis's gaze shifted between the two of them, his expression unreadable. "The Nexus does not wait for those who are unprepared," he said. "We must leave now."

Lyra's heart beat faster, a surge of resolve filling her as she glanced one last time at the orb at the center of the room, its swirling light casting shadows across the walls. Time was slipping away from them, and the danger was no longer distant. It was here, closing in around them.

"Lead the way," she said, her voice firm.

The journey to the hidden city was fraught with more questions than answers. As they left the Nexus chamber, Lyra found herself walking through corridors that seemed to stretch on forever, their paths winding through layers of reality, as if the very air around them was constantly shifting. Each step felt like it was taking her further from the world she knew and deeper into a place that existed outside time—a place where nothing was certain.

After what seemed like an eternity of walking, they arrived at a small room, no larger than a modest study. Seraphis motioned for them to enter.

"This is the starting point," he said, his voice quiet, as if speaking reverently in this strange space. The room contained only a single object—a large, ornate mirror standing against the far wall. It was unlike any mirror Lyra had seen before. The frame was intricately carved with symbols she couldn't recognize, and the surface of the mirror was clouded, swirling with dark and light. It didn't reflect the room behind them, but instead seemed to shimmer with an unknown energy, like a window into something else—another place, another time.

"This mirror will show us the path," Seraphis explained. "It is a tool of the Nexus, created long ago to guide those who are worthy of its knowledge. It will reveal the first step of our journey, but the rest will be for you to discover."

Lyra felt a strange pull toward the mirror, as though it was calling to her, beckoning her to step closer. She hesitated for only a moment before walking toward it, her breath catching in her throat as the swirling mist in the mirror began to shift.

In the glass, she saw flashes—fragments of a world she barely recognized. Solara, in ruins. Aeridor, at war. And then, amid the chaos, something else—a figure, hidden in the shadows, reaching out with an outstretched hand.

Her father.

But no—this wasn't her father as she knew him. This was something darker, something more dangerous.

And suddenly, the pieces of the puzzle clicked into place.

Her father wasn't just seeking control over time. He was trying to rewrite it, to reshape it in his image.

But in doing so, he had awakened something far worse.

And Lyra was the only one who could stop it.

The future of all worlds rested in her hands.

Sixteen

Chapter 15: A Heart in Conflict

The air in the hidden city felt heavier now, charged with an energy Lyra couldn't quite place. It was as if the very ground beneath her feet had been altered by the magic of the Nexus, the rules of time and space bending and twisting in ways that made her feel disoriented and small. Despite the urgency of their mission, she couldn't shake the feeling that she had crossed some threshold, stepping into a realm where her every decision, every action, would be scrutinized by forces far greater than her.

And yet, as she looked at Rian beside her, his steady presence was the one thing she could cling to in this strange, shifting world. They had come this far, and now, with the Heart of the Nexus within reach, they had to finish what they had started.

But even as she felt the pull of the mission, something in her heart tugged in another direction.

Her father.

Tempting the Enemy's Daughter

Lyra's stomach twisted at the thought of him. The man who had once been her hero, the one who had raised her to believe in the greatness of Solara, now stood as her greatest adversary. She had always known that his ambitions were vast, but never had she imagined that his desire to protect his kingdom would lead him down a path so dark, so destructive.

And yet, despite everything she had learned, despite the truth of what he was trying to do to time itself, there was still a part of her that didn't want to believe it.

A part of her that still wanted to see him as the father who had loved her, who had once taken her on horseback rides through the palace gardens and taught her the ways of Solara's politics, instilling in her a sense of duty and pride.

But now, standing on the brink of a reality-shattering war, she realized that the person she had loved, the person she had looked up to, was gone. In his place was a man who was willing to sacrifice everything—*everyone*—to preserve his legacy.

Her hands clenched at her sides as they walked deeper into the hidden city, the shadows of the towering structures stretching out before them. The inhabitants of the city, strange and silent, watched them with wary eyes as they passed. They had reached the heart of the city, a place that even Seraphis had described as dangerous to enter without permission. The people here held secrets of the highest order, and Lyra couldn't help but wonder what price they would demand for their assistance.

Rian's voice broke through her thoughts. "Lyra, you're quiet. What's going on in that mind of yours?"

She glanced at him, his expression a mixture of concern and curiosity. "I'm just thinking," she said softly, "about my father. About what he's become."

Chapter 15: A Heart in Conflict

Rian didn't answer right away, but his eyes softened, and he placed a hand on her shoulder, offering a small, reassuring squeeze. "I know it's hard. But we're not the only ones who have had to face difficult truths. He's *your* father, but what he's doing—what he's willing to do—is beyond anything any of us can justify. You're not the one who's failed him. He's the one who's failed all of us."

Her chest tightened at his words, but she nodded, grateful for his understanding. She had known, deep down, that she couldn't hold on to the man she had once loved, not when he was destroying everything she had worked for. But the ache in her heart, the loss of that bond, still stung more than she could admit.

Ahead of them, Seraphis stopped in front of a massive door, its surface covered in runes that pulsed with an eerie, dim light. He turned to face them, his silver mask reflecting the soft glow of the city's magic.

"We're here," he said. "Beyond this door lies the Sanctum of the Nexus. It is where the true heart of this city resides—where we will find the answers we seek."

Lyra stepped forward, her mind still caught between the two worlds she had to navigate—the one where she was the daughter of a man who was no longer the person she thought he was, and the one where she had to become something greater than she had ever imagined. She had to stop him. She had to stop *them* both—the fractured reality that he had begun to manipulate, and the forces that sought to control it.

Seraphis raised a hand, and the door groaned open with a low, resonating sound, revealing an expansive chamber inside. The walls were lined with strange, luminous symbols, casting eerie shadows across the floor. In the center of the room, a large, crystalline structure hovered above the ground, its facets shimmering with colors that seemed to shift in and out of focus. The Heart of the Nexus. Lyra could feel its power even from this distance, a magnetic pull that seemed to beckon her forward.

But as she stepped into the room, the sense of awe quickly gave way to unease. Something was wrong.

Rian's voice was low and tense beside her. "What is this place?"

Seraphis, who had been walking ahead, stopped. "This is where time is anchored," he said, his voice somber. "The Nexus is a delicate thing. It exists here—outside the normal flow of time—and inside it. It is the heart of all that is, and all that ever will be. The city is its protector, its guardian. And now, we must ask for its aid."

But even as he spoke, Lyra felt a shift in the air. Something had changed, and it was not the kind of change she had expected.

A voice, deep and ethereal, echoed from somewhere in the chamber, though no one could see its source. It wasn't Seraphis's voice. It wasn't anyone's voice. It was a *presence*, a vast intelligence beyond time.

"You seek the Heart," it intoned. "But to wield it, you must first answer a question. A question that transcends time. Are you prepared to face the consequences of your actions?"

Lyra's heart skipped a beat. "What do you mean?" she called out, her voice reverberating against the walls. "We need to stop the rift, to stop my father from unraveling reality!"

The voice echoed again, but this time there was a note of something like amusement, or perhaps pity. "The rift is but a symptom. The true danger lies in the choices that brought

Chapter 15: A Heart in Conflict

you here, in the path you are about to walk."

Lyra's chest tightened as she realized what the voice was implying. It wasn't just her father's actions that had led them here. It was hers, too. The choices she had made—her allegiance to the kingdoms, her blind loyalty to her father, even her willingness to work with Seraphis—had all led to this moment.

The question, then, was whether she could make the right choice. Whether she could truly stop her father—*and* save herself from becoming the same kind of ruler he had become.

"I'm ready," she said, her voice trembling only slightly. "What is the question?"

The voice fell silent for a moment before answering, its tone now heavy with finality. "What is your heart's true desire, Lyra of Solara? What is it you will sacrifice for the future of all?"

Lyra swallowed hard, the weight of the question settling in her gut. She had thought she knew what she wanted—to stop the rift, to save the kingdoms, to bring peace. But now, standing at the threshold of the Nexus, with the weight of history pressing down on her, she realized there was more at stake than she had ever imagined.

Her heart, her loyalties, her very future... All of it was about to be tested in ways she could never have foreseen.

The voice's question hung in the air, impossible to answer, and yet Lyra knew there was no escaping it. To save the future, she would have to make a sacrifice—a choice that would change everything.

The question was no longer whether she could stop the rift. The question was whether she could stop herself from becoming the very thing she had sworn to defeat.

And that choice was the most dangerous of all.

The chamber seemed to breathe around her. The air hummed with an energy that was ancient, alien—alive. Lyra could feel it deep in her bones, a constant pull toward the Heart of the Nexus that hovered in the center of the room like a vast, shimmering crystal. Yet, despite the mesmerizing beauty of the artifact, it wasn't its power that held her attention now, but the voice—*that voice*—that still echoed through her mind.

"What is your heart's true desire?"

The question was more than an inquiry. It felt like a judgment, a piercing look into the core of her being. Her chest tightened as the weight of it settled over her. It was no longer a question of duty or allegiance, of loyalty to her kingdom or her father. It was a question of *herself*—of who she was, and who she was willing to become.

What was her true desire?

Her thoughts tumbled over each other, her mind racing in an attempt to answer, but there was no simple solution. She had once thought she knew her purpose: to protect Solara, to preserve her father's legacy, to maintain the peace between two kingdoms that had once stood united. She had believed in the righteousness of her father's vision—until the truth of his plans, of the rift, shattered everything she thought she understood.

But now... Now, faced with the power of the Nexus, Lyra wasn't so sure of anything.

Her eyes flickered to Rian, standing beside her, his face unreadable but his posture tense. He was watching her closely, as though waiting for her to give an answer that would determine not just her fate, but his as well. She could feel the gravity of his gaze, the unspoken bond between them, growing

Chapter 15: A Heart in Conflict

stronger in the silence.

But even as her heart ached at the thought of what was at stake, she realized something: *Rian was not her father. And this moment was not hers to share with him.*

Seraphis stood a few paces behind them, his silver mask glinting in the ethereal light. He had said nothing since the voice had spoken, but his presence was unsettling—like a shadow that never quite left, watching and waiting for a mistake. He had led them here, to this crossroads, but Lyra knew that the real choice lay with her, and with her alone.

The voice spoke again, its tone soft yet filled with an unbearable weight.

"You are torn, Lyra. Between the love for your father and the truth that you have uncovered. Between the desire for power and the necessity of sacrifice. But you must choose."

Lyra's breath caught in her throat. *Choose?*

She glanced once more at Rian, who was still waiting for her answer. His expression softened, his eyes searching her face as if trying to reach her through the fog of confusion and doubt. In that moment, everything else faded—the walls of the chamber, the pulsing energy, even the presence of Seraphis and the voice of the Nexus. All that remained was the weight of the decision before her.

Her father had always preached that to rule was to make choices, but never had she imagined that the price of those choices would be so high.

Was she willing to sacrifice everything she had ever known? Was she prepared to sever the last thread that connected her to her father, to her past? To save the future of Solara, of Aeridor, and the fragile timelines of the Nexus itself?

And in that moment, a truth crystallized in Lyra's heart, one she had been running from since the day she learned of her father's betrayal:

The future was not something to be controlled. It was something to be protected.

She turned to face the shimmering Heart of the Nexus once more, her mind now steady with resolve. The Nexus—the force that governed all of time and space—was a tool, not a weapon. It wasn't something to be used to rewrite history or change the course of events for personal gain. It was something to be guarded, respected, and, above all, protected from those who would seek to alter it for selfish reasons.

Her father's vision, his plans to rewrite time, had been driven by the desire for power—a desire that had blinded him to the true cost of his ambitions. The rift was not just a danger to the present. It was a threat to all of reality. And her father, in his desperation, had become a danger to everything.

But she would stop him.

She had to. For the sake of the future, for the sake of the world, and for the sake of everything her father had once believed in.

With a deep breath, Lyra stepped forward, her gaze unwavering as she looked at the Heart. The Nexus pulsed in response to her approach, its colors shifting from a deep violet to a soft blue, as if acknowledging her decision.

"I choose to stop him," she said, her voice ringing out in the silence, carrying the weight of her resolve. "I choose to protect the future, to protect *all* of time, even if it means losing everything."

The voice of the Nexus did not answer immediately, but the air grew heavier, the space around them tightening as if waiting for her to understand the full gravity of her decision.

Chapter 15: A Heart in Conflict

"You are certain?" the voice asked. "Are you prepared to lose your place in this timeline? To sever your ties to everything you know?"

Her heart hammered in her chest, the finality of the question settling deep in her soul. The price was clear now: by choosing to stop her father, to end his manipulation of time, Lyra would likely lose everything she had ever known—her place in the kingdom, her identity as Duke Alaric's daughter, and perhaps even the life she had built in Solara. She would become an outcast, a shadow in a fractured reality, a force of disruption in the world she had once tried to protect.

But the choice was no longer difficult.

"I am prepared," Lyra said, her voice steady. "Whatever it takes."

The chamber seemed to hold its breath for a moment, before the Heart of the Nexus flared to life, its light enveloping her in a brilliant glow. The power within it surged, filling her with a rush of energy, of knowledge, of ancient wisdom—wisdom that stretched across time itself.

And then, just as quickly as it had flared, the light dimmed.

The voice of the Nexus spoke again, softer now, as if acknowledging her sacrifice.

"Your choice is made. The future is no longer in your father's hands, nor in the hands of the Nexus. It belongs to you—and to those you trust."

Lyra took a step back, feeling the weight of her decision press down upon her. The Heart of the Nexus pulsed one last time, then stilled. The chamber was silent, save for the sound of her own breath.

Rian was beside her in an instant, his hand at her back, grounding her as she stood in the aftermath of her decision.

Tempting the Enemy's Daughter

"You did it," he whispered. "You saved us all."

But as she turned to look at him, a question still lingered in her heart.

Had she?

The battle was far from over. Her father would not give up so easily. But now, Lyra had taken the first step into a new future—a future of uncertainty, but one where the consequences of her actions would be her own to bear.

And with that, she realized that no matter what lay ahead, she would never again be the person she once was.

She would be something more.

The weight of Lyra's decision hung heavily in the air, as if the very atmosphere of the hidden city had shifted along with her resolve. The chamber, once a silent, oppressive space, now seemed to pulse with an energy that was almost tangible, vibrating with the aftermath of her choice. The Heart of the Nexus had quieted, its glow dimming to a soft, steady pulse, as though it were contemplating the magnitude of what had just transpired.

Rian stood beside her, his hand still at her back, a steady presence in the sea of uncertainty she now found herself in. His touch was warm, grounding her in the moment, but even he seemed uncertain—waiting, as if he, too, was unsure of the consequences of the path they had chosen.

"I know it wasn't easy," he murmured, his voice low and filled with an unspoken understanding. "But you did what needed to be done. The future… it's in your hands now."

Lyra's chest tightened as she nodded, though her heart still carried the heavy weight of her decision. *The future.* It sounded like such a grand thing, a force beyond her comprehension. But the truth was, the future was nothing

Chapter 15: A Heart in Conflict

but a series of choices, and now she had made hers. She had chosen to stop her father, to sever the dangerous threads of his plans that had begun to unravel reality itself.

But as much as she wanted to believe in the righteousness of her decision, doubts gnawed at the edges of her mind. Was she sure? Was this really the right path? The cost of her choice was vast, and even though she had done what she believed was necessary to protect the balance of time, there was no guarantee of success. There was no guarantee that she could stop her father, or that the fractured timeline could be healed by her actions.

Her father—Duke Alaric—had always been a man of power, a man who had wielded influence over kingdoms, politics, and alliances for as long as she could remember. He had built an empire with his cunning and ambition, but now, in the face of the Nexus, his grand designs seemed small and insignificant. And yet, the fear of what he might do, the desperation she had seen in his eyes when she confronted him, gnawed at her resolve.

What if he succeeded? What if he used the Nexus for his own ends?

But that was a question for another time. The path before her was already set in motion.

Seraphis stepped forward, his silver mask catching the faint light of the Nexus as he looked at Lyra with a strange, unreadable expression. His hands were clasped behind his back, his posture straight, but there was a sharpness to his gaze that betrayed something more—something she couldn't quite place.

"You've made your decision, Lyra of Solara," he said, his voice calm, but there was a coldness beneath it. "But remember, the Heart of the Nexus does not belong to any one person. It is a force unto itself, and while your intentions may be noble, the Nexus is not swayed by desires alone. It will test you in ways you cannot anticipate."

Lyra met his gaze, unflinching. "I understand the risks," she said, her voice steady despite the turmoil inside her. "But I have no choice. If I don't act, my father will destroy everything. All of time. All of us."

Seraphis nodded, his eyes narrowing slightly, but he didn't argue. He simply turned toward the Nexus, raising his hand to touch the crystal's surface. The moment his fingers made contact, the chamber trembled, and the air seemed to thicken with a profound energy.

"Then," Seraphis said, his voice quieter now, "we must prepare."

Hours Later

They had retreated to a quiet chamber deep within the hidden city, a place carved into the very rock of the world, far from the heart of the Nexus. The walls were adorned with strange markings, symbols that Lyra didn't recognize but that resonated with the same energy that had filled the Nexus chamber.

Rian stood near the window, staring out into the horizon, his back to her. The shadows of the city stretched far and wide, the pale light of the moon casting a soft glow across the strange, crystalline landscape.

Lyra sat at a table, the weight of her thoughts pressing down on her. She had chosen the path ahead, but that didn't make the journey any easier. There was still so much she didn't understand, so much that hung in the balance. Her father.

Chapter 15: A Heart in Conflict

The Nexus. The fate of Solara and Aeridor.

Rian turned from the window and walked toward her. "You're quiet," he said, his tone gentle, as if he knew what was weighing on her. "Are you second-guessing yourself?"

She looked up at him, meeting his gaze with a small, sad smile. "Maybe," she admitted. "But I have to believe that I did the right thing. I *have* to."

He nodded, sitting down beside her. "I believe you did too. Your father's vision—what he was trying to do—it was dangerous. But now, there's no turning back. We have to stop him before it's too late."

Lyra glanced at him, her heart heavy with the complexities of their mission. "How do we stop him, Rian? How do we undo what he's already set in motion?"

Rian's expression grew serious, his eyes hardening with determination. "We find the source of the rift. It's not just your father's plans that are causing this. There's something... *someone* else involved. Someone who's been manipulating him from the shadows."

Her heart skipped a beat. "A puppet master?"

"Yes," Rian confirmed. "I don't know who it is yet, but I have my suspicions. Someone who has been pulling strings for far longer than we've realized. Someone who might have their own agenda for the Nexus."

Lyra felt a shiver run through her at his words. The idea of another player in this dangerous game was unsettling. But it also made sense. If her father had been influenced by something—or someone—else, it could explain his increasingly erratic behavior, his obsession with the Nexus.

"You think my father isn't the only one we have to stop?" Lyra asked, her voice tinged with disbelief.

Rian met her eyes, his expression grim. "I'm sure of it. But the first step is still the same: we have to stop the rift. If we don't, everything will unravel. And if your father is still determined to rewrite history, we may not have much time left."

Lyra felt a wave of fear surge through her chest, but she pushed it down. *There is no going back,* she reminded herself. *This is the path I've chosen.*

She stood up, her resolve hardening. "Then we begin. No more hesitation. We stop my father, we find out who's behind this, and we set things right."

Rian stood with her, his hand briefly brushing hers. "Together," he said simply.

Lyra nodded, and for the first time in days, a small spark of hope flickered in her heart. They might not have all the answers yet, but they were not alone. They had each other—and that was more than enough for now.

As they left the chamber to prepare for the next stage of their mission, Lyra couldn't help but feel the weight of what lay ahead. But no matter what, she knew one thing for certain: she would face it head-on. She would stop her father. And, whatever the cost, she would protect the future.

Meanwhile, far away in Solara

Duke Alaric stood on the balcony of his palace, gazing out over the vast lands of his kingdom. His expression was unreadable as the wind stirred his dark hair.

The rift had begun. And nothing—no one—would stop him now. He would rewrite time. He would rewrite everything.

Seventeen

Chapter 16: The Ultimate Betrayal

The ancient city, hidden beneath the mountains and shielded by layers of magic older than any living being could comprehend, hummed with a disquieting energy. Lyra could feel it in the very stones beneath her feet, in the air she breathed—an electric pulse that vibrated through the ground and into her bones, resonating with the deepest parts of her being.

The city had become both a sanctuary and a prison. The weight of her decision pressed heavily upon her—she had chosen to stop her father, to preserve the balance of time and space at the cost of everything she had once known. Yet, as she and Rian moved deeper into the labyrinthine streets of the hidden city, a nagging feeling lingered at the back of her mind, an unease that had no clear source.

Her decision had been made, but the consequences were far from clear.

As the two of them made their way through the city's heart,

their path illuminated by the eerie glow of the Nexus' energy, Lyra could not escape the feeling that something was wrong—something was changing.

Rian walked by her side, his expression more serious than ever. His usual easy confidence was gone, replaced by an unsettling quiet. He had been close to her, closer than anyone ever had, and yet even he seemed distant now, as though a shadow loomed between them. He wasn't speaking, but the tension was palpable, an invisible force pressing in from all sides.

Lyra could feel his discomfort, and it mirrored her own.

"We're getting closer," Rian finally spoke, breaking the silence that had stretched between them for what felt like hours. "To the heart of the city, to the Nexus itself. We need to be prepared. There's more at play here than just your father."

Lyra nodded but did not reply immediately. She had begun to suspect, ever since Rian had spoken of a "puppet master" behind her father's actions, that there was someone else orchestrating events from the shadows. But it wasn't until now, as they neared the core of the hidden city, that the full weight of his words sank in.

The Hidden City was a place of power, its energy derived from the Nexus itself. Lyra had been told that its inhabitants—those who had protected the Nexus for millennia—were beings beyond ordinary comprehension, wielders of magic and knowledge that surpassed anything Solara or Aeridor had ever known. They were the keepers of time, guardians of the flow of reality.

Yet, in that very moment, Lyra couldn't shake the feeling that she and Rian weren't the only ones who understood the importance of the Nexus. That there was something—or

Chapter 16: The Ultimate Betrayal

someone—within these walls who had been waiting, patiently, to ensure their failure.

As if on cue, Seraphis appeared from the shadows, his silver mask gleaming in the low light. His movements were deliberate, smooth, as though he had always been a part of the city itself, his presence blending with the walls around them. He was a figure of mystery, his motivations hidden beneath layers of deception, and Lyra knew now that she could no longer trust him—if she ever had.

"You're growing impatient, Lyra," Seraphis said, his voice rich with an unsettling calmness. "You think you're close to unraveling the truth, but in doing so, you're walking deeper into a trap."

Rian's hand instinctively went to the hilt of his blade, his eyes narrowing at the sudden intrusion. "What do you mean, Seraphis?"

Seraphis' eyes glinted behind his mask, his smile thin but knowing. "I mean that you've been blinded by your own sense of righteousness. You think stopping your father is the key to restoring balance, but it isn't. The Nexus doesn't *care* about your plans. It is *far* older than your petty kingdoms. It will follow its own course, no matter what you do."

Lyra felt her heart skip a beat, her throat tightening. "What are you saying? Are you telling me that everything I've done—everything we've been working toward—is in vain?"

Seraphis' expression hardened, but there was a strange sorrow in his voice as he spoke. "Not in vain, no. But misguided. You have a greater role to play, one that neither you nor your father could have ever foreseen. You are more than just a pawn in his game, Lyra. *You are the key to the Nexus itself.*"

Tempting the Enemy's Daughter

The weight of his words hit her like a physical blow, a cold rush of realization flooding through her. She had been so focused on stopping her father, on preventing the unraveling of time, that she had never stopped to consider the true purpose of the Nexus—or why it had chosen her. She had assumed she was simply the last hope, a desperate measure to stop her father's madness. But now, the truth seemed darker than she had ever imagined.

Rian stepped forward, his eyes flashing with a mixture of suspicion and anger. "What do you mean? How do you know this? What are you hiding, Seraphis?"

Seraphis took a slow step back, raising a hand to still Rian's advance. "What I'm hiding," he said, his voice soft but filled with an icy finality, "is the reason I've brought you here, Lyra. And why I've waited for so long."

Lyra felt a cold shiver run down her spine. Her instincts screamed at her, but there was no time to react. The truth was dawning on her, but it was too late.

Seraphis reached behind his back and, with a swift motion, withdrew a small object wrapped in shimmering cloth. He held it out before her, the light glinting off its surface. Lyra gasped as she recognized it: a key—one that she had seen before, a key with intricate designs, its very shape echoing the symbols of the Nexus itself.

"This," Seraphis said, his voice now a whisper, "is the key to everything. It is what your father has been seeking all along. But what he doesn't understand—and what you still don't—*is that it's mine.*"

A sickening realization spread through Lyra's chest. "No... You..."

"You're asking the wrong questions, Lyra," Seraphis con-

Chapter 16: The Ultimate Betrayal

tinued, his gaze cold and piercing. "It was never about your father. It was never about your kingdoms. It was always about me. You were never meant to stop your father. You were always meant to help me."

The world around Lyra seemed to spin, her heart racing in her chest as she finally understood the true depth of the betrayal. All this time, Seraphis had been playing them—manipulating her, manipulating Rian—and now, the true enemy had revealed itself.

Her hand went instinctively to the dagger at her waist, but Seraphis's eyes glittered with an unnatural gleam.

"You think you can stop me, Lyra?" he said, almost with amusement. "I've been pulling the strings from the beginning. Your father was merely a pawn. You, too, were never anything more than a piece in my game."

The weight of his words crashed down on her like a wave. Seraphis, the enigmatic figure who had led them to the Nexus, had orchestrated everything. The fractured timeline, the manipulation of events, the destruction of the ancient pact—it had all been part of his plan.

And now, it was too late to undo it.

Lyra drew her dagger with swift precision, but Seraphis was already moving, his body a blur as he dodged the strike. He grinned beneath his mask, his laughter cold and hollow.

"You'll see, Lyra," he said, his voice now echoing in the chamber, "In the end, there's only one way to truly control time. And that… that is the ultimate betrayal."

As his words faded into the shadows, Lyra realized that her journey—her fight—was far from over. She had been played, and now she had to face the consequences of trusting the wrong ally.

And in that moment, Lyra knew that everything she had fought for, everything she had believed, had been a lie.

The tremors that had rocked the chamber intensified, and Lyra stumbled, clutching the edge of a nearby pillar to steady herself. The Nexus at the center of the room pulsed violently, its energy flaring like a living, breathing entity. The crack in the ground widened, releasing an acrid scent of ozone and burning stone, and Lyra felt the very air around her crackle with a force she had never felt before.

Seraphis remained unfazed, his cold smile still lingering beneath the mask, though now there was something darker in his expression—an unmistakable hunger. As the ground beneath them groaned and shuddered, Lyra realized with a sinking heart that the unstable energy from the Nexus wasn't just affecting the city—it was destabilizing time itself.

"This is your doing?" she asked, her voice a harsh whisper as she struggled to regain her balance. "You've triggered this collapse. You're—*tearing time apart.*"

Seraphis's gaze flickered toward her, and for the first time, there was a faint trace of pity in his eyes. "It was always going to happen, Lyra. The Nexus has been fractured for too long. But I've sped up the process, yes. The timeline—*the very foundation of reality*—is collapsing. And in this chaos, I will reshape it. *Time itself will bend to my will.*"

The air vibrated around them as another violent tremor hit. The massive crystal at the heart of the Nexus pulsed brighter, flickering like a heartbeat, its glow turning from pale white to an eerie, unsettling shade of violet. It felt as though the room itself were tearing at the seams, and Lyra could hear the faint echoes of distorted voices—whispers from different times and places. The very fabric of reality was warping.

Chapter 16: The Ultimate Betrayal

"What do you think you're going to *do* with all this power?" Rian's voice broke through the tense silence. He had remained in the background, watching Seraphis warily, but now he stepped forward, his sword drawn and gleaming with a sharp, deadly edge. "You can't control it forever, Seraphis. The Nexus might be ancient, but it isn't bound to one man's will."

Seraphis's eyes shifted to Rian, and for a moment, there was an unsettling calmness in his gaze, as though he were speaking to a child rather than an adversary. "You misunderstand, Rian. It's not about control. It's about *understanding*. The Nexus doesn't care about the trivialities of kingdoms or borders. It exists to protect time itself, but only a few are capable of seeing that—of realizing how to unlock its true potential."

He turned his gaze back to Lyra, his voice lowering into a whisper, barely audible over the rumbling chaos. "You were always meant to be the key, Lyra. The bloodline that connects your father's realm to the Nexus. Your very existence has been tied to this moment. Don't you see? You were never just a daughter or a pawn. You were the instrument of change."

A wave of cold dread washed over her. "You're insane. You're telling me... you're telling me that everything I've done has been for nothing? My rebellion, my father's death, the alliances we've made—it's all been part of *your* plan?"

His smile widened, like a predator savoring its prey. "It was never about your father. Or your petty alliances. It was always about the Nexus. Your father was too blinded by his ambitions to see it. You were the one who was supposed to unlock it, to restore the flow of time. But now—" His eyes gleamed, and the air thickened with a rising tension. "Now, it's too late. *Time* is unraveling. And with it, I will become its master."

"No." Lyra's voice rang out, more forceful than she expected. She had been overwhelmed, yes, but she wasn't done. She couldn't be. "You've miscalculated. The Nexus may be powerful, but it's not something you can just *bend* to your will. It's ancient, far older than your petty schemes. There are forces here you don't understand. Forces that could consume you."

Seraphis paused, as though considering her words, but the grin never left his face. "The Nexus is not something to be feared, Lyra. It is something to be *embraced*. It is the key to rewriting the mistakes of the past, to seeing the true potential of the future."

Lyra could feel her heart racing in her chest, but now, it wasn't fear that drove her forward. It was defiance. Seraphis had been her mentor, her guide—but all this time, he had used her, manipulated her. And now, he was ready to sacrifice everything to obtain ultimate control over time itself.

"You are nothing more than a puppet, Seraphis," she said, her voice steady despite the chaos swirling around them. "You may have bent history to your whims, but you're not a master of time. Time can't be controlled, not by anyone. Not by you, and certainly not by me."

Rian, still standing by her side, stepped forward. "If you think you can destroy the world to remake it in your image, you're a fool," he growled, brandishing his sword. "You've already lost."

But Seraphis wasn't listening. The swirling energy in the room seemed to pulse with every word he spoke. The Nexus had grown wild, the crystal flickering dangerously, its violent, erratic glow reflecting the chaos that was tearing through the air. He turned to face it again, his posture relaxed and yet

Chapter 16: The Ultimate Betrayal

filled with an ominous finality.

"I've already won," he said, his voice now heavy with a dark, assured certainty. "You still don't understand. This world—*your world*—was never meant to last. The ancient pact between Aeridor and Solara? The balance of time? They were all destined to break. And in their place will rise a new order. An order where time bows to me. Where I can erase the mistakes and rewrite history itself. And you—both of you—will be forgotten."

Lyra's mind raced. The room felt like it was closing in around them, as the shifting energies of the Nexus grew more unstable with each passing moment. She could feel time itself warping, the air around her thick with tension, like the very threads of existence were snapping.

And then, an idea—a dangerous one—sprung into her mind. *She needed to act. She needed to take control of the Nexus. Now.*

There was no time for hesitation. The Nexus was the key—Seraphis had been right about one thing. Lyra was the only one who could unlock it. She didn't know exactly *how*, but she could feel it deep within her—a connection to something ancient, to the magic that had been passed down through generations. Her blood, her lineage, her ties to the Nexus, they were more than just a key. They were part of the very *balance* Seraphis sought to destroy.

"Rian," Lyra said, her voice low but urgent. "Distract him. I'll do the rest."

Rian nodded sharply, his eyes narrowing. "Be careful."

Without waiting for another word, Rian lunged toward Seraphis, his blade flashing in the air. Seraphis turned just in time to parry the blow, his own movements elegant and effortless. Lyra, meanwhile, didn't hesitate. She focused all her energy on the Nexus, her mind sharp and clear, her heart steady in the face of the unraveling world around her.

With every fiber of her being, she reached out to the Nexus, seeking the connection between herself and the ancient energy. It was there, buried deep within her, a spark of power passed down through her ancestors, linked to the very core of time itself.

The moment she touched it, the world around her *shattered*.

Top of Form

Bottom of Form

Eighteen

Chapter 17: A Race Against Time

The world exploded in a riot of color.

One moment, Lyra's hands were outstretched toward the Nexus, her mind filled with determination, the next, she was engulfed in a blinding light, too brilliant and pure to comprehend. It wasn't like the flashes of magic she'd felt before, the controlled, deliberate sorcery of Aeridor or Solara. No, this was *raw*, untamed energy—a force far older than anything she had ever encountered, vibrating with the resonance of ages, the pulse of history itself.

The ground beneath her feet disappeared, replaced by an endless, swirling expanse of fractured visions and flickering timelines. She saw flashes—snippets of her own past, memories twisting and warping before her eyes. Her father, sitting in the throne room of Solara, his face grave and tense. The quiet moment before the great betrayal, when she had first met Seraphis, the one who had shown her the ways of the

Nexus. Her confrontation with Duke Alaric—was that real, or had it been a memory she had *created*? The lines between past, present, and future blurred, colliding and twisting into a single, impossible moment.

Is this... what Seraphis sees? she wondered. *Is this what he's trying to control?*

She reached out instinctively, trying to anchor herself in the swirling madness, but the moment her fingers brushed the raw threads of time, she was pulled deeper into the vortex. It felt as though her very soul was being torn apart, scattered across a thousand potential futures. There was no sense of direction—no up or down, no past or future—only the dizzying pull of everything *and nothing* at once.

And then, just as quickly, the storm of light and energy ceased.

Lyra gasped, her breath sharp and ragged as she collapsed onto cold, hard ground. The dizziness from the overload of temporal energy still spun in her mind, but she forced herself to focus. Slowly, she pushed herself up, her eyes scanning the unfamiliar surroundings. The place around her was *silent*, too silent—no distant hum of the Nexus, no crackling energies, no storm. The air was still, oppressive in its stillness, and the reality around her seemed... wrong.

A faint smell of rusted metal and damp earth lingered in the air. A large, decaying stone wall stretched before her, half-buried in brambles, but the most striking thing was the landscape. It wasn't Aeridor. It wasn't Solara. The sky above her was a dull gray, heavy with clouds, as though the sun had long since forgotten how to shine. She was standing in a ruined courtyard, its stone flagstones cracked and broken, weeds pushing up through the cracks.

Chapter 17: A Race Against Time

In the distance, the faint glow of distant fires flickered along the horizon, and the air itself felt *wrong*. There was no life here, no warmth, only a hollow, pervasive sense of abandonment.

Lyra stood, her legs shaky but determined, as she surveyed the landscape. There was something deeply unsettling about this place. It didn't just feel out of place—it felt like a *memory*—something that had been erased, or buried. And yet, everything in her bones screamed that this was *real*, this was a place that existed in the fabric of time itself, a moment long lost to history.

This is what happens when time breaks, she realized with a sudden, sinking dread. *When the Nexus is unstable...*

Behind her, the air shimmered. A faint ripple distorted the space, like the air above a boiling pot. Lyra spun, her hand instinctively reaching for the dagger at her side, but the moment she did, the figure that emerged from the shimmering distortion froze her in place.

It was Rian.

But not the Rian she had known.

This Rian was older, more weathered, his features harder, more angular, like a man who had lived through countless battles. His armor was battered, blackened by smoke and time, a mismatched set that spoke of desperate fights in forgotten wars. His eyes, once so full of warmth, were now cold, like the eyes of someone who had witnessed the collapse of everything they had once loved.

"Lyra," he said softly, his voice carrying an unrecognizable sadness. His gaze swept over her, pausing only for a moment before his mouth set into a grim line. "I knew you would find your way here."

She froze, her mind racing to understand what she was

Tempting the Enemy's Daughter

seeing. *How* was this possible? How could Rian be here, looking like this—like a man from the *future*?

"You're... not real," she whispered, though even as she said it, she knew it wasn't true. He was real. He was standing in front of her, more real than the dreamlike distortion of time that surrounded them.

Rian gave a bitter laugh, the sound devoid of humor. "Oh, I'm as real as you are. Or as real as this place is. *Time is broken, Lyra.* This is where it all leads—this is what happens when you play with forces beyond your control."

Lyra felt her pulse quicken. She hadn't expected to meet him here, in this fractured version of reality. She had thought, foolishly, that by reaching the Nexus, she could somehow *correct* the time fracture. But it seemed that time had already slipped beyond repair.

"You've—seen this place before, haven't you?" Lyra asked, her voice hoarse as she looked around at the desolation. It wasn't a question. It was an understanding. She could feel that this was his world now—his future, perhaps. But it was a future devoid of hope, of life, of purpose.

"I've seen it," Rian said, his voice heavy with sorrow. "This is what happens when Seraphis gets his way. The Nexus splits reality—fragments of time are left to decay, isolated from each other. And once enough fractures form..." He trailed off, his eyes darkening. "The timeline will unravel completely. And everything will cease to exist."

Lyra felt a knot tighten in her chest. "This... this is the future?"

"Not anymore," Rian said, his eyes flashing with a bitterness that matched his words. "This is one of many possible futures. But it's the one Seraphis wants. He *planned* this—he made it

Chapter 17: A Race Against Time

so that this version of time would become inevitable. A world where only he exists, where he controls every moment. A world where nothing is real, because time is a broken illusion."

"No," Lyra said, her voice shaking with conviction. "I won't let that happen. I won't let him control everything."

Rian nodded, but his expression softened, as if he were both proud and sorrowful in equal measure. "I know you won't. But you need to understand—this isn't just about saving the kingdoms anymore. It's about saving *everything*—every possible timeline, every moment that exists, past, present, and future. The Nexus has become unstable. And if it's not fixed…"

He didn't need to finish the sentence. Lyra could feel the truth of it like a cold hand on her heart. If the Nexus couldn't be repaired—if the fractures weren't sealed—then all of reality would collapse into nothingness.

She glanced down at her hands, still trembling from the touch of the Nexus. The power coursing through her was overwhelming, but it was clear now that she had become something more than just a daughter of Solara. She had become *the last hope*, the one person who could repair the fractures in time before the collapse became permanent.

Her heart pounded in her chest, but her resolve hardened. "We need to find a way to fix the Nexus," she said, her voice steady with purpose. "We need to stop Seraphis. We can't let him control time. We have to fix this."

Rian's gaze softened just slightly, though his eyes still held the weight of a man who had seen too much. "You have no idea how much time you've lost. But there's still a chance. There's still hope."

"Then let's take it," Lyra replied, her voice firm, as she turned back toward the desolate world ahead.

And together, they began their journey to save time itself.

The broken landscape stretched out before them like the ruins of a forgotten civilization, its contours etched with the scars of time's relentless passage. The air, heavy with the weight of decay and silence, hung like a shroud. Lyra's pulse quickened as she took in the desolation—this place, this fractured moment in time, felt like a tomb for history itself.

Rian's presence beside her was a stark reminder of the stakes they faced. His eyes, once so full of warmth and life, now seemed empty—haunted by the future he'd witnessed, the timeline he'd been caught in. His armor was battered, his face weary, as if he had been fighting for far longer than anyone should have to. But there was still resolve in his eyes, a flicker of determination that hadn't completely been extinguished.

"What happened here?" Lyra asked, her voice barely above a whisper, as though speaking too loudly might disturb the fragile threads of reality around them.

"This is the result of Seraphis's victory," Rian said, his tone grim. "When the Nexus cracked, time itself began to break apart. He was never content with controlling the present. He wanted to reshape the *past*, to control the *future*. In doing so, he destroyed the continuity of time. Everything you see, everything here, is a consequence of that—the remnants of timelines that no longer make sense."

Lyra looked around, feeling a sickening knot twist in her stomach. She had always known that Seraphis was dangerous—had always known that his ambition to rewrite time could lead to catastrophic consequences—but seeing this place, this twisted, fragmented reality, brought the weight of it into sharp focus.

Chapter 17: A Race Against Time

"How do we fix it?" she asked, her voice steely with determination, though doubt lingered in the back of her mind. Could anything fix this? Could she *fix* this?

Rian turned to her, his face softening just slightly. "The first step is understanding that we're not just fighting for the present. We're fighting for every moment that came before us—and every moment that is still to come."

She nodded slowly, feeling the gravity of his words sink in. The stakes were so much higher than she had realized. It wasn't just the kingdoms of Aeridor and Solara at risk. It wasn't just her father's legacy, or even the lives of those she had once called allies. The fabric of *existence* itself was unraveling.

The Nexus, that ancient artifact of unimaginable power, was the heart of it all. If she could only reach it again, stabilize it, perhaps she could undo the damage Seraphis had caused. But Seraphis was no fool—he knew that the Nexus was the key to everything. And if the fractured timelines had taught her anything, it was that he was never far behind.

"I don't know how much time we have left," Lyra said, urgency creeping into her voice. "Seraphis must already be moving to seal his control. If he's manipulating time, even the smallest moment could shift the balance entirely."

Rian's gaze hardened as he nodded. "He's been manipulating the Nexus for far longer than we realized. The fractures you see—the ones that stretch through this broken world—they're the direct result of his interference. It's only a matter of time before his grip tightens and this entire *place* becomes his new reality."

As Rian spoke, Lyra's thoughts raced. Seraphis's obsession with rewriting history had never been about simple power—it had been about *total control*. The Nexus was more than just a tool—it was a living, breathing force that connected all points of time, past and present, in a delicate, unspoken balance. But that balance had been shattered by Seraphis's reckless tampering. And now, the reality they stood in was the result: a fractured world, teetering on the edge of destruction.

"How do we stop him?" Lyra asked, her eyes meeting Rian's with determination.

Rian's lips pressed into a thin line as he considered the question. "To stop Seraphis, we need to reach the center of the Nexus—the core of its power. It's hidden in a place that's been locked away from time. He's kept it safe, hidden in the folds of the broken timelines. If we can find it, we might be able to reverse the damage."

Lyra nodded, the weight of his words sinking in. *Locked away from time.* The thought chilled her, but she didn't hesitate. There was no time to waste.

"How do we find it?"

"We follow the fractures," Rian said. "They're the clues. The rifts in time—they can guide us."

Lyra looked at him, confused. "The fractures are all over the place. How do we know which one leads to the Nexus?"

Rian hesitated for a moment before answering. "The Nexus itself is a living thing. It responds to those who are connected to it. You felt its pull when you touched it before. *It* will guide us."

A shiver ran down her spine as she processed his words. The Nexus was a living entity, tied to her bloodline, to her very being. It was more than just magic—it was a force that responded to her. But even as she thought about it, her mind was filled with doubt. How could she trust her own connection to it after everything that had happened? How

Chapter 17: A Race Against Time

could she be sure that she wouldn't make things worse?

Rian seemed to sense her hesitation, his eyes softening. "I know it's hard to trust. But if there's one thing I've learned, Lyra, it's that time is a tricky thing. The Nexus doesn't care about our intentions. It only cares about what happens next. And right now, it needs us to stop Seraphis before it's too late."

She swallowed hard, pushing aside her doubts. There was no other choice. They had to keep moving, and they had to do it quickly.

"Alright," Lyra said, her voice steady. "We'll follow the fractures."

The ground beneath their feet shifted, and a low hum filled the air. It was faint at first, barely noticeable, but as they moved forward, the sound grew louder—a distant, almost imperceptible thrum of energy, like a heartbeat.

Rian glanced toward the horizon, where the shadows of distant mountains loomed. "The fractures will lead us to the heart of the Nexus. But there's no guarantee we'll make it in time."

A strange feeling washed over Lyra—a combination of fear and something else. Something that felt almost like *recognition*. It was as though the Nexus itself was calling to her, urging her to follow the path she had always been meant to take.

She looked to Rian. "Then we don't waste any more time."

Together, they began walking toward the distant glow, the fractured world around them pulsing with an eerie energy, as if the very earth itself was alive with the echo of a thousand possibilities. They had a long journey ahead, but one thing was clear: the fate of time itself rested on their shoulders.

As they moved, Lyra could feel the pulse of the Nexus growing stronger. Somewhere, deep within the heart of the broken world, it waited for them.

The ground beneath their feet shifted uneasily as Lyra and Rian pressed on, their footsteps echoing in the stillness of the ruined world. The air grew thick with an unnatural tension, and as they walked, the fractured landscape seemed to pulse with a life of its own. It was as though time itself were a living entity, breathing, shifting, bending, a consciousness that was aware of their presence. The cracks in reality hummed beneath the surface, drawing them forward, guiding them toward something they couldn't yet understand.

Lyra's heart beat faster with each step. She could feel the Nexus—the raw, potent force of it, as though it were tugging at her very soul, calling her name from the depths of time. But it was more than just a connection to her bloodline. It was a bond that transcended space and time. In this fractured reality, the Nexus was her ally and her enemy, both guiding and testing her, pushing her to places she had never thought possible.

She glanced at Rian, who was walking silently beside her, his eyes fixed on the path ahead. He seemed so different now, older, wearier, but still resolute. The years of struggle had hardened him, left a mark on him that she couldn't fully understand. And yet, despite everything, he was still the same Rian—her ally, her protector, and perhaps, just perhaps, something more.

"Do you feel it?" she asked, her voice low, but urgent. The pull of the Nexus was undeniable, growing stronger with every passing moment.

Rian nodded, his expression darkening. "I do. It's alive, Lyra. The Nexus... It's feeding off the fractures. It's losing its control over time, but it's still trying to reach out, still trying

Chapter 17: A Race Against Time

to repair itself. If we don't find it soon—"

"I know," she said, cutting him off. There was no need to voice the danger. It was all too clear. If the Nexus lost its grip completely, everything would fall apart. Time itself would unravel, and with it, the very fabric of existence.

They reached a clearing at the base of a jagged mountain range, the path ahead obscured by thick mist. The air here was unnaturally still, the ground cracked in unnatural patterns that twisted in on themselves, creating a disorienting maze of broken earth.

"This is it," Rian said, his voice tense. "The heart of the Nexus. Somewhere beyond this mist lies the core. If we can reach it, we might be able to stabilize the fractures."

Lyra felt a shiver run down her spine as she gazed at the swirling fog ahead. Something in the air felt wrong—distorted, as if the very laws of nature had been stretched too thin, like a thread pulled too tightly. Her instincts screamed at her to turn back, to abandon this path before it was too late. But she knew there was no other choice. This was their only chance.

They stepped forward, the mist thickening with each step, curling around their feet like tendrils of smoke. The ground beneath them seemed to shift again, as if the earth itself were alive and breathing, unwilling to allow them to pass.

A deep rumble echoed from somewhere within the mist, sending a ripple through the air. Lyra stopped, her hand instinctively reaching for the dagger at her side. Something was coming.

"What is that?" she whispered, her eyes scanning the fog.

Rian's jaw tightened, his hand hovering near the hilt of his sword. "It's not natural. We're not alone."

Before Lyra could respond, the mist parted suddenly, and

out of the swirling haze emerged a figure—tall and cloaked in shadow, its face hidden beneath a hood. The air around it seemed to warp, distorting the space and time around them, bending reality itself.

Lyra took a step back, her heart pounding in her chest. There was something unmistakably *wrong* about this figure. She had felt the presence of the Nexus earlier, but this—this was something different. This was *unnatural*. The figure was not a part of this timeline, nor any other. It was an interloper, a being that should not exist in this place.

The figure spoke, its voice a low, resonant hum that seemed to vibrate within her very bones.

"You should not have come here," it said, each word dripping with a dark power. "This place is not for mortals. The Nexus belongs to no one."

Rian stepped forward, his hand resting firmly on the sword's hilt. "And yet, we are here. And we will take it back."

The figure's form seemed to flicker, as if it were made of mist itself, twisting and reforming with each movement. Its shape became more solid, revealing a face—though its features were indistinct, a blur of shifting lines, as though it was both human and not at the same time.

"I am not here to stop you, Rian," the figure said, its voice now eerily calm. "I am here to warn you. The Nexus is not a tool to be controlled. It is a force beyond understanding, beyond time itself. You cannot *restore* what has been broken. You cannot *fix* the past. Time is not a river you can steer."

Lyra's eyes narrowed. "Who are you?" she demanded. "What do you want?"

The figure's form solidified a little more, and for the first time, Lyra saw the flash of eyes beneath the hood—eyes that

Chapter 17: A Race Against Time

burned with a cold, otherworldly fire. "I am the one who watches," it replied. "I am the guardian of the fractures. I have seen all the timelines, all the paths. And I have seen what happens when mortals attempt to rewrite history."

Rian's expression darkened. "Seraphis has already broken time. We're not here to fix the past. We're here to stop him from *destroying* everything."

The figure cocked its head, its shifting features betraying no hint of emotion. "Seraphis is but a puppet. A creature caught in a game far older than he can comprehend. You cannot stop him by forcing your will on time. You cannot save what was never meant to be saved."

Lyra felt a chill crawl up her spine. This being—whatever it was—was not a mortal. It wasn't even human. It was something ancient, something tied to the very fabric of existence. And it was right: they were playing a game with forces they didn't fully understand.

But she wasn't about to back down now.

"I don't care who you are," Lyra said, her voice firm, "and I don't care what you think. Time is broken, and we're going to fix it. We're going to stop Seraphis, even if it means going through you."

The figure studied her, the strange, shifting eyes locking onto hers. For a moment, silence hung between them, thick with the weight of unspoken truths. Then, slowly, the figure raised its hands, the mist swirling around them more violently.

"If you are determined to break the laws of time, then you will learn the cost," it said, its voice both an echo and a warning. "But know this: The Nexus will not be controlled. It will consume you. It will rewrite you. You will become part of its endless loop, caught between moments that never truly end."

Before Lyra could respond, the figure vanished, dissipating into the mist as though it had never been there at all.

A long silence followed.

Rian exhaled sharply, his grip on his sword relaxing ever so slightly. "We've come too far to turn back now," he muttered, more to himself than to Lyra.

Lyra nodded, her resolve hardening. The figure had warned them, but it had also confirmed what she had already suspected. The Nexus was alive, and it was not something to be trifled with. But they had no choice. There was no turning back.

"We'll face whatever comes," she said, her voice steady. "We have to."

Rian nodded, his expression grim. Together, they moved forward, into the heart of the mist, deeper into the fractured world. They were closer now—closer to the Nexus. And closer to a confrontation with Seraphis that would determine the fate of everything.

Top of Form

Nineteen

Chapter 18: Confronting the Enemy

The mist parted before them like a curtain being drawn back, revealing a landscape unlike anything Lyra had ever seen. Before them stood a towering structure, rising out of the fractured earth—a massive, obsidian spire that twisted into the sky like a jagged shard of night. The air around it shimmered with energy, a faint distortion that made the world feel… wrong.

Every step they took felt heavy, as though the very ground beneath them was unwilling to bear their weight. The Nexus was close now—its presence almost suffocating in its intensity. Lyra could feel it—like a pulse, like a heartbeat—pounding through her veins. It called to her.

They had arrived.

Rian moved ahead, his hand still resting on the hilt of his sword, eyes scanning the environment with the practiced vigilance of someone who had been through countless battles.

He stopped at the base of the spire, his expression taut with concentration. The air felt thick with an oppressive power, and Lyra could sense the danger they were walking into.

"Seraphis is here," Rian said quietly, his voice betraying none of the tension he was feeling. "I can feel it."

Lyra's breath caught in her throat. The name, once distant, now held weight—more weight than she'd ever imagined. She had always known Seraphis was dangerous. But now, standing at the heart of the fractured world, she understood the depth of the threat. This was no mere man. This was a force—a being who sought to control time itself. And if they didn't stop him, everything—*everything*—would be lost.

The spire loomed before them, its black stone etched with ancient symbols that glowed faintly with a sickly, pale light. The closer they got, the more she could feel it—the Nexus, pulsing from within, resonating with the very core of the structure. But it was not merely a power source; it was a wound, a tear in the fabric of time itself. The walls of the spire seemed to bend and warp with the movement of time around them, flickering like a flame caught in the wind.

Rian took a step forward, his hand tightening on his sword. "He's inside. We don't have much time."

Lyra nodded, her heart racing. They had no choice now but to face Seraphis. And she knew that once they entered, there would be no turning back. The Nexus was the key to everything, and Seraphis had already proven he would stop at nothing to control it.

Together, they crossed the threshold of the spire, the air thick with the scent of ozone and decay. Inside, the walls were lined with strange, shifting symbols, swirling like smoke, as though they were alive, breathing in the very air. The

Chapter 18: Confronting the Enemy

flickering light from the symbols cast eerie shadows across the space, and Lyra could hear the faint hum of magic reverberating in the air, vibrating through the very ground beneath her feet.

"This place," she whispered, "it's like it's part of the Nexus itself. Like it's alive."

Rian didn't respond immediately, but Lyra could see his unease in the tight set of his jaw. He was no stranger to magic, but this—this was something else. The spire was not just a structure; it was a conduit, a living extension of the Nexus, and everything within it seemed to bend to its will.

They moved deeper into the heart of the spire, the winding corridors narrowing as they descended further into the belly of the structure. The temperature dropped with each step, and the atmosphere grew more oppressive, thick with a sense of foreboding. It felt as though the spire itself was closing in around them, as if it were watching them, waiting for them to make their move.

At the far end of the chamber, a massive, circular platform rose from the ground, surrounded by a shimmering pool of liquid light. The pool seemed to ripple with energy, the surface twisting and warping like a reflection in water disturbed by a stone. At the center of the pool stood Seraphis.

He was no longer the man Lyra had once known. His form was different now, his once-human features contorted by power, by something darker. His eyes burned with an unnatural fire, and his skin seemed to shimmer with an otherworldly glow, as though he were made of the very essence of time itself. The air around him crackled with the intensity of magic—raw and unrestrained.

"Lyra," Seraphis said, his voice deep and resonant, yet tinged

Tempting the Enemy's Daughter

with something cold and distant. "You should have stayed away. You have no idea the forces you are toying with. The Nexus was never meant to be controlled by mortals."

Lyra's heart tightened in her chest, but she refused to back down. "You're wrong, Seraphis," she said, her voice steady, though her pulse thundered in her ears. "You've already broken time. You've already fractured reality itself. You're playing with forces you can't possibly understand."

Seraphis stepped forward, his eyes flickering with amusement. "I understand *more* than you know, Lyra. I've seen the timelines, watched them stretch and bend like threads of silk. I've rewritten history. I've seen what happens when the Nexus is no longer bound by time." He raised a hand, and the air around him crackled with energy. "And now, I will make time my servant."

Rian stepped forward, his hand gripping his sword tighter. "You can't control it, Seraphis. You've already destroyed everything. You've torn time apart. If you go any further, you'll tear the fabric of existence itself."

Seraphis smiled—an expression that held no warmth. "You speak as if I haven't already done that. The world is already shattered, Rian. There is no turning back. But with the Nexus, I can rebuild it. I can make it *my* world."

Lyra clenched her fists, feeling the weight of his words settle over her like a cloud of cold smoke. Seraphis had already broken time, and now he intended to remake it in his own image. But what did that mean for the kingdoms of Aeridor and Solara? For her father, for Rian, for everyone she had ever known?

There was no way she was going to let him win.

"You're wrong," she said, her voice trembling with a mix of

Chapter 18: Confronting the Enemy

anger and resolve. "We can still fix this. We can still undo the damage you've done. We *have* to."

Seraphis's gaze flickered with a hint of something—perhaps a fleeting moment of doubt, or perhaps it was merely a calculated move. But whatever it was, it didn't last long. With a cruel smile, he raised his hands, and the very air around them seemed to warp and crack.

"You still don't understand, do you?" he said, his voice growing cold. "There's nothing to undo. Time is already lost. And you," he turned his gaze to Lyra, "are the final piece of the puzzle. You are the key. You always have been."

Before Lyra could react, Seraphis made a swift motion, and the world around them began to fracture once more. The walls of the spire seemed to dissolve into light, and reality itself started to collapse in on itself.

It was happening again. Time was breaking.

This was it. The final confrontation.

And the only question that remained was whether they could stop Seraphis before the Nexus was completely consumed by his will.

The spire around them trembled, and the very air seemed to crackle with power. Lyra's heart pounded as the ground beneath her feet rippled, as though the laws of reality were unraveling before her eyes. Seraphis stood at the center of the pool, his arms raised high, the shimmering light around him pulsating with the force of something ancient and unfathomable. His eyes, burning with cold fire, locked onto hers, and the weight of his gaze felt like a chain around her chest.

"You still don't understand, do you, Lyra?" Seraphis said, his voice now an eerie calm, a stark contrast to the storm of energy swirling around them. "Time is not a thread to be sewn back together. It is a river to be redirected, a force to be bent to my will. The Nexus is not a curse. It is a gift—a key to rewriting all of existence."

Lyra's breath caught in her throat, a mix of fear and defiance rising in her chest. "You think *you* control it?" she spat, her voice trembling with anger. "You think you're the master of time, but you've only made it worse! You've broken everything—everything! And now you want to use it to make *your* world? A world where you are the god of time itself? What happens to the rest of us, Seraphis? To the kingdoms, to the people? You think they'll accept your twisted version of reality?"

Seraphis' smile was cold, devoid of any warmth or empathy. "They will accept it because they will have no choice. When I remake the world, there will be no resistance, no chaos. The fractures in time will close, and history will be mine to command. The kingdoms of Aeridor and Solara? They will be nothing more than relics of a past I will rewrite." He turned his gaze to Rian, his eyes flickering with mockery. "You, Rian. You're just as blind as she is. This is bigger than you, than both of you. You cannot stop what is inevitable."

Lyra's fingers curled into fists. She could feel the raw power of the Nexus swirling in the air, could feel its magnetic pull, like a storm trying to suck everything into its center. She could hear the faint whisper of time itself, bending and breaking with every passing moment. It was as if the very world was holding its breath, waiting for the final decision to be made.

"I *won't* let you do this," Lyra said, stepping forward, her voice steady despite the fear clawing at her insides. "You've already broken time. You've already broken *everything*. But I

Chapter 18: Confronting the Enemy

can still fix it. We can still stop this. Together."

Seraphis' eyes narrowed, his lips twisting into a grimace. "You really think you can stop me? You think your pathetic resistance will undo what's been done? You're just a pawn in this game, Lyra. A puppet. You and your father—both of you, tangled in a web of deceit and power. The Nexus isn't something that can be fixed. It was never meant to be controlled."

Rian, standing beside her, spoke then, his voice cutting through the tense air like a sword. "And yet you're trying to control it. You've already shattered the world, Seraphis. The Nexus is not a tool. It's a force, and you're playing with fire. You cannot control it. Not like this."

The room seemed to darken as Seraphis raised his arms once again, his expression hardening into something more dangerous. The energy around him intensified, the air crackling with raw, unrestrained magic. "You are wrong," Seraphis said, his voice low and dangerous. "You can't stop me. Time is already mine, and soon, it will be my *domain*. You cannot defy fate, Lyra. You were always meant to come to me. You were always meant to be the key."

Lyra felt a cold shiver creep up her spine at his words. The realization hit her like a thunderclap. *She was the key.* He wasn't speaking just about the Nexus. He wasn't just speaking about time. He was speaking about her. Her bloodline. Her power. All of it had led her to this moment, this confrontation, and Seraphis knew it. She wasn't just a pawn. She was the *final piece* he needed to complete his control over the Nexus.

But what did that mean for her? And for the kingdoms she was bound to protect?

"No," Lyra breathed, shaking her head. "I won't be your

pawn, Seraphis. I'll stop you. No matter what it takes."

Rian stepped forward, his stance solid and unwavering. "We will stop you. You can't rewrite reality."

For a moment, Seraphis' eyes flashed with something—anger? Frustration?—but it passed as quickly as it had appeared. He straightened, a malevolent calm settling over him.

"Then prepare yourselves," Seraphis said, his voice dripping with dark amusement. "I will show you just how futile your defiance truly is."

With a sudden, sweeping motion, he thrust his hands forward, and the space around them seemed to bend. The very air thickened, warping with the weight of his magic. Lyra staggered, feeling a wave of dizziness wash over her as time itself seemed to fold in on itself.

Rian grabbed her arm, steadying her, but even he looked disoriented, his eyes wide as they darted from side to side, trying to keep track of the distortion. The Nexus was becoming unstable—this wasn't just magic. This was reality itself starting to collapse.

"Hold on!" Lyra shouted to Rian, but her voice felt swallowed up by the chaotic whirlpool of energy around them.

Seraphis laughed, a dark and hollow sound, echoing off the walls of the spire. "You are too late. Time is already mine."

The distorted air around them began to warp and twist, the ground itself buckling under the strain. The spire trembled, its walls shaking as the very foundations of reality seemed to crack. Lyra fought against the disorienting pull, clutching at Rian's arm as the world around them seemed to tear open.

But she didn't let go.

She couldn't let go.

Chapter 18: Confronting the Enemy

As the energy began to surge, Lyra reached deep within herself, tapping into the power of the Nexus. She could feel it—the wild, untamed force of time that had bound her to this moment, the power that Seraphis sought to control. It pulsed through her veins, electric and untamable. But she could feel something more than just the Nexus. There was something deeper—something ancient—beneath the surface of it all.

A sudden understanding washed over her, and for a brief, terrifying moment, she saw the full scope of what Seraphis was trying to do. He wasn't just trying to control time—he was trying to *reshape* it. To become *one* with it, to erase the past, the present, and the future, and create a world entirely of his making.

"No," Lyra whispered to herself, the truth settling like stone in her heart.

She would *never* let him have that power.

With a force of will she didn't know she possessed, Lyra reached out, her hand stretched toward the heart of the Nexus, summoning the ancient magic that had called her here. The air around her crackled with power, the very fabric of time vibrating with the energy she was wielding. She didn't know if it would work, but she knew one thing—she had to try.

"Rian, now!" she shouted, her voice a command.

Rian reacted without hesitation, his sword flashing through the air in a deadly arc. Seraphis's concentration faltered for just a moment, his focus shifting toward the attack, and in that instant, Lyra unleashed the full force of the Nexus, slamming it into the center of the spire, into the heart of the fractured time.

The spire shuddered violently, as if the structure itself were alive. Seraphis let out a sharp, startled cry as the magic swirled around him, and for a brief moment, everything went *silent*.

Then—**CRACK**.

Time snapped.

The world seemed to shudder, the very fabric of time rippling like the surface of a disturbed pond. For a split second, everything—sound, motion, light—stilled. The air around them felt thick, charged, as though the universe itself had drawn a sharp, breathless pause.

Lyra's heart hammered in her chest, every muscle tense as she locked her gaze onto Seraphis. She had done it. She had *pushed back*. The Nexus had answered her call, flooding her with the power to stand against him. She felt the energy course through her—wild, untamable, like a raging river held at bay by nothing but her will.

Seraphis staggered, his eyes widening in disbelief as the force of Lyra's power crashed into him. His grip on the Nexus faltered for the briefest of moments, his control slipping just enough for her to see the cracks in his dominance.

But that moment was fleeting. A fraction of a second in time, and already Seraphis was recovering. His expression twisted into a mask of fury, his features hardening as he gathered himself.

"You *fool*," he snarled, his voice low and cold. "Do you truly believe you can stand against me? You're nothing more than a child, playing with powers you can't begin to comprehend."

Lyra gritted her teeth, the pull of the Nexus growing stronger, the power within her threatening to consume her whole. She had *felt* it—had felt the delicate thread of control that had tethered time itself, pulling it into chaos. But she also felt the weight of Seraphis' magic, thick and suffocating. He was no mere man now. He had become something far darker,

Chapter 18: Confronting the Enemy

something more powerful than she could have ever imagined.

But still, she refused to falter.

Beside her, Rian's sword gleamed with the reflected light of the Nexus, and though his face was set in a hard line, Lyra could see the uncertainty in his eyes. He wasn't sure what they were up against, what Seraphis had truly become. But he *trusted* her. That was enough.

"Rian," she whispered, her voice hoarse, "we need to destroy the core. We need to sever Seraphis' connection to the Nexus, or we'll lose everything."

Rian didn't hesitate. "I know. We'll take him down together."

But as they moved to advance, Seraphis raised his hands, and the air around them suddenly rippled, warping in unnatural ways. Lyra's pulse quickened as the space seemed to stretch, to *fold*, like a torn piece of cloth being pulled in opposite directions. Time itself wavered.

"You think you can *destroy* the Nexus?" Seraphis' laugh rang out, hollow and terrifying. "Time cannot be destroyed. It will bend to my will, as it always has. You are insignificant."

He stretched his hands wide, and with a deep, resonating growl, he summoned the full force of his power. The air began to shimmer as the ground buckled beneath them. The spire's walls seemed to liquefy, and Lyra gasped as the very structure twisted in impossible shapes. The stars outside the spire—*the very sky itself*—began to shift and waver. The world was *breaking*. She could feel it. The pull of time itself splintering.

"Hold on!" Rian shouted, reaching for her, but even his powerful grip seemed helpless against the force of Seraphis' magic.

And then, in that moment, Lyra realized—Seraphis wasn't just trying to control time anymore. He was trying to *erase* it.

He was attempting to *unmake* everything, to collapse all of reality into a singularity, a moment that existed outside of the continuum of time. Nothing would remain. Not the kingdoms, not the people, not the world itself. Only his vision would persist—a broken world, remade in his image.

"No," Lyra breathed, her voice raw. She could feel the weight of the Nexus pulling her under, but she couldn't—*wouldn't*—let him have it.

Her hands shot forward, palms outstretched toward the pulsing energy that surrounded Seraphis. Her body was shaking with the strain of wielding such immense power, but she forced herself to focus. The Nexus was still *alive*, and so was she. She was more than just a pawn in Seraphis' game.

She was the key.

With every ounce of strength, Lyra reached into the heart of the Nexus. She didn't fight against it; she *embraced* it. Her mind flared with ancient knowledge, ancient power, and for the first time, she understood it—not as an external force, but as something that flowed through her, something *she* could command.

She felt it pulse under her skin, hot and heavy, thrumming with the energy of the very fabric of reality. It wanted to break. But Lyra *pulled* it, wrenched it into alignment. She wasn't just trying to stop the Nexus—she was *controlling* it.

The world shuddered once more, a low moan of cosmic anguish, and suddenly, Lyra was no longer alone in her mind. Through the Nexus, she saw it—a vast web, threads stretching across time, reaching into the past, the future, all of it. She saw the rift, the tear Seraphis had caused, and through the Nexus, she saw the way to heal it.

But it came at a cost. The power was overwhelming, and the

Chapter 18: Confronting the Enemy

strain of holding it, of being the bridge between reality and the Nexus, made her vision blur. Her hands trembled. Every breath felt like a struggle.

Seraphis saw what she was doing. His eyes widened in fury. "No!" he bellowed. "You cannot do this! You—"

But it was too late.

Lyra let go.

With a single, shuddering breath, she released all of the power she had gathered. The Nexus surged with a violent roar, and the very air *cracked*. Time itself shattered in a blinding explosion of light and force, and the spire was torn apart, the walls collapsing as though reality itself had been wrenched from its foundations.

Seraphis screamed in agony as the light enveloped him, his body writhing in the wake of Lyra's final command. The Nexus, now freed from his influence, collapsed into a singular pulse, echoing across the fractured fabric of time. In that moment, everything *stilled*. The world held its breath.

And then—**silence.**

Lyra blinked, her mind reeling, her body numb with exhaustion. The light began to fade, and as it did, she saw the spire around her crumble into dust. The Nexus was no longer an entity of raw power, no longer something that could be manipulated by those who sought to control it.

It was simply *gone*. The rupture had been sealed.

Rian was beside her in an instant, his arms steadying her as the world around them began to solidify once more. The distortions in time were gone, the oppressive weight lifting from the air.

"You did it," Rian whispered, awe in his voice.

Lyra looked up, her heart still pounding, but something in her had changed. She wasn't the same person who had stepped into the spire hours ago. She had stopped Seraphis, stopped him from remaking reality.

But there was no time to rest. She could feel the aftermath—the balance of the world had shifted, but the final consequences of what they'd done were still to be realized.

Seraphis was gone, but the future—her future—was uncertain.

"Let's go," Lyra said, her voice steady as she turned to Rian. "We still have a kingdom to rebuild."

Twenty

Chapter 19: The Convergence

The dawn of the new world was not a glorious moment. There were no fanfares or songs, no banners raised high to signal the triumph of the united kingdoms. Instead, it was a quiet, uncertain moment—a fragile peace hanging in the balance, the calm after the storm of Seraphis' betrayal.

Lyra stood atop the crumbled ruins of the Nexus spire, her body bruised and weary, her heart still racing with the aftershocks of the power she had wielded. Her gaze swept over the desolate landscape, the air still heavy with the remnants of magic, the threads of reality still raw and exposed. Time had been fractured, remade—and though Seraphis was gone, the echoes of his actions lingered in every breath the world took.

Beside her, Rian's silhouette cut a sharp line against the shattered skyline. He stood with his arms crossed, eyes scanning the horizon, as if seeking something in the distance—

an answer, perhaps, or the next step in the long journey they had embarked upon. The tension between them was palpable, but it was different now. They had both changed, molded by the trials they had endured. They no longer spoke as adversaries or strangers, but as comrades—united by the knowledge that their worlds would never be the same again.

"Where do we go from here?" Lyra asked, her voice barely above a whisper, the weight of her words pressing down on her shoulders. "There's no going back. What Seraphis did— it's not just about time anymore. He tore a hole in reality itself. The fabric of everything we knew is…broken."

Rian turned to her, his gaze softening for a moment before hardening again. "We rebuild. Together." He paused, his eyes narrowing as he scanned the horizon once more. "But we also prepare. Seraphis may be gone, but his actions have set things in motion. There are forces at play now, Lyra—forces we don't fully understand."

Lyra nodded, a knot of unease forming in her stomach. She had always known that Seraphis' actions weren't just about his quest for control over time. They had been part of something far greater—something that threatened not only the kingdoms of Aeridor and Solara, but all of existence.

"Do you think it's over?" she asked quietly, her eyes meeting his. "Do you think that by destroying Seraphis, we've stopped the unraveling?"

Rian hesitated, then shook his head. "No. I think we've only just begun to see the consequences. The world is not the same. It's not just magic we're dealing with anymore—it's reality itself. And it's in flux."

Lyra swallowed, trying to push down the knot of fear tightening in her chest. The path ahead was uncertain, but she

Chapter 19: The Convergence

couldn't allow doubt to paralyze her. They had won—*they had won*. But the cost had been high, and the price of that victory would echo for generations.

"There's more," she said softly. "The ancient pact—between Aeridor and Solara. It was broken. But not by Seraphis. There was something else. Something... deeper. I can feel it. There's something *else* at play."

Rian looked at her sharply. "You think Seraphis was just a part of a bigger plan?"

Lyra's eyes narrowed as she turned toward him. "I don't think Seraphis was ever the real threat. He was a catalyst, yes, but someone—something else—has been pulling the strings from the beginning. And we've only scratched the surface of the truth."

A long silence stretched between them, the weight of her words hanging in the air.

Before Rian could respond, a low rumble sounded in the distance, growing louder with each passing moment. Lyra stiffened, instinctively reaching for the dagger at her side. The ground beneath them trembled, and the sky above darkened, clouds swirling ominously as if reflecting the turmoil within the world.

"Do you feel that?" she asked, her voice tense.

Rian didn't need to answer. He was already on high alert, his hand instinctively going to the hilt of his sword as he stepped closer to Lyra. Something was coming—something dangerous.

Without warning, a burst of energy erupted from the sky, a jagged streak of lightning cutting across the heavens. The bolt struck the earth with such force that the very ground beneath them shook, and the air hummed with the force of the impact.

Tempting the Enemy's Daughter

Lyra stumbled, but Rian caught her, pulling her behind him as the explosion of light and energy slowly faded, leaving an eerie stillness in its wake.

In the distance, a dark figure emerged from the lingering haze, cloaked in shadows, its form almost indistinguishable from the storm itself.

"It's not over," Lyra murmured, her eyes narrowing. The figure moved closer, its presence suffocating, like the very air had thickened around them. "It's just beginning."

The figure stopped, its outline now clearly visible. A tall, gaunt figure, wearing a cloak that rippled with the remnants of dark magic. The figure's face was obscured by the hood, but Lyra could feel its gaze—cold, unyielding—fixated on her.

And then, in a voice that seemed to come from the very core of the earth, the figure spoke.

"You've played your part, Lyra. You've done well. But you were never meant to win."

Lyra's breath caught in her throat. Her heart stuttered in her chest, her pulse quickening. The voice, cold and sharp, sounded like a whisper—but it held a power that twisted the air around them, warping reality itself.

The figure stepped forward, and as it did, the landscape around them began to *shift*—the ruins of the Nexus spire, the broken earth, the very sky—all of it began to blur, stretching and bending as though time and space were being *reformed*.

"Who are you?" Lyra demanded, her voice steady despite the fear creeping at the edges of her mind. She could feel the Nexus' residual energy pulling at her, but it was no longer under her control. This was something different. Something darker.

The figure's lips twisted into a smile, but it was not a smile of

Chapter 19: The Convergence

joy. It was a smile of something far older—far more dangerous.

"I am the one who *was*," it said, its voice deepening, as though it was speaking through layers of time itself. "I am the one who *will be*."

And in that moment, Lyra realized with a sickening jolt that whatever Seraphis had unleashed, whatever had been broken in the fabric of time—it had opened a door. And now, something far more ancient and powerful had stepped through.

"This is the Convergence," the figure intoned, its voice now shaking the ground beneath them. "The event that will bind all of creation together—or destroy it completely."

Lyra's stomach lurched, and she felt the air press against her chest, as though she were drowning in it. Time, reality, space—they were all folding in on themselves. The true enemy had finally revealed itself.

And it was far worse than anything Seraphis had ever been.

The figure stood before them, its presence bending the very air. Lyra could feel the immense pressure of its power, an oppressive weight that threatened to crush her. Her instincts screamed at her to run, to escape, but her feet were frozen in place. The world around her shifted, flickering between distorted moments in time. She could hear the faint echoes of past and future events weaving together, like a dissonant symphony.

"I... don't understand," she whispered, her voice a mixture of confusion and fear. "Who are you? What do you want?"

The figure tilted its head, the dark hood slipping back just enough to reveal a face—pale, almost translucent, with hollow, dark eyes that seemed to see through her, into something beyond her own existence. Its expression was neither malevolent nor benevolent. It simply *was*.

"I am the Overseer," the figure intoned, its voice deep, resonating through Lyra's very bones. "The one who has watched the weaving of the timelines. The one who has guided the fractures of history. You may call me Vaelor."

Rian stepped in front of Lyra, his posture protective, his hand resting on the hilt of his sword. He could sense the danger emanating from Vaelor, an energy far older than anything they had encountered before. It was like standing before a force of nature, untouchable and incomprehensible.

"You were the one pulling the strings behind Seraphis?" Rian's voice was steady, but there was a raw edge to it, the weight of the situation pressing down on him. "You've been manipulating us, all along?"

Vaelor's lips curled into a smile that held no warmth. "Manipulating? No. I simply *guided* events. I allowed certain individuals to believe they were the architects of their own destinies. But in the end, they were all simply pieces in a game far larger than their understanding."

Lyra's mind was racing. The Overseer. The one who watched the timelines. She had heard of such beings—old legends from forgotten histories, tales of entities who existed outside of time itself, who could manipulate the flow of events like a puppet master with a thousand strings. But to meet one in person—*to feel it*—was an entirely different matter.

"What do you want?" she demanded, her voice growing more defiant. "You've already broken the pact, shattered reality itself. What more do you need?"

Vaelor's eyes glinted with ancient wisdom, a knowledge that stretched back eons. "What I need is simple, child. The *Convergence* is upon us. It is the moment when all

Chapter 19: The Convergence

threads of reality—past, present, and future—bind together. The kingdoms, the magic, the Nexus, the very essence of existence... they will all be woven into a singular, unified whole."

He stepped closer, and as he did, the world around them seemed to distort even more, like they were moving through layers of time. "But that is not enough. I require something more—a sacrifice. The last fragment of the Nexus must be returned to its rightful place, or the convergence will collapse in on itself, consuming everything. Including you."

Lyra's breath caught in her throat. The final fragment. She had seen it—felt it—when she had destroyed Seraphis. It had been an echo of the Nexus, a faint remnant of its raw power, and it had vanished. She hadn't known where it had gone, or if it had been consumed in the wake of the cataclysm.

But now she understood. Vaelor was the key to the Convergence, the one who would make the world *whole* again. And to do that, he needed the last piece. The last fragment of the Nexus.

Rian's voice was low, filled with suspicion. "So you've been waiting all this time for the right moment to reclaim it? For the Convergence to happen?"

Vaelor's smile deepened. "Yes. It has always been part of my plan. The broken pact, the rift in time... all of it was merely a precursor. The Convergence was inevitable."

Lyra's mind spun. She could feel the weight of his words, the gravity of the situation settling upon her. The Nexus, the pact, the kingdoms of Aeridor and Solara—they were all tied into this grand design, this Convergence that had been set in motion long before she had even realized it.

But it was also clear that Vaelor's intentions were far from

Tempting the Enemy's Daughter

noble. He didn't just want to restore balance; he wanted to *reshape* it, to control it.

"And what happens to us?" Lyra asked, her voice hardening. "To Aeridor and Solara? To the people?"

Vaelor's gaze was piercing, his eyes flashing with a cold, almost pitying gleam. "They will be *integrated*—merged into the new order. The kingdoms, their petty conflicts, their desires for power... all of it will cease to matter. There will be only one purpose. One destiny."

He raised a hand, and the ground beneath them trembled. A pulse of energy rippled through the air, distorting the very fabric of reality, and Lyra felt the world around them *bend*, as if time itself was trying to fold in on them.

"It is already happening," Vaelor continued, his voice growing darker. "The threads are converging. The final piece is all that remains to complete the tapestry."

Lyra's pulse quickened as she looked at Rian, her mind racing. The final piece. The fragment of the Nexus. It had to be found, and it had to be kept from Vaelor at all costs.

"How do we stop this?" Lyra demanded, her voice steady despite the fear tightening her chest.

Vaelor's lips curled into an almost sorrowful smile. "You cannot stop it, child. You've already played your part. Now, you must accept the consequences."

Rian stepped forward, his hand gripping the hilt of his sword, but before he could act, Lyra grabbed his arm. There was no fight to be had here—not yet. They needed more time. More information.

"Tell me this, Vaelor," Lyra said, her voice calm but unwavering. "Why reveal yourself now? Why not just take what you need and disappear?"

Chapter 19: The Convergence

Vaelor's gaze flickered with something almost like amusement. "Because, Lady Lyra, *you* are the last key. You—your lineage, your connection to the Nexus. It was always you who would decide how the Convergence unfolds. Your choice, your actions, will determine whether the world is remade into a perfect harmony, or whether it falls into chaos."

Lyra's heart pounded in her chest. She understood now. It wasn't just about the Nexus or the Convergence. It was about *her*—her bloodline, her role in the grand scheme of things. She was tied to the Nexus in ways she hadn't fully realized, her fate woven into the very threads of time itself.

But as the weight of Vaelor's words settled upon her, she felt something stir deep within her—a spark of defiance. No matter what he said, no matter what *he* wanted to happen, she would not be a pawn in this game.

The Convergence had begun—but she still had a choice.

And she would make it.

The storm in the distance began to grow, clouds swirling, lightning crackling. The Convergence was coming, whether they were ready for it or not.

But Lyra was not afraid. Not anymore.

She knew what she had to do.

The air around Lyra and Rian pulsed with an otherworldly energy, as if the very fabric of time itself was holding its breath. Vaelor's presence loomed like a shadow over them, his words echoing in their minds, leaving a lingering chill that threatened to freeze their thoughts. The ground beneath their feet felt unstable, shifting ever so slightly as the world bent and flickered, revealing glimpses of other timelines—other possibilities.

Lyra's heart raced. She could feel the pull of the Nexus, a gnawing emptiness where the final fragment had once been. It was no longer just a relic of a broken world; it was the key to everything. To her destiny, to the fate of Aeridor, Solara, and the future itself.

But Vaelor was wrong. She *could* stop this.

She turned her gaze from the Overseer, her eyes hardening with resolve. "You think you have control over this, Vaelor," she said, her voice cutting through the tension like a blade, "but you underestimate what we've learned. What we've *become*."

Vaelor's laugh was soft, almost gentle, but it held a chilling finality. "You misunderstand, Lady Lyra. You *are* already part of this convergence. Whether you embrace it or resist it, the threads are woven around you. I've waited eons for this moment. For the right time, the right players, and the right destruction."

"You keep saying that," Rian spoke up, his voice tight with barely restrained anger. "But you've forgotten something crucial. We don't play by your rules anymore. We *never* did."

Vaelor's expression twisted with a flicker of impatience, his gaze darting to Rian. "You believe your defiance will matter? You still cling to your insignificant choices. *The timeline has been set. The world has been torn.* You are mere pawns, trying to defy the inevitable."

Rian stepped forward, his sword now drawn, its gleam flashing in the fractured light. "Maybe we're pawns," he said, his voice a low growl, "but we're not helpless ones. We know what you're trying to do. And we're going to stop you."

Vaelor's smile faded, and for the first time, a sliver of genuine annoyance passed across his features. "You still don't understand. You cannot stop the Convergence. The final

Chapter 19: The Convergence

piece of the Nexus must be restored, or all will be lost—*your world, your lives* included."

Lyra felt the weight of his words. There was truth in them. The fragments of the Nexus had been scattered, and reality itself had been fractured. If the last piece wasn't returned, there would be nothing left but a broken, disjointed existence. Time would collapse in on itself. And everyone—Aeridor, Solara, the hidden city, even the ancient powers—would be lost.

But deep within her, Lyra could feel a power stirring—something far more potent than Vaelor's manipulation. She had seen it before, when she had wielded the energy of the Nexus herself, when she had helped shatter Seraphis' hold over time. It was *her* connection to the Nexus, to the threads of time, that had always been the true power. The question was: could she control it? Could she *rewrite* the Convergence to her will?

"I'm not a pawn," Lyra said, her voice steady, as she took a step forward, mirroring Rian's stance. "I am the key."

Vaelor's eyes flickered with a brief flash of something—surprise, perhaps, or amusement. "You *think* you are the key, Lady Lyra. But in the end, you will be nothing more than a tool for the Convergence. The truth is... you've always been *mine*."

Lyra's blood ran cold at his words, but she didn't flinch. She had come to understand something deep within herself. Vaelor was right about one thing: the Nexus had always been tied to her. But she wasn't simply a tool. She was a force of her own making, forged through struggle, betrayal, and sacrifice. She had the ability to shape her own fate—she *would* shape it.

With a single, resolute motion, she raised her hand, and the air around them shimmered. The residual energy from the shattered Nexus responded to her, ripples of time bending and warping like waves in a storm. She felt the pulse of magic fill her veins, the threads of the past and future connecting in her mind's eye. She could feel them all—Aeridor's armies, Solara's forces, the hidden city—each of them caught in the swirling current of time, unable to escape.

But with the flick of her wrist, she altered their path. The threads shuddered and snapped, bending around her as she wove them into a new design.

"You're wrong," she said, her voice hard and unyielding. "I *choose* what happens next. I am not a puppet of fate. Not yours. Not anyone's."

Vaelor's face tightened. "You cannot do this. You do not understand the power you're wielding. You're toying with forces you cannot control. If you bend time now, if you pull at the fabric of reality again, you will tear it beyond repair."

But Lyra was already beyond him, her focus entirely on the Nexus' residual energy, the final fragment that had been pulled out of sync with time itself. She could feel it, hovering just beyond her reach—a shimmering essence of raw power, waiting for her to reclaim it.

"I understand more than you think," she muttered under her breath, her hand outstretched, pulling the piece back into the fold of reality.

The world trembled. The timeline shuddered violently. And then, as Lyra felt the final fragment slide back into place, the Nexus—the heart of time—flared to life once more. Its energy, vast and boundless, swirled around her, suffusing her with its radiant, all-encompassing power. It was as if the very universe had been drawn into a single point, its fractures stitching

Chapter 19: The Convergence

together in a burst of blinding light.

Vaelor's expression twisted into one of rage, his hands raised, trying to lash out, to stop her. But it was too late.

With a deafening crack, the Convergence reached its climax. Reality bent, twisted, and reformed. Time itself was *rewritten*, its fractures mended, but at a terrible cost. The once-shattered world began to heal, its broken pieces falling back into their rightful places—but the power of the Nexus, the energy required to make this possible, began to consume the very fabric of existence.

Lyra gasped as she felt herself being pulled into the storm of power, her body tugged by the immense force of the Nexus, but her mind remained intact. It was a terrifying, overwhelming sensation—but she would not let go. She would not let Vaelor win.

Her voice rang out, barely a whisper, but filled with the authority of someone who had seen the threads of fate and rejected them.

"This *isn't* your world to remake," she said, her words resonating with the power of the Nexus itself. "This is mine. This is *ours*."

As the last vestiges of the Convergence settled, the storm began to subside, leaving in its wake a world forever changed. Lyra stood, her chest heaving with the effort, the final piece of the Nexus now firmly restored, and the threads of time weaving themselves back into a new pattern—a pattern she had forged with her own hands.

Vaelor's form flickered, his expression one of disbelief. He tried to speak, but the words faltered, as if the very nature of his being was being torn apart by the shifting currents of time.

"You…" he whispered, the force of his presence weakening.

"You cannot… stop… it…"

But before he could finish, he was gone—erased, swallowed by the very magic he had sought to control.

Lyra stood alone in the silence that followed, the weight of the moment settling over her like a heavy mantle. Rian, ever at her side, stepped forward, his expression a mix of awe and relief.

"You did it," he said, his voice barely above a whisper. "You *really* did it."

Lyra nodded, her gaze drifting toward the horizon. The world around them had been remade—reformed in a way that only she could have envisioned. But as the last echoes of the Convergence faded, she realized that the work was not yet done.

The future was no longer a fixed path—it was a landscape of possibilities, and she would be its architect.

And this time, no one—no one—would decide her fate but her.

Twenty-One

Chapter 20: A New Dawn

~~~

The world was still.

For the first time in what felt like an eternity, Lyra allowed herself a moment of quiet. The storm of magic, the Convergence that had torn the fabric of time and space, had passed. The powerful force that had once bound her to fate—twisting her, shaping her into someone she never truly was—had faded, leaving her standing on the precipice of something new. Something uncertain.

She stood at the edge of the palace grounds in Aeridor, the light of the rising sun stretching across the horizon in soft, golden hues. The world around her seemed different—cleaner, somehow, as though the very air had been washed of the years of conflict and manipulation. And yet, as she stared out across the landscape, there was a heaviness to it all, a weight that hung between her and the future.

There was no going back.

Tempting the Enemy's Daughter

Rian, who had remained at her side throughout the chaos, approached slowly, his footsteps quiet on the stone path. His eyes, once filled with tension and distrust, now held a quiet understanding, though the same flicker of concern remained.

"Is it over?" he asked softly, his voice almost tentative, as if the very question could break the fragile peace that had settled over them.

Lyra's lips curled into a small, weary smile. "I don't know," she replied. "But we've done all we can."

He nodded, his gaze distant as he took in the world around them. His sword, once raised in defiance against the storm of Vaelor's magic, now hung limp at his side, its edge dull from the battles they had fought—literal and metaphorical. But there was a peace in him now, a sense of purpose that hadn't been there before.

"It feels strange," Rian said, a hint of bewilderment in his voice. "The world is still here, but it's… changed. Almost like it's waiting for something. For us."

Lyra met his eyes, her heart heavy with the weight of what they had done. "It *is* waiting. But it's not waiting for us to fix it. It's waiting for us to shape it."

She turned her gaze to the horizon, where the last vestiges of the storm clouds faded into nothingness. Time had healed, but it wasn't just the timeline that needed mending—it was the world itself. Aeridor and Solara, the kingdoms that had once been locked in conflict, would need to rebuild. The hidden city, with its ancient technology and forgotten truths, would need to decide whether it would remain hidden or emerge into the light. The people, the warriors, the scholars, the dreamers—they would need to find their place in this new world.

Chapter 20: A New Dawn

The question was, where did she fit in?

"I don't know what happens next," Lyra admitted, her voice soft, yet resolute. "But I know this: it won't be decided by anyone else. It's ours to create now."

Rian said nothing, but his presence beside her spoke volumes. The weight of all that had happened between them—their fights, their distrust, their tentative alliances—was gone. In its place was something quieter. Something more solid.

After a long silence, Lyra spoke again, her voice more steady. "I've spent so long trying to live up to what others wanted of me. First my father's vision, then Vaelor's. Even Seraphis, in a way. But I'm not just a pawn in anyone's game anymore. I *never* was. And neither are you."

Rian's lips twitched at the corner, a smile playing at the edges of his expression. "I never thought I was a pawn, Lyra. Not even when I was the one who swore to protect you. You've always had a way of seeing what others don't. I'm just glad I was there to help."

They stood together, looking out over the horizon, knowing that the path ahead would not be easy, but it would be theirs to walk. Together.

The sun rose higher, casting its light across the land as if to signify the birth of something new—a new world, a new future.

It wasn't just the Nexus that had been reshaped. It was everything. The Convergence had been the turning point, the moment when time and fate collided. But the final piece—the one that mattered most—was the choice they had made. They had the power to choose their path, to rebuild, to forge alliances where once there had been enemies, to reimagine the future they would inherit.

Lyra's thoughts returned to her father. Duke Alaric had been a man caught between duty and loyalty, his vision narrow and focused on the survival of his house. But now, in the aftermath of the Convergence, she saw him in a different light. He had been part of the ancient pact, part of the rift that had divided their worlds, but he was also a part of this new future. Whether he would see it or not, his role had changed.

And her role—her true role—was still being written.

As if on cue, a figure appeared on the horizon—an envoy, traveling on horseback, his silhouette growing clearer as he drew closer. Lyra's heart skipped a beat, her mind already calculating the possibilities. This wasn't a moment of peace. It wasn't the end of the story. It was the beginning of something else.

"Who is that?" Rian asked, his hand going instinctively to his sword.

Lyra's eyes narrowed, her pulse quickening. She recognized the crest on the rider's cloak—a symbol of Solara, but not one she had seen in years.

"It's from Solara," she said quietly, her voice filled with uncertainty. "It looks like… an emissary from my father."

Rian's gaze hardened. "Your father? After everything that's happened?"

She nodded. "Perhaps he's coming to claim his part in this new world. Or maybe he wants to stake his claim over me, once again."

The rider came closer, and Lyra took a deep breath, bracing herself for whatever this new development would bring. Her fingers tingled with the memory of the Nexus, but it was no longer a reminder of the past—it was a sign of her own power, her ability to shape the future.

Chapter 20: A New Dawn

When the emissary finally arrived, he dismounted with practiced grace, bowing low before Lyra.

"My Lady Lyra," he said with a formal tone that made her spine stiffen. "I come bearing a message from Duke Alaric. He wishes to speak with you. *He* believes the time has come for your return to Solara."

Lyra's heart thudded in her chest, and her mind raced. This was the moment, the one she had been preparing for. But what would she say? What would she do?

"I think," Lyra said slowly, "that the time has come for me to decide for myself, once and for all."

The emissary looked up, confusion and hesitation flashing across his face.

"You can tell my father," she continued, "that the world is no longer his to control. And that includes me."

The messenger stood in stunned silence, unable to comprehend the weight of her words. But Lyra, standing tall in the golden light of dawn, knew this was the first of many steps she would take in the world she had just remade. A world that would not bow to the will of the past.

She glanced at Rian, who stood beside her, a silent ally in the face of what was yet to come.

Together, they would forge a new path.

And this time, no one would define their destiny but themselves.

The sun rose higher in the sky, painting the world in hues of gold and amber—a new dawn for all.

The emissary shifted uneasily on his feet, his eyes flicking nervously between Lyra and Rian. The tension in the air was palpable—an unspoken challenge had been thrown, and the man before them wasn't sure how to respond.

Lyra's gaze did not waver. She had faced far too many challenges, too many manipulations to be intimidated now. The road ahead was uncertain, but it was hers to walk. This moment, the arrival of her father's emissary, wasn't just a diplomatic exchange—it was the first sign of what would come next. The first test of whether she, and by extension the world, would truly embrace the new reality she had helped create.

"I understand your message, but it's not enough." Lyra's voice was firm, yet calm. "I have not spent the last few months weaving together the strands of time, fighting to restore the Nexus, only to fall back into the cage my father would build for me. His time has passed."

The messenger's face flushed, and he cleared his throat, trying to regain his composure. "Lady Lyra, you misunderstand. The Duke recognizes your power, your... *importance* in the rebuilding of the kingdom. He is not asking you to return as a daughter in need of guidance, but as a partner. To rule together."

Lyra felt a flicker of something cold rise within her—a bitterness that seemed to have no end. The idea of partnership was a seductive one, certainly, but it was rooted in old power structures, old loyalties. *Her* loyalty, once shattered, would never be restored through empty promises.

"A partner?" she echoed, her voice thick with irony. "Tell your Duke that I will not be his puppet. Not now. Not ever."

Rian stepped closer, his hand resting lightly on the hilt of his sword. Not in a threatening manner, but as a silent statement of solidarity. He didn't need to speak to convey his agreement. Lyra wasn't alone. Not anymore.

The emissary recoiled, clearly caught off guard by her vehemence. "My Lady, the Duke will not be pleased with

Chapter 20: A New Dawn

such a response."

"I don't care what your Duke thinks," Lyra snapped. "Tell him that the time of old alliances is over. He must either accept the reality of this new world—one where freedom and choice are no longer bound by ancient debts—or remain in his illusions, clinging to a past that no longer exists."

She could see it in his eyes—he was torn. The man was loyal, in his way, but he was also terrified. Of his Duke. Of the unknown. And even, perhaps, of the power that now surged in her veins, the legacy of the Nexus and the shattered timelines. She didn't need to force him to make a choice. He already knew. It was only a matter of how he would respond.

With a barely audible sigh, the emissary bowed his head. "I will carry your message to the Duke. Though I fear… he will not understand. Not yet."

Lyra nodded, her expression unreadable. "Then you should prepare him. He will have no choice but to adapt. And so will everyone else."

As the emissary turned to leave, Lyra's mind raced. The decision to sever her ties with Solara was not made lightly, nor was it without consequence. Her father had always expected her to fulfill a role—one that had been dictated by bloodlines, duty, and honor. To return to him now, to accept his rule, would be to forsake everything she had become, everything she had fought for.

But was she ready to take that step? To sever herself from the past entirely and build something that could only be hers?

"Do you think he'll come for me?" Lyra asked, the question slipping from her lips before she realized it.

Rian's brow furrowed, and he turned to look at her with a steady gaze. "He may try. But Lyra, you've already proven that you can face anything. Your father is a man of power, but you've learned something far greater: the power of choice. And he'll have to reckon with that."

She nodded, her heart a mixture of defiance and uncertainty. The power of choice. It was something she'd fought for, struggled to understand. In the past, the choices she made had always felt constrained—by her father's expectations, by the manipulations of men like Vaelor, by the ancient bonds of her bloodline. But now? Now she knew the truth: her path was hers to forge.

The silence between them stretched for a moment, and Lyra found herself lost in thought. The sun was fully risen now, casting a brilliant light over the land, but the shadow of uncertainty still lingered.

"Rian," she began quietly, her voice soft but filled with conviction, "we've done something impossible. But it's not over yet. I still don't know what the world will look like tomorrow, or the day after that. But what I *do* know is that I won't be alone in this."

"You won't," Rian agreed, his voice low and steady. "Not while I'm here."

Lyra turned to him, meeting his gaze fully for the first time. There had been so much between them—so many misgivings, so many moments where trust had faltered. But now, in the wake of all they had been through, there was clarity. An understanding that had been forged not in words, but in actions, in shared experiences. They were allies, companions, and perhaps, in time, something more. But whatever happened, Lyra knew that they had one thing that could not be taken from them: a shared future.

"We've all been given a second chance," she said, her voice

Chapter 20: A New Dawn

resolute, eyes fixed on the horizon. "Not just me, or you, or the kingdoms. But the world. Time is no longer something we must bend to. We shape it now."

Rian nodded, his eyes flicking toward the distant skyline where the ruins of the past mingled with the promise of a new beginning. The ruins of the hidden city, once lost to history, were now a powerful reminder of what had been reclaimed. The nations of Aeridor and Solara, fractured by years of mistrust and old grudges, were now bound by a fragile but undeniable thread: the future.

"Do you think we can rebuild?" he asked, his voice thoughtful.

Lyra's lips quirked into a faint smile, though it was tinged with the bittersweet knowledge of how much work lay ahead. "We must. But we won't do it alone. There are people who will help us. People who *want* to help us."

The two of them stood for a long moment, watching the sun rise higher into the sky. The land before them stretched on—endless and filled with potential. Aeridor and Solara, once enemies, now had the chance to forge something better. The hidden city, with its ancient knowledge and power, would play a part in that too. And as for Lyra and Rian—they would find their place, carving a path that no one, not even fate itself, could have predicted.

"You're not just a daughter of Aeridor anymore," Rian said softly, breaking the silence.

Lyra smiled, her eyes lifting to meet his. "No. I'm something else now. Something more."

And with that, they turned together, walking side by side, into the dawn of a new world.

A Future Unwritten

The kingdoms of Aeridor and Solara would take time to heal, to rebuild from the shattered past. But the foundation was there: a shared vision, the willingness to change, and, above all, the power of choice. It would not be easy, and there would be struggles ahead, but the old cycles of conflict had been broken.

Lyra's place in this new world was yet to be fully defined, but she was no longer bound by the expectations of the past. The legacy of her father, the ancient pact, and the manipulations of Vaelor had been undone. She had reclaimed her future—not as the Duke's daughter, but as a force in her own right.

And as for the hidden city, its secrets would soon be unveiled. Its knowledge, its power, would be shared with those who were ready for it. The future would not be built on the ruins of the past, but on the choices made by those who dared to look beyond the horizon and build something new.

A new dawn had arrived.

And the world, for the first time in generations, was free.

Lyra and Rian stood in the quiet aftermath of the emissary's departure, the wind gently stirring the long grass at their feet. The sun, now fully risen, cast long golden rays across the castle grounds, illuminating the stone walls and the distant mountains beyond. It felt as though the whole world had exhaled a breath it hadn't known it was holding, but the air was thick with the weight of what still remained unsaid.

"You know what this means, right?" Lyra's voice broke the silence, sharp but steady. Her eyes lingered on the horizon, where the shadow of her father's kingdom loomed.

Rian turned his gaze towards her, his brow furrowing slightly. "You're thinking of Solara?"

Chapter 20: A New Dawn

"Solara, yes," Lyra said, her tone distant as she traced patterns in the air with her fingers. "But also the future. The world we've just reshaped—it's fragile. Everyone will be watching us. Watching me."

Rian's expression softened, and he took a step closer, his hand briefly brushing hers. "It's not just *you* they'll be watching. It's all of us. We're in this together."

She met his eyes, and for a moment, they simply stood there, both recognizing the truth of those words. Their alliance—born of necessity, yes, but strengthened through shared hardship—was more than just a partnership. It had become something far more profound, built on trust and understanding, something that couldn't be easily broken.

But even as that truth settled between them, Lyra's thoughts remained clouded by the choices yet to come. She had no illusions about what this moment meant. The choices she made now would define not just her future, but the future of Aeridor, Solara, and the remnants of the hidden city that lay in the distance. She would have to rebuild, not just the kingdoms, but herself—because the person she had been, bound by duty and bloodlines, no longer fit into the world she had helped create.

She turned to Rian, determination hardening her features. "We need to prepare. There's no telling how my father will react, or what the other powers in the kingdoms will do now. This is just the beginning of a much larger struggle."

Rian's lips tightened, and he nodded. "What do you want me to do?"

Lyra's gaze softened slightly, grateful for his unwavering loyalty. "I want you to help me reach out. We need to know who stands with us—and who we still have to convince."

"I'll do what I can," Rian said, his voice steady. "But you've already done the hard part, Lyra. The world may not know it yet, but you've set things in motion. The question now is how to keep it moving in the right direction."

She chuckled quietly, though it was tinged with weariness. "It's a long road ahead, isn't it?"

"A road worth walking," Rian replied with a slight smile, his hand brushing against hers once more. "Together."

Lyra returned the smile, but there was a quiet sadness in her eyes, something that lingered just beneath the surface. The world was no longer at war, but the wounds of the past ran deep. And though the Nexus had been healed, and the ancient rift between Aeridor and Solara had been mended, the work of rebuilding was not just a matter of politics or treaties. It was a matter of trust—trust that had been broken by years of manipulation, by betrayal, and by the shadow of the past.

"I'll need to visit Solara soon," Lyra said, her voice quieter now, more contemplative. "My father will not take kindly to being ignored. And if we are to move forward, we need to settle what remains between us. Once and for all."

Rian's expression darkened slightly, but he nodded. "I'll be there, of course. But you don't have to face him alone. Not again."

Lyra's eyes softened, and she placed a hand on his arm. "I know. But this is something I must do. I need to face him— not just as his daughter, but as something more. Something he may not be ready for."

The wind shifted again, the temperature dropping slightly as the day began to settle into its rhythm. The emissary's words still echoed in her mind, a reminder of the weight of what she had just decided. Her father would come for her. He

Chapter 20: A New Dawn

would not simply let her go, not without a fight.

But it was not just her father who would come for her. There were others—others who would see the power she had reclaimed, and who might want to use it for their own ends. The hidden city, with its untapped potential and knowledge, was an enigma that many would seek to control. And she couldn't trust that everyone who sought her help or alliance had pure intentions.

"We'll have to move carefully," Lyra murmured, more to herself than to Rian. "One wrong step, and everything we've worked for could come undone."

Rian leaned in slightly, his presence a grounding force. "Then we'll make sure that doesn't happen. Step by step."

For a long moment, they simply stood there, letting the silence wash over them. The world was full of questions now, full of possibilities. The echoes of the past still lingered in the corners of their minds, but they were no longer bound by it. The future was not a preordained path. It was a path that could be forged, one decision at a time.

Finally, Lyra turned away, her gaze lingering one last time on the horizon. "We should begin with Solara," she said quietly. "And then, we'll see who else is ready to stand with us."

Rian followed her lead, his steps confident beside her. They made their way toward the castle gates, where a new world awaited them, as fragile as it was full of hope.

The Ties That Bind

Weeks passed in a flurry of diplomatic correspondence, strategic meetings, and alliances forged in the heat of uncertainty. Lyra had traveled to Solara, her heart heavy with the weight of what she had left behind. The confrontation with her father had been everything she had feared and more. Duke

Alaric, still proud and unyielding, had demanded her return, his anger palpable as he had tried to force her into the role he had always envisioned for her.

But Lyra had stood her ground. She had refused to be controlled, to bend to the old ways that had kept her bound. And in the end, it was that very defiance that had forced her father to reconsider his stance. The Duke had left their meeting in silence, a bitter understanding hanging between them.

Alaric had been a man shaped by a world that no longer existed. But Lyra? She had become something else entirely. She was no longer just the Duke's daughter. She was a leader in her own right—a force to be reckoned with.

And though Solara's future was still uncertain, the pieces had been set in motion.

Back in Aeridor, the alliance between the two kingdoms had solidified, albeit slowly. There were those who resisted change, who clung to old prejudices, but there were also those who saw the opportunity for a new beginning. Lyra worked tirelessly to unite both sides, forging a future that was not defined by bloodlines or ancient pacts, but by the will of those who were willing to build something better.

And through it all, Rian stood beside her. Not as a protector, not as a shadow of the past, but as her equal. Together, they navigated the treacherous waters of politics, forging alliances with other kingdoms, and even with the enigmatic inhabitants of the hidden city. The world was changing—slowly, but surely.

There would be more challenges to face, more obstacles to overcome. But for the first time in a long time, Lyra felt as though the future was hers to shape. The ancient powers

Chapter 20: A New Dawn

of magic, the secrets of the hidden city, the legacy of her bloodline—they were no longer chains. They were tools. Tools she would wield with care, but with the understanding that their true power came not from domination, but from the ability to choose.

And so, the kingdoms of Aeridor and Solara, once divided by distrust and fear, began their long journey toward unity. The past could not be undone, but it could be rewritten.

And in the end, that was enough.

The dawn had come.

And this time, it would last.

Lyra's eyes scanned the horizon one last time as the sun dipped behind the peaks of distant mountains, casting long shadows across the land. The sky was awash with hues of amber and violet, as though the world itself had been painted in shades of possibility. The world, as she knew it, was changing— reshaping itself—and it was all happening under her watch.

She stood at the edge of the castle balcony, feeling the gentle breeze ruffle her hair, a sensation so simple, yet profound. There had been moments in the past when she could barely breathe beneath the weight of the throne she had never truly wanted, the responsibilities that had felt like chains. But now, standing in the wake of the battles fought, the decisions made, and the alliances forged, she was free.

Not just free from the expectations of her father or her kingdom, but free to make her own choices. Free to rebuild the broken ties between Aeridor and Solara, to heal the wounds that had festered for centuries. Free to forge a future where the past no longer defined them.

Behind her, the grand hall of Aeridor Castle was alive with

the quiet hum of celebration. The banquet that had been held to mark the end of the war, the end of an era, had not been an easy affair. The nobles and dignitaries in attendance—those who had once plotted against her, or sought to manipulate her—had been forced to accept the new order. Many had left the event with bitterness still lodged in their hearts, their ambitions thwarted by the unexpected alliances that had sprung up in the wake of the broken pact. But for Lyra, that was a victory in itself.

Rian approached her from behind, his footsteps soft but sure. She didn't need to turn to know it was him. She had come to recognize the sound of his movements as much as she had come to trust his presence in her life.

"Are you ready?" he asked quietly, standing beside her now, his gaze tracing the same horizon.

Lyra nodded slowly, her eyes fixed on the distant lands of Solara. "Ready as I'll ever be."

It wasn't just the dawn of a new day they faced—it was the dawn of an entirely new era. The kingdoms of Aeridor and Solara, once divided by years of war, suspicion, and ancient grudges, now stood at the threshold of reconciliation. The hidden city, its technology and wisdom now part of their shared future, had opened the doors to a world of possibilities neither kingdom could have imagined alone.

But Lyra knew the real work was just beginning. There were still fractures to heal, old enemies to confront, and obstacles to overcome. The alliance was fragile. Old loyalties died hard, and there would be those who would test it. But with each step they took forward, with each alliance they forged, they were building something that could not easily be undone.

"It's all happening, isn't it?" she said softly, more to herself

Chapter 20: A New Dawn

than to Rian.

"It is," Rian replied, his voice steady and sure. "And it's not going to be easy. But it's worth it. All of it."

Lyra turned to him, her eyes meeting his with a depth of gratitude that no words could truly express. They had come so far together, through danger and deceit, through manipulation and war. They had faced their demons and conquered the darkness that had once threatened to tear them apart. And now, standing at the edge of a new world, she knew that whatever came next, they would face it as equals.

"Thank you," she whispered, her voice catching slightly. "For everything."

Rian smiled, his expression warm and reassuring. "You don't have to thank me. This was always your choice. Your fight. I've just been here to help you carry it."

She nodded, knowing that he spoke the truth. This had never been about saving her—it had always been about saving the world. And together, they had done it.

There was a long silence between them, but it was not uncomfortable. They were no longer two people bound by circumstance and the ghosts of the past; they were two individuals who had found strength in each other, who had found purpose in a shared vision. Together, they had woven the threads of a new future, and now it was theirs to build, brick by brick.

Lyra took a deep breath and turned away from the balcony, her gaze shifting back toward the grand hall where the celebrations continued. "There's still work to be done," she said, her voice resolute. "The kingdoms won't change overnight. But we've set the stage. Now, it's time to make sure the world doesn't forget what we've done."

Rian's expression shifted to one of determination. "And we'll make sure of that."

They walked back toward the castle's grand hall, side by side, their shoulders touching in silent unity. As they entered the room, the sight of the gathered nobles, diplomats, and dignitaries didn't intimidate Lyra as it once had. She was no longer the uncertain daughter of a Duke, the pawn in a game of politics. She was the architect of a new world, a world of balance, of cooperation, of respect.

And though many of the faces in the room remained wary, some even resentful of the changes she had ushered in, there was no mistaking the weight of what they had all just witnessed. The once-shattered kingdoms, Aeridor and Solara, stood on the precipice of something new.

A new dawn had come—and it was one they would all have to navigate together.

As the last of the evening's festivities unfolded around them, a sense of quiet triumph settled over Lyra. This was only the beginning. There would be challenges ahead, but for the first time in her life, she knew she was prepared to face them. Not as the enemy's daughter, not as a weapon to be used, but as a woman with a vision and a future to shape. And beside her stood Rian, the one person she knew she could rely on, the one person whose loyalty would never falter.

Together, they would build the world they had fought for. And together, they would ensure that no one, no matter how powerful, could ever take it from them.

The journey ahead was uncertain, but one thing was clear:

The world was hers to shape. And she would do it with strength, with wisdom, and with a heart that had finally learned how to lead.

Chapter 20: A New Dawn

The light of a new dawn had come. And Lyra, the woman who had tempted fate, had finally claimed her place in the world.

Top of Form

Bottom of Form

Finally, Lyra turned away, her gaze lingering one last time on the horizon. "We should begin with Solara," she said quietly. "And then, we'll see who else is ready to stand with us."

Rian followed her lead, his steps confident beside her. They made their way toward the castle gates, where a new world awaited them, as fragile as it was full of hope.

The End

Tempting the Enemy's Daughter

TEMPTING THE ENEMY'S DAUGHTER

A LOVE BORN FROM RIVALRY

XANDER STEELE

Chapter 20: A New Dawn

Epilogue

Epilogue:

The world had changed.

It was a quiet evening when Lyra stood before the balcony of Aeridor Castle, watching the sun dip behind the distant mountains, painting the sky with streaks of gold and crimson. The landscape before her had transformed over the last several months—where once there had been mistrust, betrayal, and centuries of old wounds, now there was the tentative yet undeniable hope of renewal.

The world wasn't perfect. There would never be a time without conflict, without shadows lurking at the edges. But it was a world in which Lyra had reclaimed her agency—a world in which the power to shape the future no longer belonged solely to kings, dukes, and ancient pacts, but to those who had the courage to challenge the old order.

She had faced her father. She had resisted his will. She had taken her place among the leaders of the world—not as his daughter, not as the product of ancient bloodlines, but as a force in her own right. Duke Alaric had been forced to see her as she was: a woman who would not be shaped

Epilogue

by the past, but who would shape the future instead. Their confrontation had been difficult, filled with bitter words and years of accumulated hurt, but in the end, it had been the only way forward.

Alaric had left her with the weight of his disappointment, but also a begrudging respect. There had been no reconciliation—not yet. But time, Lyra knew, would erode the old barriers. The foundations of their fractured relationship had been laid in that moment of defiance. There was no going back from it. And perhaps, in time, they would find common ground again.

But that was a question for another day.

Lyra's thoughts were interrupted by a soft, familiar presence beside her. Rian. His steady presence had become a constant at her side, a pillar of strength when she needed it most.

"You're thinking about him, aren't you?" he asked, his voice gentle but perceptive.

Lyra didn't have to ask who he meant. "Yes. My father," she said, her voice distant but calm. "I thought I'd have more peace after the confrontation. But there's still so much left unfinished."

Rian stepped beside her, his arm brushing hers in a gesture of quiet support. "There always will be. The future is a messy thing, full of broken pieces and unfinished business. But you've already done what needed to be done. You've created something new—a future that's no longer bound by the past."

Lyra turned to him, her eyes searching his face. "And you? What role do you play in all of this? I couldn't have done it without you."

Rian smiled softly, his gaze holding a quiet understanding. "I'm not sure yet. But I do know one thing. I'll be here.

Whatever happens next."

For a moment, Lyra felt a flicker of uncertainty deep within her—a whisper of doubt that had always accompanied moments of change. What did the future hold for them? What would her role be now that the wars were over, the pacts broken, the ancient alliances torn apart? She had no clear answer, only the certainty that she would continue forward, choosing the path with each step, carving a future for herself and the world she had helped rebuild.

The world was full of new possibilities, and the promise of something better lingered in the air.

The hidden city, once a mystery, was now part of their shared future. Its knowledge, its technology, and its ancient secrets had been carefully integrated into the rebuilding efforts. Though it had seemed like a place of isolation and mystery, the inhabitants of the hidden city had shown Lyra that their world, though different, held the potential for progress and unity that the kingdoms of Solara and Aeridor could not have achieved alone. Their alliance was fragile, but it was real, and it would endure as long as they were willing to work for it.

Aeridor and Solara, too, had taken tentative steps toward peace. The ancient distrust between them, inherited from the long years of war and division, had not been easily erased. But with each new treaty, each new act of diplomacy, the fragile bonds between the two kingdoms grew stronger. There were still factions that resented the changes, still nobles who clung to old power structures, but they would learn to adapt or be left behind.

Lyra had forged the beginnings of a new order, one where alliances were not born from bloodlines or fear, but from

Epilogue

necessity, mutual respect, and the shared dream of a better future. She had given up her role as the Duke's daughter to become something far more dangerous in the eyes of those who had sought to control her—a leader of her own choosing.

As the last light of day faded, Rian's hand found hers, his fingers slipping between hers in a gesture that no longer felt like a promise, but a reality.

"I think," Lyra began, looking up at him, "we've only just begun. There's so much more to do. So many unknowns ahead."

Rian nodded, his gaze meeting hers with quiet understanding. "Then we'll face them together."

The silence that followed was not uncomfortable, but filled with a shared recognition. The future was a blank slate, and together, they would fill it—step by step, choice by choice.

Behind them, the castle gates stood open. Beyond the walls, the kingdoms of Aeridor and Solara would continue to rebuild, their leaders watching from the shadows, waiting for the next move. But for the first time in a long time, Lyra no longer felt the weight of their expectations bearing down on her. She had chosen her path, and she would walk it with those who had earned her trust.

It was no longer about kings and duchesses, about old pacts and broken promises. It was about freedom. About the possibility of something new. A world where the ties that bound her no longer kept her in chains, but connected her to those who would fight for a future they had created, together.

And in that moment, standing at the edge of the new dawn, Lyra realized—*this* was the world she had always wanted.

Not perfect, but full of promise.

And it was hers.